FLAME AND ASH

A WITCHBANE NOVEL

MORGAN BRICE

FLAME AND ASH

A WITCHBANE NOVEL

by Morgan Brice

ebook ISBN: 978-1-939704-95-5
Print ISBN: 978-1-939704-96-2

Cover art by Lou Harper.

Darkwind Press is an imprint of DreamSpinner Communications, LLC

1

SETH

"I'm going to miss Pittsburgh," Seth Tanner said as he and Evan Malone readied the RV to move out of the campground where they had been since November.

"We've stayed in one place longer than I expected," Evan replied, lending a hand with getting the fifth-wheeler fastened onto the back of Seth's black Silverado.

"Figured it made the best use of the winter if the next target is in the mountains of North Carolina." Seth pulled the blocks from beneath the wheels. The truck and RV had belonged to his parents and were going to be their ticket to a retirement full of exploration and adventure. Instead, they'd died in a car accident while Seth was in the hospital recovering from the trauma of his brother Jesse's gruesome murder.

The murder Seth and Evan were committed to avenge.

"It was nice having friends who know what we really do." Evan double-checked the fasteners securing the black Hayabusa motorcycle onto the back of the trailer. "I didn't have to worry about saying something I shouldn't."

"Those guys really know their stuff," Seth agreed. Travis Dominick and Brent Lawson were experienced demon hunters who had helped Seth and Evan take out their quarry not long before Christmas. Travis and Brent had welcomed Seth and Evan into their circle of found family, which made the holidays and the worst of the winter weather more comfortable and less lonely. Getting to train with the other hunters in combat skills and lore was a bonus.

"I'd like to come back when we're done." Evan sounded wistful. "It was nice having a group, you know? I haven't really had that since…" His voice trailed off, but Seth knew what his boyfriend meant. *Not since Evan's family and his church kicked him out for being gay.*

Seth slung an arm around Evan's shoulders and pulled him in for a quick kiss. "I do know. And I'm fine with visiting. They're good people."

The April wind still stung, cold and damp. Spring didn't come this early to Pittsburgh, and slate gray clouds held the threat of more snow. Seth's fingers were cold, and he was glad for his heavy coat, although he hoped he could shed it by the time they reached North Carolina.

"Do you ever think about where you might want to live when we're finally done?" Evan asked.

Seth felt a rush of warmth at Evan's casual prediction that they would survive and that they would stay together. Their relationship had moved fast, starting with a bang when Seth had saved Evan from the dark warlock who intended to kill him. Neither had expected the powerful connection between them, strong enough that Evan had gone on the run with Seth, and signed on to his dangerous quest. That meant learning to love a near-stranger, accepting that magic and monsters were real, and getting a fast-track education in how to research and fight supernatural creatures. Seth counted himself a lucky man to have found a partner like Evan.

"I figure we'll have been up and down the East Coast by the time we're through," Seth replied. "We're likely to see somewhere we want to stay, don't you think?"

Evan double-checked the lock on the RV's doors, then climbed into the cab of the truck. He ran a hand through his windswept chestnut hair, smoothing it back from his face. Seth loved the way the cold brought color to Evan's cheeks and the bed-rumpled look of his mussed hair. Seth's own blond hair was only long enough on top to be tousled by the wind, and growing up in Indiana, he was more accustomed to the cold than his Richmond-born boyfriend.

"Mountains or beach?" Evan asked as Seth got behind the wheel. They had paid the campground manager and said their goodbyes earlier in the morning, and now Seth maneuvered the truck out of the spot that had been their home for the past three months.

"Huh?"

"Where would you want to live," Evan said. "Mountains or beach?"

"Maybe somewhere we could get to both easily?" Seth turned onto the main road. Before he'd met Evan, Seth hadn't thought of what happened "after." He hadn't really expected to survive his self-appointed mission, hoping that he could destroy the dark warlocks and end their cycle of ritual killings. His previous boyfriend had dumped him when tragedy befell Seth's family, and Seth had briefly come under scrutiny by the cops. The police cleared Seth, but by that time, Ryan was long gone.

"That could be nice," Evan agreed. He turned toward Seth as much as his seatbelt would permit and unzipped his coat as the truck's powerful heater blasted warm air. "I haven't been to the beach in a long time. And it's crazy, given why we're going to Boone, but I'm actually looking forward to being in the mountains."

"Then let's plan to stay for a week or so afterward," Seth said. "Assuming the cops aren't on our tail."

"I'd like that." Evan burrowed into his puffy parka, looking sleepy and so very fuckable. Seth reached over and gave Evan's thigh a squeeze.

"As soon as I find a drive-through that's open, I'll get us more coffee," he promised. They had filled travel mugs that morning in the RV, but Seth knew it would take more than one dose of java to wake him up, especially since they were getting an early start on a long drive.

"U.S. or Europe?" Seth asked, picking up the conversation thread. "Places you'd like to visit."

"Hmm," Evan replied, sipping from his mug. "Both? Only not

Oklahoma. Been there, done that." His family had tried to flee bad luck, only for Evan to unknowingly head right back into the danger zone and return to Richmond, where his would-be killer awaited. "I want to go to Italy and eat all the food. And England, because I've read so many books set there. But I've also never seen the Grand Canyon or the Pacific Ocean, or the Rockies."

Seth grinned. "We have a house on wheels. It won't get us to Europe, but we can go anywhere you want to go in the lower forty-eight and Canada."

Evan put his mug in the cup holder, then reached out and took Seth's hand. "I like that. I'll start a bucket list."

They both left unsaid how much danger lay between now and then, with ten more witch-disciples left to kill, including the one who had murdered Seth's brother Jesse and started his plan for vengeance. But the warlock who had preyed on Evan's family was destroyed, as well as the one based in Pittsburgh. And, if their luck held, Seth hoped they'd handle the dark witch in Boone before he had the chance to go after his next sacrifice.

"Have you ever been to North Carolina before?" Seth asked.

Evan shook his head. "You?"

"Nope. But Milo and Toby have a favorite place to rent a cabin there. They've always talked about how much they love the area, how pretty it is. I'm really glad you're going to have a chance to meet them," Seth replied. Milo and Toby were older hunters, and they had taken Seth in when he'd been homeless, angry, and hell-bent on revenge against an enemy he only barely understood. They had taught him about fighting the supernatural, and trained him, changing his quest from a suicide mission to one he had a prayer of surviving. And somehow, along the way, they had become family.

"I'm excited about getting to spend time with them," Evan said. His expression sobered. "I hope they like me."

Seth gave his hand a squeeze. "You're hardly a stranger. You've spoken with them on the phone and on video calls. Trust me, they will love you. They know I'll be more careful, now that you're in the picture." Careful for Evan and for himself. Hunting didn't usually make for a long life, but Toby and Milo proved that a happy ending was possible. Now that Seth had found Evan, he wanted that same future desperately, enough to make him both fearless and more cautious.

"I know. But it's like meeting the family," Evan replied, dropping his voice.

"My mom and dad would have loved you," Seth said. "They were very chill about everything except when I went into the army. They were worried about me, and they had reason to be." He smiled, remembering. "Mom taught me to catch a football—she had five brothers—and how to ride a motorcycle. Dad helped me with my homework and taught me how to cook."

"Most of the things we did as a family centered around the church," Evan said quietly. He rarely spoke of his family. "Picnics and retreats and music festivals, that kind of thing. But one year, we did a road trip to Mount Rushmore. Mom had always wanted to see it. I guess she figured it wasn't frivolous because it was about history. It was nice. That was the year before they found out about me, and after that..." Evan turned and looked out the window. Seth kept a grip on Evan's hand, trying to curb his anger. He doubted he would ever meet the Malones, but if he did, Seth intended to give them a piece of his mind.

"I was going to come out to my parents when Jesse died, and every-thing went off the rails," Seth said. "Jesse had already figured it out. Hell, I think he knew before I did."

He struggled not to let self-recrimination color his tone, but that internal battle waxed and waned on a daily basis. After all, Seth had gone along with Jesse's idea to do a bit of amateur ghost hunting at a haunted bridge that rumor claimed was a hell gate. It was supposed to be a fun night spent drinking beers and making a hoax video to prank some of Jesse's friends.

Then one of the immortal disciples of a long-dead dark warlock grabbed Jesse as the next victim in a century-old cycle of ritual slaugh-ter, wounding Seth in the process. By the time Seth regained conscious-ness, it was too late. His wild story placed him under suspicion and briefly in a psych ward, until Seth learned to tell the doctors what they wanted to hear. By that time, his parents were dead, and his home had been destroyed in a fire. All he had left was the RV, the truck, his motorcycle, memories, and vengeance.

Until Evan.

"I wish I could have met them," Evan replied wistfully. "And I wish I could say the same about my folks, but…you know…"

"Yeah. Fuck them."

Evan nodded. "Right. Because we've got our own weird little hunter family now, and I like it that way."

Seth would be twenty-seven soon, and Evan's twenty-fifth birthday was coming up. Travis, Brent, and Mark back in Pittsburgh were a decade older, colleagues and mentors who were like the big brothers neither Seth nor Evan ever had. Toby and Milo, more than twenty years older, had made it clear that they saw Seth—and now Evan—as their sons of the heart. And other hunters or researchers whom Seth only knew online or on the phone left no doubt they had their backs.

But most importantly, Seth had Evan. As new and improbable as their relationship was, it filled a void that Seth hadn't known was there. And now that Evan was in his life, he never wanted to be without him.

He could only hope that Evan continued to feel the same.

"Do you think we can get good barbecue while we're in North Carolina?" Evan asked, changing the subject. "I've always heard about Carolina barbecue, and I'd like to try some."

"I imagine so," Seth replied, going with the shift. "There are a lot of craft breweries down there, too. You can be in charge of finding out where to go." He grinned. "Sample some local cuisine."

"If Toby and Milo have a cabin in Boone, they probably know all the good places." Evan sat back, and the earlier tension faded.

Seth laughed. "Oh, you can count on it! Toby and Milo like to eat. They're not much for fancy places, but they've got a sixth sense for local dives and sketchy roadhouses with the best food. The kind of place where you don't leave all your weapons in the truck, just in case. Just…never let them con you into darts, poker, or pool."

"They're that good?"

"Yeah. Back when they first started hunting, that's how they'd earn some cash when things got tight. Milo has a scar over one eyebrow he'll tell you was from a rougarou, but Toby swears it was a beer bottle swung by a guy who had just lost all his cash in a pool game."

"Toby didn't approve?"

"Oh, no—Toby was all-in as his accomplice," Seth replied, laughing. "I'm pretty sure they raised a lotta hell in their younger days. Still might, for all I know."

"I don't think my parents ever did anything even remotely wild," Evan said with a sigh. "If there was a church committee, they were on it. Fundraisers, covered dish dinners—no matter what was going on, my folks were helping run it, and I was expected to be involved." He ran a hand through his hair. "Looking back, it all seems kind of desperate and frantic. I guess I know why."

Evan's father had taken his family west from Richmond, fearing the family "curse" that claimed the eldest male in each generation. Going super-religious had been part of his attempt to atone for whatever had brought bad luck or for anything that might have displeased an angry god. Ironically, that religion had led to them throwing Evan out, practically serving him up on a plate for the dark warlock who wanted his next victim.

"They're far away, and they've got no hold over either of us," Seth reminded him. "So let's not think about them, okay? They're not a part of our lives." He didn't understand how parents could abandon a child, but he also knew that too many did. Seth wished he could soothe the mental scars caused by their abandonment, and he intended to try, knowing that he still had plenty of old wounds himself. He hoped he and Evan could heal together.

"At least this time, I'm pretty sure we know who the victim will be and the current identity of the witch-disciple," Evan replied. "That puts us way ahead of the game."

Usually, they lost time trying to work out one or both of those pieces to the puzzle, putting them at a disadvantage. Seth hoped that Evan was right, and their research would make the hunt safer and faster.

"Did you find out anything else about Kyle Henshaw?" Seth asked.

Evan pulled out his laptop, and Seth missed the warmth of their joined hands when Evan moved away. "I think you'd like him. He's studying programming, so you've got that in common."

Seth's computer abilities—both legal and illegal—helped with researching the witch-disciples, who changed their identities periodically to hide their immortality. Those same talents also enabled Seth to make good money as a "white hat" hacker for Toby and Milo's security company, helping companies stress-test their systems and keep out real threats. Like Evan's graphic design work, it was a job Seth could do from anywhere, making it possible to earn a living despite their nomadic life.

"His father went missing when his car went into a river—presumed dead—eleven years ago, older brother was a Marine, killed in the line of duty in Iraq. And the obituaries check out—oldest male either died or went missing, all the way back one hundred years. Direct descendant of Amos Henshaw, who was one of the deputies who helped hang Rhyfel Gremory for sorcery."

Both Seth and Evan had long-ago ancestors who had been part of that posse, whose good deed had inadvertently doomed a century of descendants to violent death.

"Brandon Clarke should have been the sacrifice in Pittsburgh, but we stopped that from happening," Seth mused as the highway opened up ahead of them, letting him pick up a little speed. "So we're messing with the cycle. Kyle shouldn't be in the witch-disciple's sights for a while yet."

"Only somehow, the warlock in Pittsburgh knew we'd killed the Richmond witch, and he moved up his timing."

Seth nodded. "Which is something I don't know how to get around. But the witch-disciples need to work the ritual to leech off more of Gremory's power since it's what keeps them alive. So they can't skip the sacrifice, and if they all decided to kill the next victim early, it just means their power wanes early, too."

"The witch-disciples scattered, and they've stayed spread out." Evan glanced through his notes on the screen. "We don't know if they ever got along well, even before Gremory died. I doubt they have board meetings."

Seth shrugged. "We can hope not. But somehow, the Pittsburgh witch got spooked by what happened in Richmond. So maybe they keep tabs on each other, even if they're not in actual contact. Even if they hated each other—or competed for power—they might want to know what the others are up to."

"I imagine it's like any other group," Evan said, staring out the windshield at the highway. "There are usually all kinds of alliances and jealousies going on, even if to outsiders they seemed like a team. And once Gremory was dead, there was no one to keep them in line. For all we know, they might be cheering for us to kill off their fellow warlocks, or waiting for the others to kill us."

Seth hadn't considered that possibility, and it sent a chill down his spine. "There's no way to know what the witch in Boone knows about us. But it's safe to assume we've lost the advantage of surprise."

Evan nodded. "Yeah, I agree. At least we know who the witch is this time. Current name is Ira Sturdevant, the founder of a non-profit that takes young people on wilderness adventures."

Seth snorted. "That's awfully ironic."

"That's what I thought. I traced the identities all the way back. The original witch-disciple, Albert Olsen, was a doctor. He stayed in the general area and got away with reinventing himself under other names and sticking with medicine until modern record-keeping made that too hard," Evan said.

"From there, he faked credentials to be a private nurse, an ambulance driver, and a therapist, among other jobs. Olsen—or, I guess I should say Sturdevant—seems to have stuck close to medical-related work. That made him easier to trace than the guy in Pittsburgh, who tried out a bunch of different jobs."

"Anything else about Henshaw?" Seth asked.

"Other than somewhat dropping out of school to help with the family business, his boyfriend, Steve Williams, is a trail guide. I couldn't find much on either of them online, outside of their jobs," Evan supplied. "I'm just hoping that we can still get a signal when we get to Boone, or any follow-up research is going to have to be done the old fashioned way."

"I have a feeling that Toby and Milo will have it covered," Seth assured him. "Even on vacation, I can't imagine them not having a way to connect. After all, they're hunters."

2

EVAN

Despite Seth's reassurances, Evan's stomach churned with nervousness. He knew how much Toby and Milo meant to his boyfriend, and Evan worried that the two older hunters might find him to be an unsuitable match for the man they'd clearly claimed as a son.

After all, Evan thought, *what value do I bring to the situation?* Six months of training had improved his skills, taught him a few more rote spells, and helped him understand more about the kinds of things that went bump in the night. Despite it all, Evan knew he had a long way to go before he could match Seth's abilities, and he worried that he could be the weak link that cost Seth his life.

The trip from Pittsburgh to Boone would take most of the day, and while Evan offered to take a turn behind the wheel, he knew that Seth preferred to drive. When he wasn't chasing down loose ends about the Boone situation on his computer, Evan planned to doze in the passenger seat, but dark dreams woke him more than once, earning him worried glances from Seth.

"Hey." Seth's voice roused Evan from his thoughts. "Whatever you're thinking—let me in. Don't keep it to yourself."

"I just don't want to let you down," Evan admitted.

"You won't."

"You don't know that."

"I know that you've saved my ass more than once," Seth replied. "And that was before we spent the last three months doing more training." He reached out to take Evan's hand. "I trust you. I believe in you. There's no one I'd rather have beside me in a fight. And I love you."

Evan's throat tightened. "I love you, too. And I want to be here, doing this, with you. It's just…I'm not really the action hero type."

Seth chuckled. "And I am?"

"You were in the army. You're a soldier. So, yeah."

Seth sighed. "I went into the army to get away from a bad breakup. Not exactly the most noble reason. I did okay, I guess. I was lucky enough to come home. But I knew I wasn't going to make a career out of it. Some guys, they get in, and they know that's where they're supposed to be. It becomes their home and family, like they were born for it." He shook his head. "It was never that for me."

"I made okay money, working at the bar." Evan looked at the road instead of at Seth. "But something was always missing, you know? What I did didn't really matter. This…" He gestured to mean the two of them, hunting, the search for the witch-disciples. "It makes a difference. Saves lives. Stops a hundred years of killing. It just seems like fate could have picked someone who was better prepared."

Seth laid his hand on Evan's thigh, solid and warm. "Hunting doesn't work like that. You've talked to Travis and Brent and Mark. They didn't train to be a hunter from the time they were kids. They lost people, and it changed them. And from that point on, they learned on the job," Seth said. "Just like you."

Evan managed a wan smile. "If this were a TV show, I'd want to skip to the finale, where we ride off into the sunset."

"I wish we could," Seth admitted. "But I'm afraid there's no fast-forward on real life."

The day grew warmer as they drove south, though that proved to be relative since Boone was in the North Carolina mountains. When they stopped for fuel and to stretch their legs, Evan still wanted his coat, although the wind had died down and the air no longer held a bitter chill. Evan went to get hot coffee and takeout burgers for them, while Seth pumped gas. As he walked back across the truck stop plaza, he couldn't help admiring how good Seth looked.

Seth's jeans set off his long, muscular legs, and the parka rode up in the back, giving Evan a glimpse of his fine ass. Even a down coat couldn't hide those broad shoulders, and the wind sent blond strands of hair flying. He marveled again at his luck, finding a man like Seth to share his life with, despite the craziness and danger.

"How much longer?" Evan asked as they got back into the cab.

Seth checked the app on his phone. "About two hours. Unless we hit traffic, we should be there in time to meet up with Milo and Toby for supper."

"Have you heard from them?" Evan sipped his coffee, enjoying the warmth. He liked the days they spent driving, cocooned in the bubble of the truck cab, like their own private world. Even as a child, he'd enjoyed long car rides, preferring the trip, in some cases, to actually arriving at the destination.

"They squabble like the old married couple that they are." Seth fondly rolled his eyes. "They're both around fifty, and while they're definitely in good shape, they worry about each other. When they called me from the road, Milo was telling Toby he needed to pull off and let him have a turn to drive. Toby was on Milo's case about not taking some medicine on time. I swear they forgot they even had me on the phone."

"Are they both okay?" Evan hadn't met Seth's surrogate fathers yet, but he'd enjoyed the calls and video chats, and he knew how much they meant to his boyfriend.

"You know that quote on how it's not the years, it's the mileage? Hunting goes hard on people. Fifty is old for a hunter," Seth replied. "It's not a job that comes with a retirement plan." He cast a sidelong glance at Evan as if he thought about adding to his comment and then changed his mind.

"You're not scaring me off," Evan replied. "I told you—I'm in this for the long haul." Parts of his new life terrified Evan, and he knew that Seth had his own fears, though he hid them well.

"It's like any combat role," Seth said. "After a while, the injuries add up. You can only break bones or dislocate joints so many times before they don't ever fix quite right. Scar tissue, concussions—the body can only take so much. Both of them have gotten mauled, bitten, stabbed—Toby's got enough scars on his back that it looks like a highway map." He let out a long breath. "And that's on top of the normal things that start going wrong when you hit your fifties and onward."

"Why don't they retire?"

"I think Milo wants to," Seth replied. "At least, I think he's ready to scale back on hunts. They have the security business and could still help the hunting community with lore and research, like Simon Kincaide does. But Toby's stubborn, and he's been doing this for so long, I don't know if he can imagine not doing it."

"You're worried about them."

"Of course I am." Seth looked uncomfortable as if he were breaking trust giving voice to his concerns. "But there's only so much I can say. As much as it's nice to have backup, and as much as I want to see them, I tried to talk them out of coming to Boone because I don't want them getting hurt." He grimaced. "If you hadn't noticed, I lost that argument."

Evan searched for the right words to frame his thoughts. "Maybe you just have to trust them to make the right decision at the right time."

Seth glared at him. "You're supposed to be on my side."

Evan held up his hands in a "don't shoot" gesture. "Hear me out. I had one grandfather who planned his retirement date, and the other one got laid off a year before he was supposed to finish up. The one who got to finish his projects, say goodbye, have a party, and leave on his own terms did just fine. Moved to Florida with my grandmother and as far as I know, they're still living the good life."

"And the other one?" Seth's tone suggested he already guessed where this story was heading.

"Not so much. It bothered him that they didn't think he could cut it anymore—his words for it—and he had to leave in the middle of things he'd been working on without being able to wrap them up or hand them off," Evan said. "He was angry and bitter, and he started drinking too much, and then his health went downhill. He was dead in a year."

Seth looked away, and Evan wondered if he'd spoken out of turn. Finally, Seth nodded, and some of the tension left his shoulders. "I guess you're right," he conceded. "I just want them to get a chance to enjoy themselves a little and not be in danger."

"I imagine they feel the same way about you," Evan replied, arching an eyebrow. "Did you ever think that maybe they won't feel like they can really quit completely while we're still hunting the witch-disciples? Even if they aren't part of the hands-on hunt again?"

The look on Seth's face told Evan that hadn't crossed his mind. "You really think that's it?"

Evan shrugged. "Could be. And I get that you're worried about old injuries catching up to them, slowing them down, but don't forget that they've been at this long enough to know how to use brains instead of brawn. After all, I don't imagine it's easy for them to let you go off and do this, knowing what they know."

Seth looked like he might argue, and then he let out a long breath. "It's just that...you and them, it's all I've got. I don't want to lose any of you. Sometimes I think maybe I should let this go, just walk away. Let someone else hunt the witch-disciples." He didn't look at Evan, and the tension in his jaw suggested how hard it was to talk about this.

"But then I realize that they'll just come after both of us again if we don't put an end to this. And all the other descendants, for maybe another hundred years. God help me, I can't let that happen, and I don't think I'd survive losing any of you, and it twists me up so I can't sleep."

This time, Evan placed a reassuring hand on Seth's leg. "We're going to see this through, you and me, and probably Milo and Toby too. But we've got friends. Resources. We're not going to do it alone. And then, when it's over, we'll figure out where we go from there."

He gave Seth's thigh a squeeze. "And the next time you can't sleep, let me know. I have some ideas on how to burn off all that nervous energy."

They rolled into Boone in the late afternoon, and Evan gawked at the mountains and the picturesque tourist town. "This is a really beautiful place. Hard to believe Sturdevant's been here under everyone's noses, killing people."

"I love the mountains," Seth agreed. "Where I grew up in Indiana, it's all flat cornfields. Anything's better than that."

"That's why I came east, after getting dragged off to Oklahoma," Evan said. "I'm not really into tumbleweeds."

Seth followed the directions Milo had sent, leading them out of town and down a side road toward a campground with cabins and RV spots that offered a great view of the mountains. "There it is," Evan said, pointing. "Cabin 22. So I guess that's the camper spot next to it that they snagged for us."

Seth maneuvered the RV into position and parked the truck. In minutes, Evan had the trailer hookups connected, while Seth uncoupled the truck. Just as they finished, two men hurried out of the cabin.

"Seth! Evan! You made good time." The speaker was a tall, broad-shouldered bear of a man whose dark hair and beard were peppered with gray. Evan guessed that was Milo. Beside him was a slightly shorter, but equally fit, dark-skinned man with a shaved head, full beard, and the wary gaze of a soldier, who had to be Toby.

Milo and Toby took turns folding Seth into a bone-crushing hug complete with back slaps, while Evan stood to one side, unsure what to do. Seth broke from Toby's embrace and stepped away, closer to Evan.

"Milo, Toby—this is Evan Malone."

Evan expected handshakes but was instead swept into Milo's strong arms that gripped him like iron bands. He'd barely caught his breath before Toby did the same.

"Evan. So good to finally meet you," Milo said, as if Evan and Seth had been together years instead of months. Then again, it felt as if they had packed a lifetime of experiences into that short time.

"Likewise," Evan replied, feeling a bit overwhelmed, although he was pleased by the warmth and welcome.

"Come on in," Toby said, as Milo led the way into the cabin. "I've got chili in the slow cooker, and cornbread in the oven. We figured that way dinner would be ready whenever you arrived."

The cozy rental cabin had a more home-like feel than Evan expected. A large mission-style couch and matching chairs and coffee table created an inviting space in the living room, while a farm table with benches in the kitchen provided both dining and workspace. He took a deep breath and felt his stomach rumble at the smell of the food.

"You're set up already?" Seth asked as Toby and Milo worked around each other with practiced ease in the small kitchen, reminding Evan of how he and his boyfriend navigated the RV's tight spaces.

"Yep. We put the main computer in the bedroom, out of sight," Toby replied with a smirk. "I know it looks like we're miles from civilization, but we picked this spot because there's a cell phone tower disguised as a pine tree about a mile away, and with a little finagling, we've got all the juice we need."

Whatever dubious legality might be involved with that "finagling" obviously didn't bother ex-cop Milo, who ladled chili into bowls as Toby set out salad and toppings. "Get what you want to drink out of the fridge, will you, Seth?" Toby asked. "We've got soda and beer chilled. Brought some hard stuff for later, or medicinal purposes, whichever comes first."

Seth grabbed cold beers for the four of them, and they settled at the table. Seth sat close enough for his thigh to press against Evan's, silently reassuring him. Evan bumped his shoulder, appreciating the gesture. They dug into the chili, and Evan realized just how hungry he was.

"The chili is delicious," Evan said. "And so is the cornbread."

"The cornbread is my grandma's family recipe," Toby replied. "Milo got the chili recipe from someone he used to work with."

"So what did you think of Pittsburgh?" Milo asked, directing his question to Evan.

"It was cold," he replied. "I think I might like it better in the summer. We did a little sightseeing, once the work was done, but I imagine there's a lot more to do in better weather."

Milo nodded. "I'm from Buffalo, so I always thought of Pittsburgh as 'south,' but I guess it's a bit of a change for you."

Evan nodded, realizing that even a safe topic like the weather could be a minefield. "I grew up in Oklahoma, and it gets plenty cold there. Richmond was a lot warmer, but it had its own problems." *Like a psycho immortal warlock set on sacrificing me to a dark witch.*

"There was a lot less wind than in Indiana," Seth added, "at least if you stayed away from the rivers. But still damn cold."

Toby took a swig from his beer. "I'm from Georgia, and I swear I only get warm enough in July most places."

Milo gave his husband a wink. "I'll warm you up any time."

Evan noted the matching silver bands the two men wore. Seth had told him that Milo and Toby had been together for more than twenty years, an admirable accomplishment for any couple, but particularly given the danger of being hunters.

Seth cleared his throat. "We had a good drive down," he said, getting Evan off the conversational hook and proceeded to talk about the noteworthy sights they'd seen on the way and recount a few funny things that had happened at the truck stops.

"We worked a hunt in Boone about fifteen years ago," Milo recalled, setting his empty bowl aside. "Vampire. It was autumn, and the mountains were so beautiful, we always said we'd come back sometime just for fun."

Toby savored a bite of buttered cornbread before answering. "And since this is still technically a hunt, I'm holding you to that," he reminded his partner. "I want to come back in high summer when everything's green. Sit on that deck and look out over the mountains and read all day."

"You mean like that time we went up to the Finger Lakes in New York?" Milo raised an eyebrow. "To the campground you promised me was not haunted?"

Toby groaned. "You're never going to let me forget that, are you?"

Milo grinned. "Nope." He turned to Seth and Evan. "We had just finished up a job around Ithaca—in those days, we traveled all over the place—and Toby got it into his head that he wanted to stay a while. Pretty countryside, so I didn't mind. We needed some downtime."

Toby snorted. "You'd been bitten by a ghoul, and I'd been clawed by a wendigo, so we were in pretty sorry shape. You left that part out."

Milo's eyes narrowed. "It was included in the idea of 'downtime.'"

"Yeah, sure it was." Toby's eyes glinted with fondness even if his tone held a challenge.

"Am I telling this story, or are you?"

Toby finished his beer. "Fine with me if you do the telling—just get it right, old man."

Milo's eye roll was positively dramatic. "Anyhow," he said with emphasis, "as I was saying…" he glanced at Toby as if expecting a challenge, but Toby's expression was the picture of innocence. "My dear husband here said he'd find us a nice, quiet place to stay. A lot of small towns didn't have their rentals on the internet yet, back then—this wasn't too long after we got together. So Toby called around to some agencies. Told me he got us a great deal on a little cabin off the beaten track." He gave Toby another look that Evan could only classify as the stink eye.

"That much was true," Toby replied, unperturbed.

"So we get there," Milo continued, "And the place is nice, but it doesn't look like anyone's been there in a long time. We take a look around—everything's in working order, the location is good if a bit remote, and we can't figure out why the rental agent practically gave it away."

"You have to understand, this was before you could log in from anywhere," Toby interjected. "So it wasn't like it is now, where you can just Google everything. And as it turned out, the rental agent had been less than truthful with me."

Milo made an unflattering noise. "Yeah, you could call it that."

Toby ignored him. "Once all the equipment in the house checked out, we figured maybe it was just the location that made it less popular. We were tired and hurting, so all we wanted was to sit on the deck, drink some beer, and put our feet up."

"But?" Seth prompted.

"Everything went well while the sun was up. We'd brought groceries with us, and I'm in the kitchen fixing dinner, while Milo took a walk."

"No, I went out to gather wood for the fire," Milo corrected.

"Whatever. Milo was outside the cabin, I was inside," Toby continued. "Then I heard sounds on the back porch, and I yelled for him that dinner was almost ready. A minute later, he comes through the front door and asks if the food is done yet. I thought he was pulling my leg."

"I'd been around back and hadn't seen anyone on the porch. But I thought I heard a car pull up in the front and thought maybe a neighbor came to check on the place, since it didn't get used much," Milo added.

"That was just the beginning," Toby took up the tale. "Nobody around back, no car in the front. I went into the kitchen, and all the burners on the stove had been turned off, and the water was running in the sink."

"And I went out to get the wood I'd chopped, and my axe was sticking out of a tree, instead of on the ground where I'd left it," Milo said.

"Which is where we figured out that we got the place dirt cheap because it was haunted," Toby admitted. "Though, of course, the rental lady didn't know we were hunters."

"Then, as soon as the sun started to go down, the spookapalooza really got underway," Milo interrupted. "We heard someone whistling down the hallway, but no one was there. The electric lights flickered. The radio suddenly came on, blaring. It was like a horror movie that decided to hit every cheesy kind of ghost activity."

"Which just goes to prove that some ghosts aren't very original," Toby said. "But it was also clear that the 'pranks' were shifting from just trying to scare us away to threatening us, and we were both just on our last nerve."

"We had all our stuff out in the truck, because we always carry it," Milo continued. "And at this point, we were pissed. I put down the salt and iron filings, while Toby broke out the holy water, and we start going through the house with an EMF meter, looking for spikes. We finally zeroed in on this wooden duck decoy that must have belonged to the former owner. Toby threw it in the fireplace and lit it up, and this old guy came out of the wall and went for his throat."

"While I'm being force-choked by a fucking ghost, my dear husband is trying to keep the fire from going out on that bloody duck," Toby supplied. "And dinner is starting to char in the oven."

"The stupid carved duck wouldn't burn," Milo protested. "I ran into the kitchen, grabbed a bottle of vegetable oil, and poured it all over the decoy, then tossed in my lighter. I'm pretty sure that the flames went all the way to the top of the chimney, and I thought it might burn the cabin down in the process."

"Then he grabs one of the iron fireplace pokers and slashes it through the ghost, which means I can breathe again. But since the duck hasn't turned to ashes and the old guy was a stubborn coot, he keeps popping up in one place or another all over the living room, and Milo is swinging at him like it's some kind of ghostly Whack-A-Mole," Toby added.

"By the time that fucking duck was finally gone, I felt like I'd played the World Series all by myself," Milo complained. "Toby was trying to help, but every time the old man would pop out and pop back in again, he'd manage to slug Toby. I don't know why he focused on Toby when I set that damned duck on fire."

"And every time the ghost grabbed me, I got colder and colder," Toby said, "like he was leeching all my body heat. I'm shaking and shivering and having my own personal winter, while the fireplace is roaring like an inferno."

"Just as the ghost bastard gets his hands on Toby's neck again, the last bit of duck went up in smoke, and the ghost went with it," Milo recounted.

"But since he'd been almost solid a moment before, and I was trying to fight him off, I was suddenly pushing back against nothing, and fell flat on my ass," Toby finished.

"What did you do once the ghost was gone?" Evan asked as he and Seth gasped for air, after laughing hard enough to bring tears.

Milo gave him a look like it was the dumbest question in the world. "We salvaged what was left of dinner and cleaned up the mess in the living room. Then I put down a nice thick salt line, and Toby burned protective herbs in the fire and said an exorcism, for good measure."

"You stayed?" Seth asked, eyes wide.

"Of course we stayed!" Toby replied. "We'd gotten the place dirt cheap, and now we had sweat equity."

"But then the rental agent called on the second day, and she said she was checking to make sure everything was in order. But I'm sure she wanted to see if we'd run for the hills," Milo said, laughing. "We told her it was perfect—quiet and very peaceful. I wish I could have seen her face, because I bet she was wishing that she'd charged us more."

"I didn't lose any sleep about getting a good deal, because we un-haunted the cabin for her, which meant she'd be able to rent it for more money and more often," Toby finished.

Milo slipped an arm around his husband. "Of course, by the time the old duck guy was taken care of, Toby looked like he'd gone ten rounds with a boxer, and I'd opened up my stitches. Not to mention Toby also had the beginnings of hypothermia."

Toby leaned into Milo's side and gave him a peck on the cheek. "You warmed me up just fine."

Milo gave him a fond look with a wicked gleam in his eye. "I did, didn't I?"

"TMI, guys," Seth protested, wiping the tears from his eyes. He reached under the table and took Evan's hand. Evan finished off his beer and sat back, happily full from the delicious meal and finally losing the edge of worry about being accepted by the two older hunters that had dogged him since they started out from Pittsburgh. "Before you ask, we've already checked out the whole campground," Toby told them. "No spooks. But we set wards and put down salt lines in the cabin and around your site, too, just in case. We'll put wards on the RV too, now that you're settled." He gave them a wink. "For the record, Milo booked us here, so if you have any complaints, it's not my fault."

After dinner, they moved into the living room. Seth and Evan took turns updating Milo and Toby on what they had learned about Ira Sturdevant and Kyle Henshaw.

"Sturdevant has moved around from town to town in his different lifetimes," Seth added. "Right now, he's got a reputation as a publicity-shy do-gooder, so he's going to be impossible to attack directly. If we can persuade Kyle that he's in danger, we might be able to draw Sturdevant out, get him to make a move so we can take care of him out of the public eye."

"That's all good intel," Toby said, leaning against Milo on the couch. "As far as we've been able to tell, no one has tried hunting these warlocks before, so how they'll react is a wild card, and a lot of it is going to come down to individual personality. If Sturdevant was a doctor, he might be more confident than some, and that could make him bolder in response to a threat."

"More dangerous?" Evan asked.

Milo shrugged. "They're all dangerous. The trick is going to be figuring out the individual disciple's most likely response to a threat. Now that we're in town, sniffing around, we'll have to make our move fairly soon, before he knows we're after him."

"And hope the witch-disciples don't keep tabs on each other," Toby added.

They made plans for the next day and finished a second round of beer. Evan found himself starting to drift off, and it looked like Milo was also losing his battle to stay awake.

"I think we're going to call it a night." Seth stood and pulled Evan up with him from the love seat where they'd been sitting. "We can get a jump on things early in the morning."

"See you at eight." Toby waved goodbye and gently poked Milo to let him know it was time to close up. Evan and Seth set their empty bottles in the kitchen and let themselves out.

The campground was quiet, and while the temperature had fallen, Evan still felt warm from dinner and the beer. "Look at those stars," he marveled craning his neck to see the clear sky. "You can see so many more of them out here."

Seth wrapped an arm around Evan's shoulders and looked up. "Jesse and I used to camp in our backyard when we were kids," he said softly. "Our town was small enough that we could still get a good view, especially late at night. He'd have loved it here."

"I wish I could have met him. He sounds like he was a great guy."

Seth nodded. "He was. You'd have gotten along well. I think about him all the time. Still can't believe he's gone."

Evan threaded his arm around Seth's waist. "It's okay to talk about him," he said, realizing that in the time they'd been together, Seth had shared almost nothing about Jesse except the circumstances of his death.

"We were always so close, growing up. He wasn't happy about me going off to the army. Thought it was an extreme reaction to a breakup, and I guess it was. I wonder, sometimes, if anything would have gone differently if I'd stayed in town. Maybe Gremory's disciple would have been able to tell us apart, and he wouldn't have gotten the wrong brother."

Evan shivered, but not from the cold. He knew Seth still blamed himself for Jesse's death, even more so because as the eldest, Seth was the intended target. But as much as Evan wished Jesse could have been saved, he couldn't bring himself to wish under any circumstances that Seth had died instead. *Maybe that makes me a bad person. Seth would have offered his life in exchange for Jesse's in a heartbeat. Seth would have died, we'd have never met, and I'd be dead now, too.*

"Because of that mix-up, you're going to stop the killing," Evan said quietly, choosing his words carefully. "Hundreds of people will live—and go on to have children of their own who won't need to be afraid of the family 'curse.' And as one of those people, I'm very grateful."

He reached up to touch Seth's cheek, and Seth pulled them together, dropping his head for a kiss. His lips were warm, and his mouth closed over Evan's, seeking comfort, reassurance, absolution. Evan slipped his hand into Seth's short hair, as the kiss grew more urgent. He tried to let his reaction be the affirmation Seth needed, reminding him that they were alive and together.

"Come inside," Evan murmured. "I can take your mind off the hunt for a while."

The RV was only a few steps away. Seth fumbled with the key, and Evan slipped close behind him, rutting against Seth's ass. Coats and jeans got in the way, but he knew his boyfriend got the message. The door opened and they practically fell inside.

"Bedroom," Evan murmured. He came up for air from a heated kiss, realizing how desperate Seth was for the distraction of lovemaking. "I'll make you feel real good."

They slowed down just long enough to leave coats and boots by the door, locking up behind themselves. The trailer's heat had kicked on, so the interior held only a slight chill. Evan led Seth toward the bedroom in the front, and pushed him down onto the mattress, crawling on his hands and knees until he could lie down over Seth.

Evan bucked his hips, feeling Seth's erection through his jeans, knowing Seth could feel his own hard cock. He ground against Seth's pelvis, keeping his lover pinned with his body. Evan claimed Seth's mouth with his own, nipping at his lips.

He pushed his hand down between them, working open their jeans, shoving down fabric until he could wrap his fingers around their hard and leaking cocks. Evan let the pre-come slick his palm and set a hot, desperate pace. He loved the way Seth kissed back like he was starving, and how he dug the fingers of one hand into Evan's ass to pull them together.

They were both close, breathing hard, covered in a sheen of sweat despite the cool night outside. Seth's face was flushed, and his eyes darkened with arousal. This wasn't the time for slow and gentle. Evan knew they both needed release and connection, hard and fast, primal confirmation that they were alive.

Seth came first, arching beneath Evan, rutting into the channel of his grip. His eyes narrowed, and his mouth opened as release rushed through him. Just seeing Seth's expression of ecstasy brought Evan the rest of the way, and his thrusts lost their rhythm until he cried out and felt the warmth of his own come add to Seth's cooling spend.

Evan waited until Seth was watching, and then withdrew his hand, running his tongue up his seed-slicked fingers, sucking them into his mouth. All the while he kept eye contact, rewarded by the moan Seth let out as his eyes widened. Feeling bold, Evan reached between them again and scooped more onto his fingers, then pressed them into Seth's mouth. Seth closed his lips and sucked, running his tongue up and down Evan's fingers. It was so damn sexy that Evan felt his spent cock twitch.

Seth pulled him close and kissed him tenderly, a coda to the rough coupling from minutes before. Evan saw a tear slip from Seth's eye and brushed it away.

"Here. Now. Us. Together," Evan said, his voice huskier than usual.

"We'll get your vengeance. But we deserve something for ourselves when it's all over. We've earned this. And I'm going to move heaven and hell to keep it."

3

SETH

"THAT'S SOME VIEW." SETH HELD ON TO THE METAL RAILING AT THE TOP OF Flat Top fire tower, as the wind gusted around them. The steel framework creaked but held steady. Next to him, Toby looked a little green around the gills, and Seth remembered that his mentor hated heights.

"I guess so," Toby agreed half-heartedly. "Not sure how much good something like this does anymore, what with satellites and drones and airplanes now."

"Back in the day, there were rangers who lived at these towers during the high-risk season, and they kept watch in case a fire broke out," Seth replied, from the information he and Evan had researched online.

"So they could call for reinforcements? Like in that movie about the cursed ring?" Toby grinned.

Seth rolled his eyes. He knew Toby was pulling his leg. "Yes. Just like that," he replied sarcastically. "More like they could sound an alarm, get people out of the area, and maybe dig a big fire break trench to try to contain the blaze."

He turned slowly in a circle to see the countryside, which was just beginning to wake from winter slumber. Even now, forest sprawled to the horizon, mostly unbroken by towns and roads. It didn't take much to imagine how isolated this spot had been a hundred years ago, and the solitude the rangers of that time must have prized to take such a posting.

"It's beautiful, but I don't even want to think how cold it is in the winter." Seth pulled his coat tighter as the wind whipped past them.

"Maybe that seemed like sanctuary to Amos Henshaw, back in the day," Toby mused. "It's a long way from Brazil, Indiana."

"There was a forestry school around that time, down near town, and there's always been logging in these mountains," Seth replied, his attention still captured by the view. "Probably let ol' Amos earn a living, and he must have thought he'd run to the ends of the earth."

"Too bad it wasn't far enough."

"Sturdevant showed up as a doctor for the logging company," Seth said absently. "Amos probably never got a good look at him when they hanged Gremory. We don't even know for sure the witch-disciples were nearby. Probably weren't—or they didn't try too hard to save their boss."

"Wouldn't be surprised if they ran away to save their own skins," Toby replied. "And they wouldn't care now about Gremory if he wasn't the key for them to live forever."

Another moment passed as they looked out over the Blue Ridge Mountains. After growing up in the flat cornfields of Indiana, Seth found mountains of any kind to be a wonder.

"This is a great place to take pictures, but it's too public for Sturdevant to use for his murders," Seth said. "Although I bet you can see an awesome sunset."

"Too damn cold to be romantic, if you ask me," Toby groused. "Freeze your nuts off."

There wasn't really a good reply to that, so Seth led the way down the open metal stairs toward where they had left his truck. "We can drive closer to the old forestry school, but we'll still have to hike in the last mile or so."

Toby shrugged. "Fine with me. Beats sitting around." Neither Milo nor Toby looked like they spent much time sitting, but Seth knew better than to argue.

They climbed into the truck, and Seth started the engine. A few other cars had pulled into the fire tower's lot, and a line of tourists and hikers formed at the base of the steps. He suspected that their next destination would be far enough out of memory and absent from the hiking guides to give them plenty of privacy to investigate.

"So…you and Evan. How's that going?" Toby's casual tone and the way he looked out the passenger window told Seth his friend was trying not to put him on the spot.

"Good. Really good." Seth hoped Toby read the sincerity in his tone. "You know how he stepped up to the plate on training, and I told you how he saved my ass in Pittsburgh."

"I didn't ask about the hunting, son," Toby said. "I meant, between the two of you."

Seth nodded. "You know I don't have a lot of experience with relationships," he answered. "At least, not good ones. But…he keeps talking about making plans for what we want to do after we track down all of Gremory's disciples. Where we might want to settle, or whether we keep on traveling and hunting. Future stuff. That's a good sign, right?"

Toby smiled. "I'd say so. When Milo and I first paired up, it took me a while to figure out whether he was in it just for the hunt, or me."

"That's not how he tells it."

Toby's snort surprised Seth. "Yeah—not how he tells it *now*. But he was a cop when I met him, and times were different back then. He was so far in the closet his best friend was a talking lion."

That made Seth grin. "Really?" It was hard to imagine his out-and-proud surrogate father ever being different.

"Fortunately, you can't really imagine how it was. That's a good thing. But twenty years ago, it wasn't just that Milo couldn't have been a gay cop; he probably wouldn't have been alive if anyone suspected. He had a lot to make peace with, taking up with me. Finding out that monsters were real. Hunting them. And then navigating feelings he'd spent a lifetime locking in a box and burying as deep as he could."

That made Seth catch his breath. At least Evan hadn't had any qualms about being gay and out. He knew that guys like Milo and Toby had fought for every win. He knew that—but every time he heard the stories, they made him angry and humble and sad.

"How did he decide? You know. To come out?"

Toby's smile was sad. "To me? Or to the world? Because those are two different things. I had accepted who I was and who I loved, but that didn't mean I was wearing rainbow shirts. There were places you could do that and lots more where you couldn't. I don't think it had ever occurred to Milo that he could let that side of himself out anywhere. He didn't expect me to pick the lock on that closet door of his."

Seth wasn't sure he wanted to know whether Toby had seduced Milo—that was a little TMI.

Toby seemed to guess his thoughts. "No, not like that," he said, growing a bit red in the face. "At least, not at first. But there were places I took him where we could be honest about hunting, and some where we could be honest about being gay. A few where we could do both. I think that once he got a taste of not having to hide, he liked it. And after you've had a bit of freedom, it gets real hard to go back."

Seth nodded. "How long were you together before you were...together."

A fond smile lit up Toby's face. "About six months. I pushed, but not too hard. Didn't want to spook him. He had a lot on his plate, adjusting. There were times when it was helpful, what he knew as a cop, but it went hard on him when we had to break the law for the greater good. I'm not a patient man. But for Milo, I figured I could wait a lifetime." His smile changed to a smirk. "Fortunately for both of us, he's not a patient man, either."

They drove in silence for a few minutes. "I love Evan."

"Kinda figured that."

Seth shook his head. "No, I mean, this is different. He's it for me. Forever." He snuck a glance in Toby's direction. "I want the kind of forever you and Milo have. What my parents had. Rings, certificate, the whole enchilada." He chuckled. "Maybe no white picket fence. At least, not for a long time."

When Toby didn't say anything, Seth went on. "I can't believe I went into the army because I thought Ryan broke my heart. After what Evan and I have been through, when I thought I lost him..." Seth's voice trailed off, but he knew Toby took his meaning. "It's just not the same at all. Not even close."

"It's like that, when you meet the right one," Toby said with a wistful tone. "I think I knew after the first few weeks with Milo. He says now that he did, too, but it took him a helluva long time to come around to doing something about it. I'd pretty much figured that it wasn't going to happen."

"What changed?"

Toby sighed. "We fought off a creature, out in Illinois. Weren't sure what it was, beast of some kind. The thing got away, but it bit me. I thought it was a werewolf, and I told Milo he had to put me down, so I didn't hurt anyone."

Seth's raised eyebrow spoke volumes.

"He wouldn't do it. And he wouldn't let me do it myself. Damn fool locked me up in an abandoned jail until he could track the monster and kill it, to figure out what it was."

"Since I've never seen you go furry during a full moon, I assume it wasn't a were."

"Nope. It was a Black Shuck—a dog creature—we'd never seen before. I was stunned. Milo, apparently, had a moment of truth, because he let me out of that jail, grabbed me by the collar, and kissed me on the lips." He laughed. "I don't know which one of us was more surprised. But once Milo makes up his mind, he sticks with it. We were together."

Seth smiled. "That makes a great story."

"Yeah, it does," Toby agreed. "And most of the time, we get along pretty damn well for a couple of old codgers."

"You're not old."

"Hunter-years are like dog-years," Toby said. "We age fast in this business, between what we see and can't forget, the things we have to do sometimes, and the damage we take. Goes hard on a man. If you stay in the game as long as we have—and I hope you don't—you'll see. Too many of us go it alone, and if the monsters don't get us, the alcohol will. Having a hunting partner helps a lot. Having a life partner— that's like winning the lotto."

"Yeah. It is. And I want to give Evan that happily ever after he keeps talking about," Seth replied, speaking those thoughts aloud for the first time. "When I got into this, I didn't really plan to outlive the witch-disciples."

"I know that," Toby said, giving him a stern look. "Milo and I both knew."

Seth swallowed hard. "I thought I was a better liar than that."

"Not hardly, son."

"Now, with Evan, it's different. Everything's different. I think…I think I can let Jesse go, finally, when this is done."

"You don't have to do it all yourselves," Toby replied. "If you haven't figured that out already."

"It was good, working with Travis and Brent and Mark in Pittsburgh," Seth replied. "Great to have you and Milo here. And that guy in Myrtle Beach, Simon Kincaide, he knows everything about the lore. It helps a lot."

Toby grinned. "It's family. Not the regular kind, the kind you find for yourself. And the hunters that live long enough to retire—like I said, they don't do it on their own. You're on the right track."

A few minutes later, Seth pulled off the main road onto a barely-there dirt road and went as far as he could, with weeds scraping the undercarriage. He stopped when the saplings in the middle of the road became too sturdy to drive over. "I guess we go on foot from here."

They got out of the truck, and Seth slipped his Glock into the waistband of his jeans. Seth had steel and iron knives in sheaths on his belt, and the pockets of his jacket were filled with salt and iron filings, plus a flask of holy water. Those tools wouldn't keep them safe from everything, but combined with whatever Toby might be packing, Seth felt sure they could cover most of what was likely to be lurking in the woods if the rumors of hauntings were true.

"The forestry compound was a spin-off from the school over in Asheville," Seth said. "When the guy who started it had a big falling out with his patron, he came over here and tried to do it on his own. He even found a new supporter."

"Let me guess. A doctor."

"Yep. One of Sturdevant's old identities," Seth confirmed. "The school ran for about twenty years, although there were reports of some deaths." He shrugged. "Nobody thought too much about it at the time. After all, logging is dangerous, and the woods are, too."

"And in that time, one or two of the Henshaw men died?"

"One went missing in 1912, and another died in a logging accident in 1924–poor fellow had completely bled out by the time they found his body, and he'd been gnawed on by enough critters it was impossible to identify him." His tone made the sarcasm clear.

"You think this might be where Sturdevant kept dumping bodies when he changed identities?" Toby asked, fighting his way through kudzu and brambles.

"It's possible. That's what we've seen with the other two disciples. They use somewhere familiar for their burying grounds."

Toby slapped a hand against his neck. "Damn bugs. I doused myself with spray, and they're still biting."

"Welcome to the wilds of North Carolina."

If the hike had been just for fun, Seth could have let himself appreciate the scenery. The woods were quiet, just starting to come into leaf but still far ahead from how things had been in Pittsburgh. He took in a deep breath, loving the smell of loam and leaves. When he wasn't chasing monsters, he actually enjoyed a walk in the forest. Seth couldn't remember the last time he'd done that, just for fun. Maybe when they caught Sturdevant, he and Evan could come back here for a day.

"Up there," Toby said, his voice quiet.

Seth snapped back to watchfulness, although he didn't pull his gun yet. He'd rather not have to explain his weapon to any park rangers who might be around, although he really didn't expect to see any out here. They stepped over the rusted remains of an iron fence, barely a collection of a few remaining uprights and cross pieces.

"Doesn't look like anyone's used the place in a while."

The "school" was a rustic collection of wooden buildings that were well on their way to collapse after a century of disuse. Two of the smaller sheds had already fallen in on themselves. The main classroom stood, weathered and gray, though it listed to one side as its foundation gave way.

"Seems like a strange place to run a school," Toby mused.

"Forestry was all the rage, after George Vanderbilt and Frederick Law Olmstead showed the world what a planned landscape could look like over at Biltmore," Seth said. "Olmstead is the guy who designed Central Park in New York City. They made nature look better than it did naturally, and the idea caught on. Everyone wanted to learn about it, and work for the next rich guy with money to spend."

"And Sturdevant sold them a bill of goods."

Seth went around one side of the rickety school as they talked, while Toby circled around the other. "Yes and no. We know he was here to keep tabs on the Henshaws. But the guy he hired to teach actually did turn out a few students who did big things. Of course, most of them just ended up being gardeners or working for the Park Service. But maybe even that was a step up. There wasn't much around here in those days."

The lightheartedness Seth felt on the walk had vanished, replaced by a sense of foreboding. They'd had no indication that they had been followed, but Seth couldn't shake the feeling they were being watched.

He and Toby fell back into a comfortable habit, not needing words to coordinate. Gestures and glances were enough, born of long practice. An hour later, they had covered the old school grounds thoroughly, even sneaking a peek inside the buildings that hadn't collapsed.

"Nothing," Toby said when he met up with Seth in the middle of the grounds. "No bloodstains on the floor, and it doesn't look like anyone's torn up the vegetation to get a vehicle around here in a long time."

Seth took a canister of salt from his pocket and tramped down a large enough circle in the grass that he and Toby could stand inside. He walked clockwise around the circle, laying down a solid line of salt for protection.

"Time for step two. Gonna talk to some ghosts. Cover me." Seth closed his eyes and concentrated. Part of his training with Milo and Toby had been learning some rote magic—spells that didn't require any special talent, just will and intent, plus plenty of practice.

He spoke the words he had memorized that made his will a weapon. A frisson of energy ran through him as he cast the summoning spell into the forest, seeking restless spirits. The spirits couldn't cross the salt line, so—at least in theory—he and Toby were safe.

If everything went right.

"Look," Toby whispered. Orbs of light danced in the shadowy spots as the afternoon sun waned. *Fairy lights. Will-o-the-wisp.* Over the centuries, orbs like that went by many names. Seth's spell wouldn't hold the spirits long, but he hoped it would be sufficient to learn more about the dark witch they planned to kill.

"We want to stop the murders," Seth said as at least a dozen orbs bounced in the air. "We know about Ira Sturdevant…and his other names. We're here to end this. But we need your help."

The balls of light stretched and changed shape until gray ghosts ringed Seth and Toby. All men, most in their twenties or thirties, some older. "They can't all be related to Henshaw," Toby murmured. "There are too many of them for the twelve-year cycle."

"Unless he found some other way to steal energy from murder, in between," Seth replied. "Blood magic, death magic. He wouldn't be the first."

"Holy shit. There are a lot of them."

"Maybe they aren't all victims," Seth suggested. "Maybe some of them are witnesses."

Seth turned back to the ghosts. "I'm sorry to have woken you," he said. "I'm sorry that you died before your time. But I need to talk to the ones who were murdered by the doctor. The rest of you—go in peace."

All but six ghosts blinked out of sight. "There should be eight, maybe nine," Toby said. "If he's kept to the cycle."

"None of them look like Kyle. They might not be Henshaw men."

"Some ghosts hang around where they were buried," Toby said. "Others stay close to where they died. The Henshaw men could be near where the ritual is done."

Seth looked to the spirits who had moved closer to the salt circle. "The man who killed you, he's a dark witch. Your deaths made him stronger. He's going to kill again, unless we stop him. Please— anything you can tell us, it could help."

The ghosts regarded them with unreadable expressions, not hostile but definitely unwelcoming. This place no longer belonged to the living. Seth and Toby were trespassers.

A cold wind whipped through the clearing, rustling the branches and stirring the tall grass. Seth worried for a moment that the ghosts intended to break the salt line and attack them, but when he blinked, the spirits had changed, presenting themselves with their death wounds, their clothing dark with blood.

The ghosts drew back, then closed ranks and lost definition until they were a gray cloud. The spirit cloud moved toward the old school building, and for a moment, they massed just outside the door, then vanished.

"Well, would you look at that?" Toby said, pointing.

Crudely carved into the weathered wood was the word *"Nowhere."*

"I don't know what that means, but I think we've worn out our welcome," Seth said, as all his instincts urged him to flee.

"I think you're right."

The salt circle was safe, but they couldn't stay there forever. The late afternoon sun wouldn't last much longer, and Seth had no desire to be out in the woods at night. While he hoped the ghosts of the forestry school weren't dangerous, they'd all met violent deaths— whether by accident or intent. That could make for vengeful spirits, too many for Seth and Toby to easily handle on their own.

Seth didn't feel like testing their luck.

"If we're both carrying salt and iron in our pockets like I taught you," Toby said, arching an eyebrow, "it's going to be hard for ghosts to touch us. That should get us back to the truck." He pulled his iron knife, and Seth did the same, knowing that iron disrupted the ghosts' limited energy.

"Just in case," Toby added, raising his blade.

A low growl sounded from the forest beyond the school buildings, where the shadows were deepest. A pair of red eyes glowed, and Seth could just make out the darker silhouette of an unnaturally big black dog.

"Damn. That's a Shuck, can't ever forget that beast. This just keeps getting better," Toby muttered.

"How do you want to play this?" Seth glanced between Toby, the Shuck's red eyes, and the path back to the truck.

"Lead the way, I'll cover our asses." Toby pulled a sawed-off shotgun from the inside of his jacket.

"Will that work?"

"It damn well better. Run!"

Seth sprinted toward the lane, mindful not to outpace Toby. He held a fistful of salt in one hand and the iron knife in the other. Three ghosts closed on them from the front, none of them Henshaw men. Maybe they were bitter about the circumstances of their deaths, but that wasn't anything Seth or Toby had a hand in, and Seth felt no guilt slicing through their gray shapes as they tried to block his path.

Contact with the ghosts made his skin tingle and chilled him to the bone, nearly making him drop the knife. He gritted his teeth, tightened his grip on the salt, and spun just as a spectral hand reached out toward his throat. The knife cut through the apparition, and it winked out, only to appear on the other side, waiting for another chance.

The shotgun boomed behind him as Toby took aim at the Shuck. Seth didn't dare turn; he had three vengeful ghosts waiting for his attention to lapse.

"Keep running!" Toby yelled as he blasted the monster again. Seth could have sworn he heard the snick of teeth and then the rumble of a deep growl.

Seth nearly tripped over the old broken fence when inspiration struck. He yanked one of the iron uprights from the ground and held it in front of him lengthwise, creating a barrier between him and the ghosts. "Come on!" he yelled to Toby. In response, Toby racked more rounds.

Toby let out a yelp as the black beast howled. Seth turned just in time to see the creature sprint at Toby, knocking him to the ground. The shotgun blast went wild.

Seth threw the handful of salt at the ghosts, then swung the iron rod and threw his knife. The rod struck the creature in the head, and the knife buried itself in its shoulder. The monster growled and stalked toward Seth, bleeding and unsteady but still dangerous. It tensed, ready to attack when the shotgun fired once more.

This time, Toby's aim caught the creature in the head, and the red eyes lost their gleam. The big, hairy beast stumbled, then fell to one side.

"Run!" Toby shouted as Seth reached out a hand to help him to his feet.

Both men sprinted toward the truck, which seemed farther away than Seth remembered parking. Briars tore at their clothing and tendrils of kudzu snagged their feet. They were panting and winded when they reached the truck, but by then their spectral pursuers had vanished. To Seth's relief, the monstrous Shuck did not resume the chase.

Seth and Toby threw themselves into the cab. Seth started the truck and slammed it into reverse, turning around to see where they were going as he steered.

"Try not to get us killed!" Toby warned.

Seth ignored him until they were halfway back to the main road when he finally slowed. "Do you think you killed it? The creature?"

Toby shrugged. "Not sure you can kill something like that, not for good. Maybe if we'd have stopped and cut off the head, burned the carcass. I didn't feel like hanging around." He wiped his forehead. "The body probably just vanished. It's more of a manifestation than a real animal—doesn't mean they aren't just as dangerous before you put them down."

Seth took deep breaths, trying to still his thudding heart. "Why would something like that be at the forestry school?"

"For all we know, it was there long before the school was built. There's a lot of strange things out in the woods, stuff that was there long before people came. Most of the old tribes, they knew the bad places to avoid, and they steered clear. We're not usually that smart."

Seth didn't relax until he pulled onto the asphalt. "Do you think it meant something? The word the ghosts wrote. 'Nowhere'?"

"I hate how dead people can't speak in whole sentences," Toby grumbled. "It's always riddles. I imagine 'nowhere' has a meaning, at least to ghosts. But to us? It could be anything."

Seth watched the road. Out here, the night was darker than he was used to, without streetlights or a city on the horizon. The blacktop ribbon vanished into the shadows just beyond the reach of the headlights.

"If I were a ghost, and someone said they were going to off my killer, and I had one shot to send a message, I wouldn't waste it," Seth said. "So 'nowhere' is a message. Maybe Evan can make something of it."

The sunset meant some light remained in the sky, but tall trees on either side of the lonely road made it much darker where Seth and Toby drove. They still had several miles to go before they returned to a main road, and in the mountains that still didn't guarantee a full interstate highway.

In some places the road squeezed between massive clefts blasted into the mountainside. On other stretches, the highway hugged the rocky cliff while the other side dropped off to the bottom of the valley. Seth's black Silverado truck felt like it took up the whole lane, with little space to spare, and more than once he found himself holding his breath as if that would make the big vehicle narrower.

Just past the fire tower lane the road angled down. The last of the light had faded, and Seth's headlights were the only illumination. He didn't see any headlights in his rearview mirror, and nothing ahead as the road wound its way down the mountain. Seth turned to say something to Toby when bright high beams nearly blinded him. All he could make out were the lights and the shadowy shape of a semi-truck.

"It's on the wrong side of the road!" Toby yelled.

"Hang on!"

If he tried to veer around the truck, Seth knew they stood a good chance of going off the side of the road or slamming into the rock wall. This stretch of road had no shoulder, no pull-offs.

"What are you doing? Are you trying to get us killed?"

Seth didn't answer. He gripped the wheel white-knuckled, narrowed his eyes against the bright lights, and drove a collision course with the big truck, hoping Toby wouldn't try to grab the wheel.

The lights bore down on them, filling the cab with light. Toby muttered prayers and curses. In the last seconds, Seth hoped his hunch was right and braced for impact.

The headlights vanished, and a cold, dark shadow passed over the Silverado like the hand of Death. The truck disappeared.

"What the everlasting fuck!" Toby exploded.

Seth knew if he eased his grip, his hands would shake, and he didn't dare take his eyes off the winding road. It had been challenging by day, and now was treacherous in the dark. His heart pounded, and he had held his breath for so long he felt light-headed. When a scenic pull-off finally opened off to one side, Seth pulled in and leaned forward, resting his forehead against the steering wheel.

"How did you know?"

Seth didn't have to ask what Toby meant. "There were a few spots where I could see the road ahead, and I hadn't seen a semi. No lights, no place for one to come on from a side road. And I knew if I jerked the wheel, we'd go over the side. I bet on it being a manifestation, and hoped for the best."

"You're just damn lucky I don't have prostate problems," Toby said, wiping the sweat from his forehead. "Or you'd need to clean the upholstery."

Seth didn't want to linger in the pull-off, but he needed to quell his nerves so he didn't cause a wreck. He grabbed a bottle of water from the back seat and chugged it, then took a few more deep breaths before heading back to the road. A glance at Toby confirmed that the other man still looked shaken.

"Damn. That was good driving, but once was definitely enough," Toby said when the road flattened out again.

"Agreed." Seth paused. "I want to see what we can find about tractor-trailer accidents on that stretch. We had ghosts, a Shuck, and a phantom-semi try to kill us today. That's three too many in my book."

"No argument from me on that. But the real question is, why? Did we just run into a bunch of surly spirits, or did someone sic them on us?"

"I don't know," Seth admitted. "But I'm going to find out."

4

EVAN

"I NEVER REALLY THOUGHT ABOUT WHERE CHRISTMAS TREES COME FROM," Evan admitted as he and Milo drove into the countryside.

"Welcome to North Carolina, one of the biggest growers of Christmas trees in the U.S.," Milo replied.

"Not exactly a quick turnaround," Evan mused. "I guess that's why Otter Creek Nurseries sells a lot of other stuff."

"Family business—multiple generations, on Kyle Henshaw's mother's side. As long as they keep planting new trees, there should be more to replace what's used."

Milo drove and pulled the blue pickup into the gravel lot. "Follow my lead," he murmured as they walked through the gate into the rows of plants. April in the mountains was still cold, so the rows weren't as full of flowers as they would be in a few weeks, but Evan and Milo had taken that into consideration.

"Can I help you find something?" A red-haired young man close to Evan's age strode out to meet them. He wore a canvas jacket bearing the name of the nursery over worn Levis and scuffed work boots. The hard work of hauling heavy plants and landscaping materials made for good exercise; he looked lean and solid. Evan recognized Kyle Henshaw immediately from the pictures they'd found online.

When Seth researched me, I thought he was stalking. Now I do the same thing for a good cause. Funny how perspective changes.

"I'm Kyle. What are you looking for today?" Kyle's smile was sincere, but Evan didn't miss the dark circles under the man's eyes. He hoped Kyle had plenty of family help running the business.

Milo shook hands, as did Evan. "I'm Milo, and this is my nephew, Evan," he said. "My sister-in-law wants to get a jump on her container gardening this year, and we wanted to see if you had some herbs and lettuce plants she could nurture in her sunroom until she can move them outside."

Kyle's smile brightened. "Sure thing. What kind of herbs does she like to cook with?"

Evan trailed behind, letting Milo keep up the conversation about his fictional relative and her love for making homemade marinara sauce. As Milo kept Kyle talking, Evan kept his eyes open, observing Kyle and getting a feel for the nursery.

Evan's mom had never done much gardening beyond a few bedding plants and window boxes, but he'd helped out a neighbor once who needed to bring back garden supplies. Otter Creek was a medium-sized nursery, Evan supposed. Not as huge as the big commercial growers, but large enough to give the national chain hardware stores a run for their money with healthier plants and more selection.

A wooden house had been repurposed into the nursery office as well as a shop for decorative wares like birdbaths and wind chimes. In the distance, Evan could see neat rows of pine trees and various types of bushes. He caught a glimpse of several people hard at work tending the plants and moving wheelbarrows full of mulch, and he wondered if they were all related.

"You're right that it's early to plant outdoors," Kyle was saying to Milo, "That's why we still cover everything at night. But in a few weeks, you should be fine, as soon as we're past the risk of frost."

Milo asked questions about basil and oregano, bibb lettuce, and arugula. Kyle answered knowledgeably, offering helpful tips and making suggestions, clearly at home with the topic. A brown mutt padded out from between the bushes to trot alongside Kyle, who reached down to scratch the dog's ears without losing a beat in the conversation.

Still, Evan thought he saw signs of strain. The old house-office could use a coat of paint. The sign by the road was weather-beaten, and the parking lot had bare spots needing a new load of gravel. Evan figured that the family likely reinvested just about everything they made into the business, and cosmetic touches weren't at the top of their priorities.

Was Kyle's father hands-on with the nursery? How much strain had it added when he was killed? Evan's father had said little about the deaths and disappearances in their own family, but the impact couldn't be hidden. The dead men left behind struggling families, leading to tales of debt or hardscrabble efforts to avoid bankruptcy. Seth hadn't said much about what the witch-disciples' murders had done to his extended family, but Evan suspected the stories would be similar.

Generations of hardship wrought on the descendants of the unlucky posse that killed Rhyfel Gremory, a hundred years of lives upended, families damaged. All because the witch-disciples considered immortality to be their due.

"It's is the first time I've been out here. Nice place," Milo said, making conversation as he lugged a wagon with a big bag of potting soil and a dozen plants Evan couldn't identify toward the little gatehouse that served as the checkout.

"Thanks," Kyle replied, and his pride in the business shone in his eyes. "It's been in my mom's family for fifty years. We're not as big as some, but we treat our plants like family," he said, and while he blushed a bit at the hokey tagline, Evan had the feeling it was true.

"You really know your stuff," Milo said. "Were you an Ag major?"

Kyle shook his head. "Actually, I was a computer science major. But I...took some time off. Working on finishing up online."

Evan read between the lines on what Kyle didn't say. His other brother had died in the line of duty in Iraq five years ago when Kyle would have been a sophomore in college. Evan wasn't surprised that the tragedy brought Kyle home to console his mother and help with the business. Kyle's willingness to do so, at the expense of his own dreams, made Evan think even more highly of him. He resolved to keep Sturdevant from causing any more heartache for the Henshaws ever again.

They all looked up when a motorcycle's engine sounded from the parking lot. A few minutes later, a young man with short black hair walked into the nursery grounds with the familiarity of someone who belonged there. Evan didn't miss the glance that passed between Kyle and the newcomer. Too much heat in that gaze to be a family member. This had to be Steve Williams, Kyle's boyfriend.

"Good morning," the biker said, including Milo and Evan in his greeting as well as Kyle. "I came to help unload when the truck gets here. And whatever else."

Kyle's smile slipped. "Steve, you don't have to use your day off—"

"I told you, I want to help," Steve answered, squaring his shoulders to make it clear he wouldn't be dissuaded. He held out a box. "I brought doughnuts," he added, offering some to Milo and Evan first, and then to Kyle. Kyle sighed and rolled his eyes, then took one and bit into it, rewarding Steve with a blissful smile.

"Okay. You can stay. But just because you brought doughnuts," Kyle teased. He glanced toward Milo's wagon. "Let me get them rung up and loaded into their car. The delivery truck should be here soon."

Steve headed into the office, clearly at home. He had an athlete's build, with broad shoulders and a trim waist, a bit shorter and more heavily muscled than Kyle.

"I'm sure Evan and I can manage if there's a shipment you need to unload," Milo said as he handed several bills across the counter to pay for their purchase.

"The truck isn't here yet, so it's all good," Kyle assured him. "Besides, helping you load is part of the Otter Creek experience," he added with a grin.

The three of them chatted about the weather as they loaded Milo's truck, making short work of the task. Evan found himself genuinely liking Kyle, who seemed like a good guy. That just made him more determined to find Sturdevant and put an end to the murders.

Kyle waved goodbye from the parking lot as Milo and Evan pulled away. Evan couldn't resist waving back.

"We've got to save him," Evan said, turning toward Milo.

"I agree."

"Nephew, huh?" Evan teased.

Milo grinned. "I figured it raised more questions not to say something. That's my answer, and I'm sticking to it."

"What's Toby going to say when we show up with plants and dirt?" Evan glanced back through the window at the load in the bed of the truck.

"What he always says when I go out unsupervised with money," Milo replied. "A string of impolite words starting with 'fuck.'"

"Where to, now?" Evan settled back into his seat.

"We drop off the plants at the cabin, and then swing by the local Historical Archive," Milo answered. "With Boone and Blowing Rock being small towns, there's less information online than in big cities. I want to see what we can turn up on Sturdevant and his former aliases that might help us nail the bastard."

"You have a cover story in mind?"

"Sure do. We arrive separately, pretend we don't know each other. I'm a reporter who is up from Charlotte, working on an article about the old forestry school for some kind of anniversary write-up. You came over from Asheville because you promised your grandmother you'd do some genealogy research for her on family that had been in this area, and she doesn't get around so well anymore, the poor dear."

"I'm starting to see where Seth gets his penchant for stretching the truth."

Milo let out an exaggerated sigh. "You wound me!" He favored Evan with a big smile. "I knew I'd find a way to use my high school drama experience."

The Archive was an old brick building that looked like it might have begun life as a store. They parked a distance away and took different routes to get there, with Evan pausing to get a cup of coffee before ambling over.

He forced himself not to look for Milo when he approached the archivist. A woman who looked like his grandmother sat behind the desk. She peered at him over her reading glasses, which were connected to a beaded lanyard around her neck. A nameplate in a brass holder said she was "Mrs. Albritton."

"May I help you?"

Evan hoped he managed to look charmingly confused instead of just clueless. "I sure hope so. I promised my grandma that I would try to find records for her stepmother's side of the family. They used to live in this area." He dropped his voice confidentially. "She did all this herself until she fell last winter and, you know how that goes."

Mrs. Albritton warmed a bit at that. "I understand. And I hope she's up and around soon. It's nice of you to do the legwork for her."

Evan tried for an aw-shucks shrug. "She's my grandma," he replied as if that explained everything. "She wanted me to look up births, deaths, and marriages. I guess she lost track of that side of the family, and she really wants to be able to fill out the family tree."

"Depending on how far back you need to go, that's going to be in the microfiche room," Mrs. Albritton told him.

"She wanted me to go from 1900 on, and she gave me some names to start with," Evan replied. "Campbell, Lee, and Henshaw," he added, having pulled two of the most common local names from an online directory to obscure the real target.

"Do you know how to use microfiche?" A thin, painted-on eyebrow arched in challenge.

Before he had started hanging around with Seth, the answer would have been "no." But part of his training during the winter months had been ways to tease out information from all kinds of sources, including ancient technology like microfiche and card catalogs.

"Grandma taught me," Evan said, pleased that he seemed to have surprised her. Mrs. Albritton didn't fool him. She reminded Evan a lot of his sixth-grade teacher, and he bet she could be a real dragon if she didn't like someone.

"Good for her," Mrs. Albritton replied. "Doing real research is almost a lost skill these days."

"Where is the microfiche room?"

She pointed toward the far corner. "Microfiche is down those stairs, in the basement. That's where you'll also find the newspaper 'morgue,' but you shouldn't need to handle any of the old papers, since every-thing from 1898 on is on film, and we've had an intern digitizing the papers from 1980 forward."

That was more progressive than Evan had expected, for a small town that couldn't have a big budget for such things. Then again, volunteers could move mountains. "Do you have a map of the building? In case I need to find something else?"

She handed him a photocopied floorplan. "First floor is rotating exhibits, local art displays, and the video archives. There's also a computer tied into all our digitized resources. Second floor has books by local authors, census, and scientific data, and photo archives. I'd suggest starting with microfiche, and then making a list of things you want to look for in census and photos, depending on how much time you have."

"I'll take your advice." Evan hoped the smile he used to finagle extra dessert out of his grandmother worked on Mrs. Albritton. She didn't quite return the expression, but the stern set of her mouth softened just a bit, so he took that as a win.

He glanced from side to side. "Is it always this quiet?"

"Except when there's a school project due," she replied, not hiding her distaste. "Or the Genealogy Club has its monthly meeting and group research time. There's a reporter around here somewhere, so don't be startled if you run into him." She eyed Evan's backpack. "And I'll have to look in your bag on your way out. Just a precaution."

"Of course," he agreed, happy for the heads up so he could remove his knife, salt, and holy water flask.

Despite getting access to the inner sanctum, Evan felt Mrs. Albritton's gaze follow him as he headed for the steps. He wondered if the old building was haunted and whether ghosts liked the solitude or got bored. *I'd much rather haunt a movie theater. At least there'd be something to do.*

The basement was a single room with industrial-grade vinyl floor tiles and white walls. Metal shelves lined the perimeter, with shelves full of binders that he assumed held old newspapers, and dated containers of microfiche. Two huge, ancient machines for reading the film hunched against the far wall. The overhead fluorescent light gave everything a harsh, blue cast.

Milo definitely wasn't on this floor, so Evan figured he had gone straight to the census data and photo files. He pulled some of the containers of microfiche from the shelves and powered up one of the reading machines, which worked like an old-fashioned projector coupled with a magnifier. As much as he wanted the distraction of background music, Evan didn't want to be caught unawares if someone else—friend or foe—approached, so he only slipped one earbud in, and kept the volume low. It was enough to cancel out the hum of the machine and the rattle-clank of the old heating system and water pipes.

Back in school, Evan hadn't been much for research, even when a project demanded it. But Seth had shown him how to find all kinds of interesting tidbits, while Brent Lawson, a private investigator, had taught both of them the kinds of things to look for that sent up a red flag. Travis Dominick had helpfully taught both Seth and Evan a rote spell for neutralizing a cursed book, which Evan fervently hoped he never had to use.

Since Milo had promised to text when he thought they should go, Evan settled in without worrying about the time. He had brought his tablet to take notes; after a few awkward fumbles with the dials and knobs, he managed to get the hang of paging through the old sheets of film.

At first, nothing jumped out at him. The old newspapers transferred to film were readable, even if the tiny print made his eyes tear. Day after day revealed the kind of mundane news Evan expected from a small town—births, deaths, marriages, businesses openings, community events, and potluck dinners. Evan knew the key events he was looking for—Henshaw deaths on the twelve-year anniversary date, information about the forestry school, and anything he might turn up about Sturdevant's other personas of the places he worked.

Evan faced the challenge like a scavenger hunt, one with a life-or-death prize at the end. Time passed quickly, and it wasn't until he reached the papers for 1924 that he realized that some of the consecutive issues were missing.

"Shit," he muttered, backing up to 1912, and then jumping ahead to 1936, all years where there should have been a Henshaw death. In each case, the key section of film was either too damaged to read or missing.

"That's not good," he grumbled. His online research had given him a few other dates for things he hoped he could find more information about—especially the tuberculosis hospital Sturdevant had worked at back in the 1920s, and a local mansion reportedly built by one of his early alter egos. Once again, the film was blurred beyond legibility or gone.

"Once is a coincidence. Every friggin' time is a conspiracy." Evan noted the missing dates, growing more frustrated. Just in case, he checked the physical newspaper files with their fragile, yellowed sheets. He found that they included copies that were more recent than Mrs. Albritton had suggested, but even so, crucial pages had been removed.

To be safe, Evan checked all of the twelve-year murder dates, allowing a cushion of a few months. In every case, the information had been purged.

"Son of a bitch," he growled, gathering his things and powering down the machine. Evan texted Toby that he was wrapping up and headed upstairs. A glance at the time told him it was past noon, which explained why he was so hungry.

"Find what you needed?" Mrs. Albritton didn't look up from the papers on her desk, but she watched him out of the corner of her eye.

"I found a few things," he said, "but I was surprised that so many records were either missing or damaged."

"I don't know what you're talking about. Our collection is complete." The sharp denial—without even asking for details—told Evan that she either knew or suspected something she didn't want to tell.

"Maybe I just didn't do it right," Evan covered, giving his best peace-keeping smile. "I'll check with Nonna and maybe I'll be back." He let her peer into his backpack and hoped she didn't ask him to turn out his coat pockets, since he had stashed his weapons and questionable items there. She dismissed him with a nod.

"That room is set to close for renovations starting this weekend," Mrs. Albritton told him. "I'm not sure how long that will take."

Oddly convenient, Evan thought. "Oh well. Then I guess I'll have to wait until it opens back up," he said. "Thanks a lot."

He forced himself not to hurry out the door, but he could feel Mrs.

Albritton's gaze boring into his back as he retreated, and wondered if Milo had any better luck.

Milo met him at the truck. "Any luck?" he asked as they got in.

"Yeah, but most of it's bad," Evan replied. He told Milo about the missing and smudged films, and the older man nodded.

"There were items missing out of the census and photo archives. In some cases, the whole page had just been ripped out. Other times, there was a listing in the catalog, but the picture was gone."

"You think Sturdevant is trying to erase himself?"

Milo shrugged. "Seems the likeliest possibility. He wouldn't have had to do it all at once. Could have done it a bit at a time, or had someone else take care of it."

"The other two disciples didn't bother," Evan pointed out.

Milo thought on that for a moment while he drove. "They were in bigger cities. Easier to blend in, get lost, be overlooked. A place like this, that's harder to do. While you can laugh off a resemblance, it would be more likely someone would turn up with a photo or awkward questions. It might just be because Sturdevant had to hide in plain sight."

"I don't understand why the witch-disciples stick around," Evan said. "Why not just come in, kill the descendant, then leave town for twelve years? Safer that way."

"I've got a theory about that," Milo replied. "Don't know how we'd prove it. My bet is that the witch-disciple has to stay within a certain distance of where the ritual is performed to keep the benefits. Might even be that the ritual space becomes more powerful over time, the more the rite is done there. It's just a guess, but magic often has a built-in little gotcha that limits the effects."

Evan considered that, then nodded. "Could be. I figured that they might just also want to keep a close eye on their next victim. That way they could interfere if necessary, to keep him nearby."

"Which the warlock in Richmond didn't do when your father moved to Oklahoma."

"I've wondered about that. Maybe that warlock wasn't as good about details. Or maybe somehow, he figured he could influence me to go back." Evan stared out of the window. "I thought it was my idea to go back to Richmond. But I guess I'll never know for sure."

"It doesn't matter." Milo spared a glance in Evan's direction. "He's dead and you're not. Don't spin your wheels worrying about it."

"Sturdevant probably moved around just enough to keep people from being suspicious," Evan said, not wanting to think too hard about the other issue. "And he's better than average at covering his tracks. But we still don't know whether the disciples communicate with each other—and know we're gunning for them."

"I'd be surprised if the witch-disciples were best friends," Milo said. "The kind of people who gravitate to a leader like Gremory want power. And that means they don't share well or play nicely with others if the boss isn't around to make them behave. My bet is that they cooperated while Gremory rode herd on them, and they went every man for himself when Gremory died. More so for some than others, maybe."

"Guess we'll find out," Evan replied.

Conversation paused as they pulled up to order at a burger joint. Once they had their food, Milo found a parking lot where they could have a view of the mountains while they ate.

"So how are things going, with you and Seth?" Milo asked with his mouth full.

Evan smiled. "Good. Really good. At least, I think so. Why?" He didn't know Milo and Toby well, and he hoped they thought he was good enough for the man they'd taken in as their almost-son.

"Just checking in, that's all. No reason to be worried. The thing is… I know what it's like, trying to make a go of a relationship with a hunter."

"Yeah, I guess so." Evan sighed. "Was it complicated, when you and Toby got together?"

Milo snorted. "Before or after he kept trying to drive off and leave me?"

"After."

Milo finished his burger and wadded up the paper wrapper. He pulled a French fry from the bag and ate it before he spoke again.

"Toby got into hunting after his first husband was killed by a rougarou."

"I didn't know that he'd been widowed," Evan said. He frowned. "But how? That was more than twenty years ago."

Milo made a face. "Yeah, okay. Not legal 'husband' back then, but as close as people could get. Commitment ceremony. To Toby and Ray, it was the same as being married." He paused. "They'd gone hiking, and the rougarou stalked them. Killed Ray—Toby's husband. Clawed up Toby, too, but he managed to call for help. The rangers and the police tried to tell Toby it was a bear, but Toby knew what he'd seen. He found some old-timers who trained him and went after it. Killed the sucker, too," Milo added, a note of pride in his voice. "And kept on hunting. Sound familiar?"

Evan nodded.

"That was a couple of years before I met Toby. He saved my bacon, because the disturbance I thought was a kegger turned out to be ghouls," Milo said.

Evan had heard this part. Milo used to be a cop, and he'd met Toby when a routine call turned out to be anything but.

"Toby had gotten hurt real bad, and he needed help, but the damn fool wouldn't go to a hospital—you know why." Too many questions and answers no one would believe. "So I had a split second to decide what to do. Turn him in, and go about my life? Or leave my cruiser behind, patch him up, aid and abet, break a bunch of laws, deep-six my career, and hare off with a total stranger to hunt creatures no one else thought was real." He flashed a big grin. "Guess which one I picked?"

"I know the feeling." Evan had done something similar, taking off with Seth after only knowing him for four days in the wake of killing the witch-disciple.

"Thing is, Toby had walls up when I met him. I'm talking twelve-foot-thick stone walls with electrified razor wire on top," Milo replied. "He didn't want to get anyone else killed, and he didn't want to care about anyone like he cared for Ray."

"What happened?"

"Well, once he figured out that I wasn't going away, he graciously allowed me to stay as his hunting partner. I wanted more from the beginning, but I knew he wasn't ready for that. He pretended he didn't notice any of my hints. I let him think I was still in the closet. That gave him 'plausible deniability,'" Milo added, smirking.

"What changed?" Evan found himself leaning forward, totally into the story.

"A werewolf—or at least, that's what we thought it was," Milo replied, sobering. His eyes took on a haunted expression. "We were hunting something else—can't remember what—and the son of a bitch attacked us out of nowhere. It was Toby's worst nightmare, happening all over again. Only this time, he saved me—but he got bitten in the process."

"By a werewolf?"

"We weren't sure. Never got a good look at it. But it was around the right size. Toby, the damn fool, went all self-sacrificing on me. Wanted me to shoot him before he could turn and hurt anyone. I didn't like that idea. So he offered to do it himself. I liked that idea less."

"I'm guessing you had a better plan?"

Milo shook his head. "I was fucking terrified. And I had no idea what to do. I'd fallen hard for the guy, and he just wanted to give up. I locked his ass in an old abandoned jail and went out to hunt the thing. I needed to be sure." He sighed. "Thank God I did, because it turned out to be a Shuck—a black dog creature. I brought the body back to show him. And when I let him out of the cell, I kissed that man within an inch of his life." A smile touched his lips. "And he kissed me back."

"Would you have shot him? If it had really been a werewolf?"

The question hung in the air between them. "I don't rightly know," Milo finally answered. "I seriously thought about letting him bite me and going off to be wolves together. Maybe we could have managed. Toby wouldn't have agreed to it. He would have done the job himself if I didn't. I'm glad I didn't have to make that choice—because I don't believe I would have walked away, either."

Milo was silent for a moment, and he kept his gaze out the windshield at the mountains. "Toby was in a bad place when I met him. I've always thought that if we hadn't started hunting together he might not have made it too much longer. A lot of hunters are really looking for 'suicide by monster.' I'm certain Toby was." He turned to meet Evan's gaze. "Pretty sure Seth was, too, before he met you."

Evan caught his breath. *Was that true?* He searched his memories, but the whole thing had happened so fast, it hadn't left time for introspection.

"Maybe you didn't see it at the time," Milo went on, "but when he showed up at our place, early on, he was nothing but rage, vengeance, and pain. We trained him as best we could, but we were both afraid for him. I think Toby saw himself in Seth and knew how dangerous he was to himself. Let me tell you, we're both very happy you and Seth are together. You're good for him."

"I love him, Milo," Evan confessed. "I know we came together fast, and sometimes we argue, but I really think he's my forever guy. I want that bad enough to fight for it."

"You think he doesn't?"

Evan shook his head. "That's not what I meant. I think he does. I really hope so. Sometimes, we talk about what we'll do…after." Milo would know what he meant. After the witch-disciples were dead. When the hunt was over. "Maybe get out of hunting, or just help with training and information. I mean, monsters aren't going to just go away. But…we'd be together. For good."

He caught the glint of Milo's wedding ring when the other man shifted in his seat. Evan knew it was too soon to want that, but it didn't change how he felt. After all, he and Seth hadn't even been together for a full year, and there had been plenty of…distractions…in that time. But maybe someday…

"I'd like to see both of you get out and stay out when this is all done," Milo said. "Too many guys push their luck. They hate to give up the thrill, and then one day the luck runs out. Toby and I argue about this a lot."

"You do?"

Milo nodded. "Well, I argue. Toby grunts at intervals to make me think he's listening. He knows I'm not going anywhere without him. But fifty-something isn't kind to hunters. Body doesn't bounce back the way it used to. We get slower, but the monsters don't. There's a lot we could do to help from the sidelines. Research. Teach. Create a better network among hunters so people don't have to keep reinventing the wheel. Maybe run a store for hard-to-find stuff hunters need."

He shrugged. "You get my drift. We could still be involved, but leave the ninja stuff to you young guys," he added with a grin that didn't quite reach his eyes.

"Is it a bad thing that I'm not sure I want to keep hunting until I'm fifty?" Evan couldn't imagine spending the next quarter-century chasing monsters.

"I'd say that proves you're a smart man," Milo said. "Finish off the job, do some hunts on the side in between, but when you're done with the witch-disciples, be done. You'll have earned your right to live out the rest of your life in peace."

Evan chuckled self-consciously. "Some days Seth seems to agree. Other days, I'm not sure."

"Let's see where he is when you've gotten the last of those warlock assholes," Milo answered. "I'm also real glad you've started to pull in help. I had trouble getting Toby to do that, and we barely squeaked out of some situations because of it. Working with Travis and Brent, getting help with lore from Simon and connecting with that Mark guy up in Pennsylvania—that improves the odds for your surviving this mess."

"It's kinda nice to be able to hang out with people who really understand," Evan agreed.

"Yeah. Sorta like the way combat vets stick together. No one else knows, unless they've been in the trenches."

Their next stop was a place called Mystery Mountain. Evan hadn't expected the side trip, and he gave Milo a puzzled glance.

"There are a bunch of these places in tourist areas all over," Milo said as he locked the truck. "Most of them are just optical illusions that make people think they're seeing things that can't be true. Like when the shorter person looks taller, or water looks like it's flowing uphill."

"So why are we here?" Evan remembered seeing brochures in restaurants about places like this, and he had to admit that he was curious to visit knowing what he now did as a hunter.

"Toby and I make a point of checking them out. It's usually harmless fun. House of mirrors stuff, sleight of hand," Milo replied. "But sometimes it's more. Bones. Relics. Cursed or haunted objects. That's a danger. Then we make arrangements to take care of the problem, so no one gets hurt."

"Arrangements?" Evan's first thoughts ran to burglary, and he thought Toby seemed very off-handed about breaking and entering.

"Yeah. Simon knows a guy who buys the bad stuff and makes it disappear. All on the up-and-up. Before you ask—I don't know what he does with it, and I don't think I want to know."

The building had a carnival air to it as they approached the front door, with signs and banners promising amazement. *"You will BELIEVE!"* *"#1 Place to visit."* *"Feel the Wonder."*

"Wouldn't it make more sense to have a real medium with you?" Evan asked in a whisper. "Someone like Simon or Travis? I'm not going to be much good."

"You've got eyes, and you know the kinds of things to look for," Milo replied. "And if nothing's wrong, we'll have a good laugh about it when we meet up with Seth and Toby."

"Welcome to the place where time stands still. Make your vacation last forever!" The brightly colored sign next to the ticket booth seemed ominous to Evan instead of enticing, and he was glad for the salt in the pocket of his sweatshirt and the small iron knife in a sheath on his belt.

Milo paid for their tickets and a teenage boy ushered them into a hallway that was really a suspended wooden path with railings that led through a rotating metal drum. The inside of the drum was black, splattered with glow-in-the-dark paint and illuminated by black light. Evan had to admit the low-tech effect was pretty trippy.

"What makes the Mystery Mountain different?" A sign just inside the door read. *"Is it a magma vortex? An alien spaceship buried deep underground? High levels of dielectric bicosmic radiation? We don't know why the rules of physics don't work here—but we do know that you will be amazed and astounded!"*

Inside, the attraction was part oddity museum and part weird science. Milo headed for the oddities, leaving Evan to wander through the illusions. Despite the tacky-tourist signs outside, the interior was clean and painted in fun—if garish—designs. Still, he couldn't shake the feeling that something wasn't quite right. The upbeat eighties song on the PA system sent a shiver down his spine.

Since Milo had wandered off, Evan had to use the cardboard standee provided to help visitors get the illusion experience of their relative heights being wrong or a weird sense of moving when he was standing still. He dropped a tennis ball, and sure enough, it appeared to roll uphill. The attraction delivered on its promises, and Evan couldn't figure out how.

Part of hunting, Seth taught him, was learning to trust his instincts. Right now, Evan's gut told him to get the hell out.

With a confused last glance at the illusions he couldn't explain, Evan hurried to catch up with Milo.

He found the museum of oddities to be even creepier.

Some of the items he recognized as flat-out fakes—"mermaids" made of taxidermied fish and animal parts, "voodoo" dolls that were nothing of the sort, and "alien" skeletons exploiting the remains of deformed animals. Two tarnished metal cones, each about two feet tall, sat next to a placard explaining how they had been buried millennia ago by extraterrestrials as locating beacons.

"I think we need to leave," Evan murmured.

Milo used his phone to take a picture of one of the least remarkable items in the big glass display case. An old coin appeared to stand on end inside a small bamboo cage. Unlike all the other displays with attention-grabbing signage that made liberal use of all-caps, the little cage tucked toward the back seemed designed to be overlooked.

"I agree," Milo said. "But I'm going to send the pictures to Simon."

Evan nodded goodbye to the teenager in the ticket booth as he and Milo walked back to the truck. Once they were out of the parking lot, he realized he had been holding his breath.

"So, what's the deal? There was something weird in there, but I can't figure out what it was or how it worked."

Milo nodded. "And if we hadn't been carrying salt and iron, we might have spent a lot more time there, entranced by the displays. And all the while, that Brigadoon Coin would have siphoned off our energy."

"Brigadoon Coin?" Evan frowned. "That little coin in the cage?"

"Yep. It's old magic, and dark because it steals life force. The coin creates a minor temporal anomaly in a small radius around it. That's why you couldn't figure out how the illusions were done. They weren't illusions. The effect is so subtle, we don't have scientific tools to measure it," Milo said. "And the 'tricks' look like the ones at all the harmless tourist traps."

"Why would anyone build an attraction around something like that?"

Milo turned to look at him. "Might be exactly what you wanted if you were a dark witch hedging your bet on immortality."

"Shit. You think Sturdevant is behind it?"

"I know he is. The ownership is tangled up and complicated—as you'd expect for a person with something to hide. The attraction's been there since 1912."

Evan didn't need the slight emphasis on the date to get the hint. "Since the first round of sacrifices," he said. "You think Sturdevant is trying to stretch out his time? Or storing up extra power?"

Milo shrugged. "Don't know. Don't care. I doubt most visitors stay long enough to suffer much harm. But that kid at the ticket booth, or anyone else with long-term exposure—that's another matter."

"You're going to give Simon a call?"

"Already sent him the picture and the address, asked him to hold off until I give him the go-ahead. I doubt Sturdevant is going to want to part with his little marvel willingly, no matter how much money he's offered. And we don't want to tip our hand. But once we take care of the witch-disciple problem, I'll make sure the Brigadoon Coin is handled."

Evan didn't recognize the landmarks as Milo drove out of town. "Where to now?"

"It's still early. Seth and Toby won't be back for a while yet. I left lasagna in the slow cooker for dinner, and there's salad in the fridge, so dinner is covered. I thought we might stop in to see a friend of mine in Blowing Rock, next town over."

Evan took in the sights as they drove through Boone's downtown. Charming cafés and gift shops sat shoulder to shoulder with independent book stores, outfitters, and resort real estate brokers. Arts and

Crafts-style architecture mingled with Victorian homes and log cabins to give a rustic, upscale feel.

Driving from Boone toward Blowing Rock meant more winding roads. Evan caught his breath at the sight of a huge white and green Victorian hotel perched on the side of the mountain, and other signs enticed visitors to indulge at a famous spa resort.

"This isn't exactly like my uncle's fishing camp," Evan observed.

Milo chuckled. "Oh, there's stuff for regular folks here, too, if you know where to look. Like the cabin and campground where we're at. Pretty normal, easy on the wallet. Lots of folks have had cabins and property up here since World War Two, at least. Before that, people came here to take the 'cure' for bad lungs—which is where the Victorian stuff comes in. And the pricy new places—that's pretty recent."

Billboards off to one side advertised a local Wild West amusement park, guided rafting tours, and treetop zip lines that made Evan's stomach pitch.

"That doesn't look like fun to you?" Milo joked.

"Hell to the no."

Milo laughed, throwing his head back. "You know, I'd probably do it. Seth might, too. But Toby? No way."

Before long, they passed a *"Welcome to Blowing Rock"* sign. Evan spotted a couple more cafés that looked good and a coffee shop amid the boutiques and specialty stores. "That coffee shop has a bakery," he said. "I vote for getting some coffee for the road and dessert for after dinner."

"I like the way you think," Milo replied with a hearty chuckle. "I want to touch base with the chief of police here. He and I go back a ways."

"Does he know what we do?"

"Uh-huh. Sure does. At least, the hunting creatures part. Some of the things that go into it…I might not have mentioned."

Evan understood. Hunting required some "creative interpretation" of the law on occasion, like Seth's hacking and the many times they had technically committed trespassing or breaking and entering for the greater good. Then again, no one was going to give them a warrant to look for a wendigo.

"How did that happen?" Evan liked hearing the stories Toby and Milo told. One of the best parts of spending the winter in Pittsburgh had been the nights he and Seth had spent with Travis and Brent, swapping hunting stories. Nobody needed to exaggerate to have tales worthy of legends.

"Toby and I were out this way, long before we met Seth or knew about the witch-disciples. We were hunting a Santer, which is a type of vampire-beast," Milo replied. "It's native to these mountains. We were asking a lot of questions, and Chief Williams decided to see what we were up to. He thought we were with some kind of paranormal TV show. I thought he was going to run us out of town."

"I'm guessing not, if we're going out of our way to say hello."

"Surprised the hell of out of me," Milo admitted. "Turns out Scott is a born-and-raised mountain boy. His great-granddaddy might have been a moonshiner, and his great-grandmama was definitely a witch. God-fearing, of course," he added with a wink. "He suspected a Santer was on the loose, he just didn't know what to do about it. He threw in with Toby and me, and we lit that fucker up."

"Are you going to tell him about Sturdevant?" Evan could come up with all kinds of reasons that might be a bad idea, but he trusted Milo's lead.

"Not in so many words. At least, not now," Milo replied. "Mostly because it's one thing to hunt a monster and another thing to hunt down a human. But I'd like to have him keeping an ear open for us. It never hurts to have an ally who knows the area."

Milo had gambled that Chief Williams might be home on a Saturday in the late afternoon. He pulled the truck to the curb in front of a tidy bungalow-style house. Evan followed him up the steps to the porch. Footsteps came to the door quickly after Milo rang the bell.

"My God, Milo Cornell! What brings you here?" Scott Williams looked to be in his late forties or early fifties, close to the same age as Milo and Toby. He had short, thinning dark hair, sharp hazel eyes, and hadn't completely lost a hint of color from last year's tan. The broad shoulders and fit body told Evan that Scott took keeping in shape seriously. Definitely not a doughnut cop.

"Scott? Is there someone at the door?" A woman called from inside the house.

"Some old friends from out of town stopped in, Liz," Scott yelled back.

A trim, brown-haired woman showed up at Scott's shoulder. "Don't just leave them on the porch, sweetie. Ask them in." She looked to Milo. "Can you stay for dinner?"

Milo grinned. "Thank you kindly, Liz. But my husband'll be waiting for me, and he might take offense if I eat without him."

"Maybe another time then," she said, with a smile that made Evan think she meant it. "I'm in the middle of something, so I'll leave you boys to it. There's fresh coffee in the kitchen." With that, she left them alone, but Evan felt like he'd been in the presence of a blue-eyed cyclone.

"Come on in," Scott welcomed them. "You've weathered 'Hurricane Liz,'" he added with a laugh. "I wish I had half her energy, even on one of her slow days!" He led them into a comfortable living room. Evan glanced around and felt a pang. The house looked cozy and normal, and it made him miss the home he used to have before he'd been disowned.

"Scott, this is Evan Malone. Evan, Chief Williams," Milo made introductions. He turned back to Scott. "You remember I told you about Seth—the young man who lived with Toby and me for a while? Evan's his partner. We're all up here taking a break from the big city." He and Evan settled onto the sofa, while Scott took a seat in the armchair facing them.

Scott gave Milo a shrewd look. "You don't live in the big city, Milo. Cut the bull. What are you guys hunting?"

Milo managed a sheepish grin. "You got me. There's a creature that we think is linked to a curse on a local family. Caused a lot of hardship over the years. Saw a twin of it elsewhere, and tracked this one here. Thought we'd take care of it."

"Curse?" Scott's eyes narrowed. "As in bad luck? Real bad luck?"

Milo's grin faded, and he was all business when he met Scott's gaze. "Like nine men dead bad luck, and we don't want there to be a tenth."

Scott's breath caught. "You're talking about the Henshaws. Aren't you." He didn't make it a question.

Milo hesitated, then nodded. Evan found himself holding his breath. "You know?" Milo asked.

"What I know is that a good family has had an unusual amount of bad luck and lost a lot of men too young," Scott replied. "I was friends with Jack Henshaw. We went to school together. I was at his wedding. Been to barbecues at his house. When his car went into that ravine, I didn't believe it was an accident for a minute. But it didn't happen in my jurisdiction, and the other chief of police was not…helpful." He cleared his throat, making the point that he didn't care much for the Boone chief.

"Point taken," Milo replied.

"I looked into the accident myself at the time," Scott said. "Unofficially. This was about eleven years ago, give or take. It didn't make any sense to me. The road was dry that night. Family said there was nothing wrong with the car. Jack was a very responsible man. He wouldn't have been speeding or taking chances. No other vehicle was involved. So why did the car go down the embankment and catch fire? There was hardly enough left of him to bury, all burned up."

Evan felt bile rise. He wondered if the charred corpse had really been Jack Henshaw, or whether another body had been put in his place to cover Sturdevant's sacrifice.

"And I'm guessing the Boone chief didn't find anything unusual?"

Scott's expression darkened. "Paul Bondell couldn't find his ass with both hands. Still, I expected better. The Henshaws are an old Boone family. Been here for a long time. Own that nursery out on the road apiece. Not that every accident shouldn't get the full attention of the police, but hell, if you're going to gloss over something, his was an odd one to skimp on."

"What about the county sheriff?" Evan asked. "Will he be any help?"

Scott shook his head. "Dan Peters is a good guy, but he's only a few years from retirement. He's no fan of Bondell's, and he's had a low-key investigation going to get rid of him, but I'm not sure how far along it is. One thing I do know is that Peters is very traditional in his religious beliefs. He's not going to be open to anything about magic or the supernatural, and he's not real open-minded about LGBTQ."

"Are we going to be harassed here?" Milo asked.

Scott sighed. "I don't think so. Bad for tourism. And in my experience, Dan tries to be fair. But if he knew—he might not give you the benefit of the doubt."

"How hard will it be to work around Peters and Bondell?" Evan didn't like the idea of a potentially hostile sheriff, on top of a corrupt chief of police.

"Told you, he's already got one foot out the door. Spends as much time as he can get away with going to law enforcement conventions and training classes," Scott replied. "I wouldn't be surprised if he retires right after he nails Bondell for something that will stick. I don't think Peters will get in our way. Last I heard, he was going to be gone for two weeks at some conference in Raleigh."

Evan was already sure they needed to give Chief Bondell a wide berth. He sounded like trouble. Could he be in cahoots with Sturdevant? From the look in Milo's eyes, Evan bet the older man had already made that leap.

"That's what made me do a little digging. Something real bad seems to happen to the Henshaws every dozen year or so," Scott went on. "And it'll be eleven years this June since Jack died." He paused. "You think whatever this thing is, if you catch it, you can stop the killing?"

"Pretty damn sure," Milo replied.

The back door opened, bringing the conversation to a halt. Steve, the young man they'd seen at the nursery, the guy Evan was almost certain was Kyle Henshaw's boyfriend, burst in. He looked sweaty and disheveled, and the streaks of mud on his arms plus the dirt on his T-shirt suggested that he'd been successful in getting Kyle to let him help out at the shop.

"Hey dad—" Steve stopped in his tracks, staring at Milo and Evan. "Weren't you at the nursery this afternoon?"

Scott gave Milo a look, then returned his attention to his son. "Milo's an old friend. He and Evan just stopped in to say hello."

Steve shrugged. "Oh. Okay. Thought I recognized the truck. Anyhow, I need a shower." He darted off.

Scott waited until they heard the water turn on. "Explain," he said to Milo. His expression had shifted to what Evan thought of as "cop eyes."

Milo didn't blink. "I told you we came here to save that boy's life. Wanted to get a feel for who he was. Seems like a good kid."

Scott glanced back toward the hallway where Steve had gone and then brought his attention back to Evan and Milo. "Kyle's a great boy. When Kyle's dad died, and then his brother got killed in the war, it was a real blow to the family. Kyle pitched in wherever he could. He's a hard worker. Changed his plans about going to college. He's been trying to pick up classes online, or at the community college. He's supposed to go to UNC Asheville part-time this fall. I don't think his mother, Carla, would survive losing Kyle, too."

"We're going to do our damnedest to keep him safe, and end the curse," Milo promised.

Scott suddenly looked older and worn. "Steve and Kyle went to school together. Somewhere along the line, they went from best friends to… more. Steve thinks Kyle hung the moon," Scott confessed. "If he thinks Kyle's in danger, he'll be right beside him. Don't let anything happen to my boys—either of them."

Milo nodded, accepting the duty. "We won't." Milo stood, ready to go, and Evan followed his lead. Scott walked them to the door.

"Anything I can do—unofficially—just let me know. I might not have jurisdiction in Boone, but I do have friends. And resources. Just watch your back," he warned. "Bondell's a mean SOB. Not everyone on his force is like him, but he's got a few who are. That's another reason why Peters wants to get rid of him. Bondell's not going to like outsiders sniffing around his territory."

"We'll be careful," Milo said. They shook hands with Scott and headed for the truck. Evan didn't speak until they were back on the road.

"You think Chief Bondell's working for Sturdevant?" Evan asked, remembering the cop who had betrayed him back in Richmond.

"Probably. Whether or not he knows about the witch part, he's probably at least on the take to keep an eye out for threats and run off people who are asking too many questions."

"We need to warn Seth."

"We will," Milo assured him. "But he's with Toby, and Toby will watch out for both of them. Toby doesn't trust most cops. Present company excepted," he added with a grin.

5

SETH

From the way Evan greeted him when he made it back to the cabin, Seth knew his boyfriend had been worried. Still jittery from the phantom truck incident, Seth welcomed the solid anchor of Evan's embrace. Evan kissed him like they had been parted for days instead of hours, giving Seth the impression that whatever Evan and Milo had discovered had unsettled him.

"You okay?" Seth asked, brushing a lock of dark hair out of Evan's face.

Evan nodded but tightened his grip. "Yeah. Sorta." They walked into the kitchen with their arms around each other's waists, unwilling to move apart. Toby and Milo spoke in low tones in the kitchen as Toby plated the lasagna and got the salad out of the fridge.

"Sit down," Toby ordered. "Let's eat." He didn't comment when Milo grabbed the Jack Daniels and four glasses, plunking them down next to the salad dressing.

The lasagna smelled amazing, and despite everything Seth discovered he was hungry. Conversation was put on hold while they dug into the meal, which the four of them polished off in record time. They all helped clean up while Toby put leftovers away, then moved into the living room. Milo brought the whiskey with him and poured them all shots.

"So here's what we found out today." Milo went first, recounting everything that had happened, as Seth and Toby listened intently. Evan jumped in from time to time to add his impressions. He stayed next to Seth, sitting close enough that they touched from shoulder to knee. Both of them seemed to need the connection more than usual. Toby drew a chair up to sit beside Milo's armchair and laid a hand on his forearm.

"You're sure about the Brigadoon Coin?" Toby took a sip of his whiskey as if the revelation rattled him.

"As sure as I can be without examining it," Milo replied. "Everything we experienced—it all adds up. I'd like to get the coin out of there before we take on Sturdevant. But if Simon's person makes a move, that'll be sure to throw up red flags, and we don't need to give the witch any more of an advantage than he already has."

Toby and Seth grew concerned when Milo and Evan told them about Chief Williams's input, especially his warning concerning the Boone police.

"Scott Williams was a big help the last time," Toby said. "I wish we didn't have to work around the other asshole, but I'll take all the help we can get."

"How about you?" Milo asked, holding his shot of whiskey without drinking it yet. "Find out anything good?"

Toby knocked the rest of his drink back before answering. Seth also took a slug, although he didn't pound the whole shot.

"That good, huh?" Milo raised an eyebrow.

Evan must have figured he'd need a little fortification himself and took a drink as well.

Milo's expression turned from a concerned frown to an outright scowl as Toby and Seth tag-teamed their recap. Evan laid a hand on Seth's thigh as Seth told about the creature that had chased them, tightening his grip when Toby explained their near-miss with the phantom truck. Seth thought he might have bruises from Evan's fingers, but he didn't mind at all. He was alive, and Evan was next to him, grounding Seth in the here and now.

"I'd like to know more about that truck," Milo growled. "Are there any other accounts of a ghost truck on that road? Any fatal truck wrecks?"

Toby cocked his head and looked at Milo, puzzled. "You think it's not a ghost?"

"I don't know what I think," Milo replied, his voice sharp. Seth figured it was Milo's reaction to their close call. "But this witch-disciple seems like he's got more on the ball than the last two, and I don't want to make assumptions."

"I'll do some digging tomorrow," Seth promised. "The truck wasn't a very old model, so I don't think I'd need to go back too far to find the wreck." He glanced at Evan. "And if you tell me what you think was missing from the archive records, I can take another shot to see if I can turn up something online."

"We ended up at the archive because we couldn't find anything online," Evan replied, still remembering how frosty Mrs. Albritton had turned at the end. "But it's worth a try."

"Tomorrow, I want to see what we can learn about Sturdevant," Milo said. "I know we've got to be low-key about it, particularly if he's got this police chief in his pocket. But if we're right about his past aliases, then Sturdevant also spent some of his time in Asheville and Banner Elk—close enough to keep tabs on the Henshaws, but far enough away that people didn't notice he was changing his name. We might hit pay dirt."

"I thought Evan and I could go take a look at the old tuberculosis hospital," Seth said, taking Evan's hand in his. "It's one of Sturdevant's stomping grounds, and since it's abandoned, it might be a ritual site. There's also an old mansion that he built in one of his prior identities that probably bears looking at."

Toby and Milo put in a superhero movie they had all seen before. Seth and Evan left halfway through the flick, needing time alone to sort out everything that had happened. Seth had the impression that Toby and Milo needed some space as well.

"Missed you today," Seth said, as he and Evan walked back to the RV hand-in-hand.

"I missed you, too."

"I mean, it was good getting to spend some time with Toby. Like the old days. But you and I have a rhythm going, you know what I mean?" Seth didn't quite know how to explain.

Over the past few months Evan had filled the empty places in Seth's life, not just as a lover, but as a friend and a hunting partner. They'd learned to work together, depend on each other, read one another's signals. He'd never experienced that kind of synchronicity, not even when he was with his team in the army. Deep down, Seth knew just how special that was, how rare. He hoped he could keep that bond forever.

"Yeah, I do," Evan agreed as Seth turned the key in the lock. "It was nice to get to know Milo better. But he's not you."

"Of course not. He's twice my age, surly, and with less hair," Seth replied with a smirk.

Evan backhanded him on the shoulder. "You know what I mean. I tried to follow his lead, but I couldn't guess where he was going with things. Not like with us."

Seth locked the door behind them, flicked on the lights. He peeled out of his coat, then toed out of his boots as Evan did the same. "I like how things are with us," he said, pulling Evan toward him and kissing him, hard. Evan kissed back, with just as much fervor.

"Not here," Seth murmured, letting go reluctantly and leading Evan up the few steps to the bedroom. They fell together onto the king-size bed, both of them stripping fast until they were naked.

Seth never tired of admiring Evan's body. They were the same height, but Seth had more muscle. Evan was leaner, toned but not as bulky. A dark trail led down to Evan's hard, cut cock which jutted from a darker thatch of hair, glistening with pre-come. Evan gave him a sexy smile, knowing Seth was looking, taking Seth's own erection as proof that Seth got off on the view.

"So...you want to watch?" Evan asked in a sultry voice, reaching down to stroke himself. He spread his legs wider to give Seth a better look.

Seth felt his cock twitch, thinking that the show Evan was putting on was the sexiest thing he'd ever seen. He licked his lips. "Touch your nipples."

Evan kept eye contact as one hand slipped up his chest, slowly circling first one pink nipple and then the next. Circles turned to pinches and then to tugs. More pre-come leaked from his cock, slicking his hand, and Evan gave a throaty groan of pleasure that went right to Seth's balls.

"Take your time," Seth said, moving to the end of the bed. The small room smelled of Evan's shampoo, sweat, and arousal. Evan drew his knees up, keeping his feet flat on the comforter, exposing himself to Seth's view.

Evan's fist pumped more slowly, and Seth fought the urge to touch himself. He wondered if he could watch Evan get off and then make him come a second time when they fucked. All Seth could think about was being buried balls deep inside Evan, losing himself in their connection.

"Open yourself up for me," Seth said, loving the lust darkening Evan's eyes. "Get yourself ready for my cock."

They'd never played around like this before. Seth wasn't quite sure where it was all coming from. Maybe they'd picked up some ideas from the videos they'd watched recently, although those tended to be better for suggesting positions and toys than for seduction. Wherever this new boldness came from, they both seemed to be all in. Evan's cock was dark red and so very hard, and his own prick felt like steel.

Evan reached for the lube on the nightstand and flicked it open one-handed, managing to squirt some on his fingers without losing his rhythm with the other hand. He rose to his knees languidly, performing for Seth's attention. Then he turned to the side, so Seth could watch while Evan reached around and started to finger himself.

This performance was a whole new side of Evan that Seth hadn't seen, and he hoped to see it again. Maybe they'd finally gotten comfortable enough with each other to take risks. Seth would have to figure out how to repay Evan in kind—later, because right now, he could hardly think past his own aching balls.

Evan let his head fall back, getting lost in the sensation as he worked himself both ways. Seth thought it was the sexiest thing he'd ever seen, and he was torn between watching the show and wanting to join in.

"You are so beautiful," Seth murmured, and it took all of his self-control not to stroke himself too. Evan's smile made it clear he knew what he was doing to Seth.

"So close," Evan gasped. He gave Seth a challenging look. "Want me to take this all the way, or would you like to step in and finish things off?"

Seth didn't need to be asked twice. He crawled across the bed as Evan folded forward, offering up his ass to Seth as he continued jacking himself with one hand.

Seth knelt behind him, reaching for the lube with one hand and taking hold of Evan's hip with the other. He bit gently on each ass cheek, just enough to pinch, then pulled them apart to expose Evan's glistening hole.

He leaned in, running the tip of his tongue around the sensitive skin, rewarded when Evan's moan said his lover couldn't hold out much longer. Seth alternated between the tip, a bit of delicious teasing, and the flat of his tongue, then pushed the tip into the loosened furl just to make Evan squirm.

"Seth…please." Evan's breathy voice nearly made Seth come.

Seth grabbed the lube, slicked his cock, and lined himself up. He pressed in, holding tight to Evan's hips with both hands. He bottomed out, unable to muffle the groan that slipped out as Evan's tight channel gripped him. "Not going to last long," he breathed.

"Make me come."

Seth pulled back, then thrust in, a few short strokes and then fast and deep, feeling his balls slap against Evan's ass, loving the way Evan gasped beneath him. They were both so close, teetering on the edge. He shifted so his next stroke pegged Evan's spot, and Evan cried out as he spent, pushing back to take Seth as deep as he could go, trembling with his release.

Seth couldn't hold out any longer, and he felt his climax rush through him, finishing off with a few more hard thrusts.

They fell forward with Seth rolling them so they stayed connected but keeping his full weight off Evan. Both of them were breathing hard, sweat-slicked, and sated. Seth slipped an arm over Evan's chest, drawing him back, holding him tight. Evan leaned against him, letting his head loll on Seth's shoulder.

"That was...the sexiest thing I've ever seen," Seth whispered against Evan's ear. "You were magnificent."

"That was okay?"

Seth could hear the vulnerability in Evan's voice, second-guessing himself. He realized that putting on the show for his benefit had really pushed Evan out of his comfort zone, and now that they were spent, doubt crept in.

"So much more than okay," Seth assured him. "You are amazing." He kissed Evan's temple and licked at the edge of his ear. "I don't know what I'm going to have to do to return the favor. I'll have to think on that a while."

"Mm," Evan murmured. "I like that idea. Can't wait to see what you come up with."

Seth's dick slipped free, and cooling come reminded him that cleanup was needed. He kissed Evan again and untangled himself, then headed to the bathroom. He returned with a warm, wet cloth and cleaned Evan up, something that always struck him as being as intimate as the act itself.

"Need to wash the comforter again," Evan said with a rueful look at the wet spot.

"Worth it!" Seth laughed. He tossed the cloth toward the bathroom as Evan rolled to one side, and they both crawled underneath the covers. Evan snuggled against him, resting his head on Seth's shoulder, and Seth combed his fingers slowly through Evan's hair.

"I love you," Seth said quietly.

Evan twined their fingers together. "Love you, too."

Seth heard a twinge of something in Evan's voice. "What's wrong?"

Evan squirmed, uncomfortable with the shift in topic. "It's scary, knowing that you and Toby could have been hurt—or worse—by that ghost truck. I know it goes with the job, but I don't have to like it."

Seth nodded. "I know. I don't like it either. Even less when you're the one in danger. But…like you said. It goes with the job."

Evan was silent for a few moments, but Seth knew he hadn't fallen asleep. "When we met Kyle at the nursery he just seemed like such a nice guy. And if we can't stop Sturdevant, he'll die bloody."

"Like Jesse."

Evan's arm slipped around Seth's waist, pulling them close. "Like what was going to happen to me. And I was so angry—at Sturdevant and all the rest of the witch-disciples. It just reminded me why what we're doing matters."

Seth hugged him tight. "I want that. But even more, I want us. Safe. Together."

Evan nodded, and Seth nuzzled against his hair, taking in his scent. "So do I."

THE NEXT MORNING, THEY DROVE TOWARD BLACK MOUNTAIN AND THE old sanatorium grounds. "Did anyone really get cured at one of these places?" Evan wondered aloud as they parked and walked along the cracked driveway.

"They didn't know how tuberculosis spread or what caused it at the beginning," Seth replied with a shrug. "Bad air seemed like as good an answer as any. Probably also included a bunch of people with asthma, COPD, everything else. I mean, all that coal smoke? In the big cities, the sky was dark at noon."

"I read up on this place," Evan said. "It was huge." He pulled a printout and a picture from his pocket and held them up, trying to orient them with what remained.

The original building was brick with white wood trim, with a central three-story section and two long, matching wings. The chain-link fence warned away trespassers. Tall grass suggested that no one bothered to mow the lawn. "I mean, it's still big," Evan went on. "But back in the day, there were plenty of outbuildings. When TB patients stopped coming, it got changed into a prison hospital. They closed it down back in 2010."

The old building looked to be in good shape, considering the years of neglect. "They built things to last, that's for sure," Seth said. "And with that history, it's got to be haunted as all hell."

"Ya think?" Evan asked. "One of the online sites said that none of the guards that supposedly patrol the place will go up to the third floor. I thought all the bad stuff happened in the basement."

"A place like that, I'm pretty sure bad stuff happened everywhere."

"Sturdevant did a gig here as a doctor after he left Boone," Evan said. "But it doesn't look like any of the Henshaw men were patients. Sturdevant used it as a hiding place, but it didn't give him access to Kyle's ancestors."

"Not to them." Seth scaled the chain-link fence and dropped over the other side. Evan did the same, landing in a crouch. "But that's not to say the sick bastard didn't find ways to use the patients to amp up his power."

"Maybe he's a better witch than the others were," Evan mused. "He seems to be working all the angles. Brigadoon Coin, paying off the cops, maybe killing extra people to gain more power."

"That's a scary thought." Killing the witch-disciples in Richmond and Pittsburgh had nearly done them both in, and the idea that Sturdevant might be an even more formidable enemy chilled Seth.

"No kidding."

They fell silent as they walked through the tall grass toward the imposing old hospital. Seth knew they probably had more to fear from ticks than ghosts, but that didn't quell the fear that slithered down his spine. The dark windows stared down ominously, and it didn't take much imagination to suppose that the tortured souls of patients and prisoners never really left.

"If the place has only been closed since 2010, then Sturdevant wasn't using it for his dumping ground before that," Evan said. "Now maybe, but not then."

"I'm not sure that doing a summoning spell here is a good idea." Seth remembered what happened back at the forestry school. Facing down the angry revenants of Sturdevant's victims was bad enough, but waking up the ghosts of the hospital couldn't end well. There were plenty of victims here, not all of them the witch-disciple's.

"Not going to argue with you on that," Evan said. "But there's only been one Henshaw murder since this place closed. It won't sit empty forever."

"The forestry school has."

"It's out in the middle of the woods. This," Seth replied, waving his hand at the large, empty building, "Someone will eventually figure out a way to turn it into something."

"Condos? Nursing home?" Evan shivered. "What could possibly go wrong?" His voice was thick with sarcasm.

They made a circle around the old hospital and noted where crumbling foundations and tumbled piles of bricks marked the location of the smaller outbuildings. Nothing stirred in the tall grass and no guards appeared, yet Seth couldn't shake a sense of foreboding.

"I hope we don't have to go through that place room by room," Evan said when they stood on the front steps. "Because I don't intend to be here after dark."

Seth shook his head. "I don't think that's going to be necessary. From what Milo found, Sturdevant reinvented himself as Doctor William Conroy after he left the forestry company. Probably faked his paperwork. Must have made quite an impression, because by the time he 'retired' a dozen or so years later, they named a treatment suite after him."

"And you think that might be an anchor of some kind?" Evan asked.

"If it is, and we can disrupt that, maybe we can weaken Sturdevant, make him easier to kill," Seth said. "Like taking care of the Brigadoon Coin. By the way, I put in a call to Simon—his guy must have a private plane or something, because he said to let him know when we need the coin gone and he'd make it happen."

"Helpful and a little scary," Evan acknowledged.

Seth shrugged. "I'm not sure it's someone Simon actually knows. Some friend of his cousin in Charleston."

"Still. Nice connection to have."

"Yeah. That's what I thought."

"What do you think Sturdevant might have left as an anchor?" Evan asked as they climbed the steps. Seth carried a gear bag filled with salt, holy water, iron filings, and a variety of weapons. Evan had a sawed-off shotgun with salt rounds in his coat, and steel and iron knives in sheathes on his belt. They'd be totally fucked if the guards caught them, but they might stand a chance if the ghosts of Black Mountain turned surly.

"I don't know," Seth admitted. The large front doors did not open when he tried them. A simple rote opening spell took less time than picking the clunky old lock. Seth pushed the door open—just enough for them to enter—and closed it behind them without letting it quite latch.

The entrance had the feeling of a grand lobby retrofitted for hospital intake. The original sanatorium had been built more on the order of a big hotel or a huge lodge to make its well-off patients feel more at home.

"The brochures about these tuberculosis hospitals made it sound like a vacation staffed by nurses." Evan kept his voice hushed although they were alone. "I'm sure the reality wasn't quite like that, but the thought was nice."

The spring chill clung to the old rooms. Peeling paint and bubbled plaster showed the effects of being left to the elements. Most of the windows were intact, but a few were broken, and Seth saw where leaves and debris had blown in and birds and animals had made nests. The white and green paint might have once been bright and crisp, but now mildew and dripping water left streaks and stains. Seth didn't have to be psychic to pick up the sense of despair that filled the empty rooms.

"Where's the Conroy suite?" Evan pulled out his shotgun, ready for trouble.

"Second floor, turn right. Halfway down the wing." Seth headed up the stairs, with Evan watching his back.

Seth had learned what he knew about lore and monsters from other hunters. But the army had taught him tactics—how to clear a room, how to take a hill. He'd fought insurgents in Iraq and Afghanistan, but the principles remained the same. He taught everything he could to Evan, hoping that the knowledge would keep them both safe, and keep Evan alive.

Now, they moved up the stairs, wordlessly in tune with each other. A long hallway stretched in both directions, so far that he couldn't see either end. Doors opened off the corridor, gaping black holes. Dust motes danced in the light that filtered in from dirty windows in the central atrium. Shadows filled the hallways, broken only by the weak rays that struggled in from the smudged glass in each room.

He paused, listening. In the distance, rats scurried. Seth started down the right-hand hall, with Evan behind him.

The doors slammed shut, one after another, with a series of bangs like gunfire.

"What the fuck?" Evan asked under his breath.

"I'm guessing we might not be welcome."

Seth stared down the now-darkened hallway. "We mean you no harm," Seth called out to the spirits that had never left Black Mountain. "Let us pass. We're trying to stop the charlatan who hurt you. Keep him from hurting anyone ever again. But we need to get to the Conroy room. Let us in and out, and we'll leave you in peace."

They waited, listening to the old building. A cool breeze out of nowhere wafted past them, and like someone had pressed a button, the closed doors all opened to stand ajar.

"I'm going to take that for a yes," Seth said, with a nod to Evan.

He didn't have to tell Evan not to trust the ghosts. His partner stayed alert, still behind him, weapon ready. Seth was so friggin' proud of Evan, but now wasn't the time for praise. Later, once they were both safe, he'd let Evan know. Now they needed to get what they came for and leave before the ghosts changed their minds.

One hand went to check his pockets. They both had salt and iron, as well as the silver and onyx amulets they'd given each other for Christmas. As he'd seen at the forestry school, salt couldn't keep them completely safe, but it could certainly force ghosts to keep their distance.

"Get your light." Seth and Evan pulled their military-grade flashlights from their pockets, and Seth felt a surge of pride as Evan automatically fell into the stance he'd taught him.

The old building held the damp, cooler than the chilly day outside.

But the hallway's temperature had fallen just since they climbed the stairs, and Seth could see his breath.

"Stay sharp," he murmured.

"Right behind you."

Seth and Evan kicked each door open, sweeping the rooms one by one. Seth wasn't about to let anything have an easy way to sneak up on them, although with ghosts, an empty room wasn't a guarantee.

The Conroy suite was in the middle of the wing, as the floorplan showed. Evan stayed on guard at the door watching the hallway while Seth moved into the room cautiously. His flashlight didn't completely light up the big space, and the dirty windows provided little help. Still, he could make out the important parts.

When Seth had seen the word "suite" he hadn't been sure what it meant. Now he knew. It was an operatory, a surgical suite with six stainless steel tables and the ragged remains of curtains hanging between them. Green metal cabinets with frosted glass center panes hung above lower cupboards with stainless countertops. For as long as it had been abandoned, the equipment looked new, though dated. *Built to last.*

"Cover me." Seth opened the cabinet doors and searched through the lower cupboards. They were empty of everything except mouse nests and cobwebs. He stood, brushing the dust off his knees and played his light over the walls. Seth thought he might find some personal item left behind as an anchor—a diploma, a photograph, even a coin. The walls were bare, and the drawers and storage areas empty.

"Seth. Come look at this."

He hurried to where Evan stood just outside the door, shining his light on a bronze plaque affixed to the wall. *"In gratitude to Dr. William Conroy, for service and philanthropy,"* it read, with an etched likeness of the man Seth recognized as Ira Sturdevant.

"That's got to be it," Evan said, meeting Seth's gaze. "He would have been proud of it. Emotional resonance."

Seth nodded. "Yeah. You're probably right." He pulled a squeeze bottle of salted holy water from his pocket and doused the metal plaque, then withdrew a grease pencil and drew a null symbol on the bronze plate to temper any magic that might have been linked to it.

Evan withdrew a crowbar from the gear bag and handed it to Seth. "Go for it."

Seth turned toward the plaque, and Evan turned away, on guard. The hallway had gotten cold enough that Seth's nose and lips were chilled, and he could see how Evan shivered from the tremor in the flashlight's beam. Best to get this over with.

He wedged the tongue of the crowbar beneath the plaque and threw his weight against the bar. The old plaster cracked and crumbled, then the fasteners tore loose. The bronze plate clattered to the floor, sounding unnaturally loud in the silent old hospital.

"Let's get the hell out of here," he said, grabbing the plaque and shoving it into the gear bag.

"We've got company!" Evan warned.

Seth turned just as a gray shape swept down the hallway from the dark end. He could barely make out a face and a long dressing gown as the apparition rushed past him.

"Steal your breath," a disembodied voice whispered.

Before Seth could move, the spirit struck Evan right in the chest, knocking him to the ground and vanishing.

"Evan!"

Evan gasped for air. His body bucked, and his heels scrabbled against the dirty tile. Evan's eyes widened with panic, and he coughed, deep, racking wheezes for air, followed by sharp, painful hacks. Flecks of blood colored his pale lips, and he'd gone as white as his T-shirt.

"Let him go!" Seth ordered. Evan convulsed, curling in on himself as the painful cycle of wheezing and hacking repeated, bringing up more blood.

Evan rocked from side to side, and Seth pulled out the salted holy water, spraying a stream of it onto Evan as he began to recite the banishing ritual Toby had taught him. Evan's eyes widened, and his hands tore at his throat as if there were an invisible noose cutting off his air. Seth hurled a handful of salt onto Evan, and Evan's whole form shuddered. For a second, Seth saw two images, lightly off-set like a bad 3-D picture, of Evan and the spirit that fought to control him.

Seth fought panic and kept saying the ritual, willing all of his love and protectiveness for Evan into the words. Evan thrashed, fighting for breath, growing paler as blood turned his lips crimson.

Consumption. Tuberculosis. The victims couldn't breathe. They coughed up blood. Oh, God. That's what it meant about stealing his breath.

Seth shouted the final words in terror and defiance, hoping that Evan could hear him and that he knew Seth was fighting for him. Praying that Evan would survive. Terrified and out of options, Seth tore his protective medallions over his head and threw them onto Evan's convulsing body.

"Depart!" Seth cried, his voice raw.

Evan collapsed and lay still and bloodied.

"Evan!" Seth had the presence of mind to lay down a salt circle around the two of them before he dropped to his knees beside his boyfriend. "Come on. Breathe for me, baby. Please, Evan. Don't go like this."

Evan gave a deep gasp that ended in an ominous rattle, but his eyes opened wide, and no coughing fit followed. He licked his lips and then grimaced in distaste at the blood.

Seth helped him sit up, watching him closely. "Can you breathe?"

Evan drew one breath and then another, normal and deep, then nodded. "Yeah. What happened?"

"You got carjacked." Seth hugged him fiercely and kept his tears inside. He pulled Evan up. Some of the color had begun to come back to Evan's face, and he looked steadier as the minutes ticked by.

"Ready to get out of here?" Seth asked. All he wanted was to pull Evan into his arms and kiss away the fear, but they needed to get away before the psycho ghost tried again, or one of the other spirits got copycat ideas.

"Yeah," Evan said, nodding. "Let's go." He handed back the medallions to Seth. "You need to wear these. Doesn't do us any good if they get you instead of me."

Reluctantly, Seth complied, then he hefted his gear bag, keeping out the bottle of holy water. Evan picked up the shotgun from where it had fallen, looking shaken but determined.

"Together," Seth growled, keeping an arm around Evan as they left the salt circle and headed for the stairs. The ghosts maintained their distance when Seth and Evan entered the old hospital, but now they made themselves visible in the doorways of the darkened rooms or standing along the hallway.

"Don't look at them," he told Evan. "Keep your eyes on the steps, on the door. Just move."

Seth walked them past the revenants, feeling the silent judgment of the scowling ghosts who envied them life and air. He clenched his jaw so hard it ached, holding a fistful of Evan's jacket to keep him close and upright.

Evan stumbled on the stairs but caught the railing before he fell. They hurried as fast as they dared and rushed toward the doors, eager to be out in daylight and away from the desolate souls of the old hospital.

Seth pushed the doors open and pulled Evan through, not bothering to close them. He didn't know whether Evan could make it over the fence, but Seth resolved to get him safely back to the car even if he had to carry him.

"I can climb," Evan said, though his throat sounded raw and his words were just above a whisper.

"I'll boost you."

Seth gave him a leg up and steadied Evan as he climbed. He waited until Evan crawled over the top and fell gracelessly to the other side. Seth scrambled up behind him and dropped down beside Evan to help him up.

"Just a little farther," he said, slipping his arm around Evan again and practically carrying him the rest of the distance to the truck.

Despite the chill in the air, Seth's shirt clung to his back, damp with sweat beneath his coat by the time he threw himself into the driver's seat and pulled out at top speed. He glanced at Evan, who still looked too pale and shaky.

"I'm...okay," Evan assured him in a voice that sounded as if he'd gargled broken glass, raw from the painful coughing.

"Like hell you are."

Evan slumped against the seat. "Better than I was."

Seth knew the attack in the old hospital would haunt his nightmares. "That ghost tried to kill you."

Evan shook his head. "She wasn't *trying* to kill me. She was desperate to breathe. But when she took me over, I think I relived her last moments." He closed his eyes. "My God. If that's the way they suffered…"

"Milo said most of the victims were young, back then. Teens and twenties." Seth kept his eyes on the road, repeating facts from the research to drive the awful images of Evan struggling for breath from his mind. "People treated it as tragically romantic because of the pale skin and dark lips, the whole goth look."

"Gothic," Evan said. "Not goth. And yeah, I saw *Moulin Rouge*."

Seth slowed once they reached the main road. He didn't want to force Evan to talk with a raw throat, but he snuck glances in his direction to assure that his boyfriend was breathing and conscious.

"I'm okay," Evan said, reaching over to lay a hand on Seth's thigh. "Nothing some saltwater gargling can't fix."

"I was scared," Seth admitted. "I wasn't sure I could make her let go of you in time."

"I was scared, too," Evan replied. "But I knew if there was a way you'd save me." Evan's simple trust made Seth's heart squeeze, and he desperately hoped he would always be worthy of Evan's faith in him.

"We've done enough today. Let's head back." The other stops Seth had originally planned to make could wait.

"What are you going to do with the plaque?"

With all the near-death excitement, Seth had almost forgotten about the bronze marker. "I figured I'd ask Milo and Toby about that. We might be better off neutralizing it for now, if destroying it would tip off Sturdevant. Maybe we send it off with Simon's friend, along with the Brigadoon Coin."

Evan nodded, lapsing into silence for a while. They had about an hour's drive back to the RV. Seth turned on the radio, keeping the volume low in case Evan wanted to sleep. He thought his partner had drifted off when Evan spoke again.

"Her name was Alice. She was twenty-four."

Seth frowned. "Who?"

"The ghost who hurt me. When she…took me over…I could see her memories. Some of them, anyhow. So, yeah."

"Did she know anything about Conroy?" Seth asked, using the witch-disciple's old name.

Evan's eyes took on a far-away look as he thought. "She was afraid," he said quietly. "Her family was far away, and she knew she was dying. People didn't visit—they were scared of catching the disease. She was lonely. She got chosen for a 'new treatment' by Dr. Conroy. Some of his patients had miraculous recoveries. But for her, it didn't work."

Seth wondered whether Conroy was a charlatan by the time he went to Black Mountain, or whether his prior medical training remained relevant. Could he have healed patients with his magic? Maybe he did—just enough to look like a hero, but not too many to raise suspicions.

Which to Seth was tantamount to murder.

"Do you know her last name?" Seth asked. "Because as sad as her story is, she's a vengeful ghost and the next person she attacks might not be so lucky."

"Gillespie," Evan answered. "She's buried in the cemetery behind the hospital. Her family never claimed her body."

"Another reason she's still there and pissed off."

"You're probably right."

Evan fell asleep, and Seth let him doze. He tried to pay attention to the music and let it distract him, but he kept seeing the attack at the hospital replay in his mind. He'd been so proud of the way Evan had learned military tactics and hunter skills. Both were necessary to survive in Seth's world. But he felt a pang at the way adapting had changed Evan in the short time they'd been together.

Yes, Evan had gained enough confidence to stand up to an abusive ex-lover, and he had learned how to protect himself. That was a plus. But the job they did gradually shattered any innocence that remained, and killing the monsters they encountered required a certain bloody-mindedness usually seen only in cops and soldiers. Seth hated to see Evan's goodness tainted, no matter how much he craved his boyfriend's company and wanted him by his side.

"Quit thinking so loud," Evan said without opening his eyes. "What happened wasn't your fault. And so help me, if you try to overprotect me 'for my own good' I will beat your ass, and not in a fun way."

Despite his dark thoughts, Seth had to smile. Evan knew him so well. "I just don't want to drag you into something that you'll regret later."

Evan glared at him. "I choose to be with you, and I choose to hunt. These witch-disciple sons of bitches have been killing my family for a hundred years, too, don't forget. It's as much my fight as it is yours. Don't you dare try to make that choice for me or take it away from me. I am exactly where I want to be."

When they got back to the campground, Seth steered Evan toward the cabin rather than the RV. "Where are we going?" Evan protested. "I really just want to lie down."

"I want Toby to look you over, make sure you're really okay," Seth explained. "He's not a medic, but he's been hunting long enough that he knows more than I do. Please. Indulge me."

Evan sighed. "All right. But we make an early night of it. Even if you need to come back once I'm asleep. I'm whupped."

"I promise." Seth noted that, despite Evan's protests, he still leaned on Seth harder than usual as they walked up the steps to the cabin door.

Milo met them and cast a worried glance at Evan. "What happened?"

Seth helped Evan to the couch before answering. "We ran into a vengeful ghost out at the old tuberculosis sanatorium. She tried to...I don't know...*possess* Evan. He couldn't breathe. Started coughing up blood. I got her to let go, and he says he's all right but—"

Toby had come in while Seth gave the recap. He walked out and returned a few moments later with a medical kit. "I don't have a degree to prove it, but I've had a lot of off-the-books training," Toby said to Evan as he approached with a stethoscope. "Comes in handy. Now, let's listen to you breathe."

Evan tolerated being poked and prodded and answered all of Toby's questions. Milo brought in a whiskey for Seth and a hot tea for Evan's sore throat, along with a handful of lozenges.

"Could she have made him sick, for real?" Seth found the nerve to ask the question that he feared most.

Toby raised an eyebrow. "I've never heard of catching something from a ghost," he replied. "His lungs sound fine. Whatever happened when the ghost controlled him wouldn't have exposed him to TB."

Seth hadn't realized he'd been holding his breath. "How about his throat? He was coughing up blood."

"My throat's sore from all the hard coughing, but there hasn't been any more blood," Evan said, glancing anxiously between Seth and Toby.

Just to be sure, Toby used a light to check Evan's throat, then laid a hand on his shoulder reassuringly. "It's a little red, but that's it." He glanced at Seth. "I suspect that the ghost manifested her own symptoms when she possessed you. That's what caused the coughing and the blood, but those symptoms went away when her spirit let go."

"Smart thinking on your part, Seth," Toby praised as he stood and packed up his kit. "Sounds like you got rid of the ghost as fast as possible."

Seth still blamed himself for not having prevented the possession, but he knew better than to argue.

"Dinner's not quite ready," Milo said. "Do you want to lie down on the couch and we'll call you when it is?" he asked Evan.

Seth opened his mouth to protest when Evan cut him off. "If you wouldn't mind, that would be great." He looked at Seth with a lopsided, apologetic smile. "That way we both eat, and you don't end up coming back over later for leftovers."

Seth chuckled since that had been his plan. "Mind reader."

"Nah," Evan said, already stretching out on the couch. "I could hear your stomach rumbling." He looked like he would fall asleep as soon as he got comfortable. "Just wake me when the food's on the table," he murmured in a sleepy voice.

Seth stayed beside Evan while Milo and Toby headed for the kitchen. He watched Evan's chest rise and fall, grateful that the breaths came easily. Evan's color had returned, and his rest seemed untroubled.

Toby quietly cleared his throat from the kitchen doorway and gestured for Seth to come. Seth cast one more look at his sleeping boyfriend and then tip-toed out of the room to join them.

"Let him sleep," Milo said. "You can take leftovers with you and heat something for him when he wakes up."

"Yeah, that's what I was thinking." Seth sat down at the table across from his friends. "God, he scared me to death today."

"But you're both all right," Toby reminded him. "That's what counts. Any day you can say that, it's a win."

6

EVAN

Evan woke in their bed back in the RV, with only a vague memory of how he had gotten there. He remembered falling asleep on the couch in the cabin, had a fuzzy recollection of Seth trundling him to the door, and then nothing until late morning. Since he was wearing only a T-shirt and his briefs, he'd also managed to sleep through Seth stripping him, something Evan hadn't thought possible.

The spot next to him had been slept in but was already cold, and a glance at his phone told Evan why. "Shit, it's ten," he muttered, rolling onto his feet. His throat still ached, but gargling and a hot shower helped a lot, and by the time Evan got dressed, he felt mostly recovered from the previous day's ordeal. He heard voices and smelled coffee, so he headed to the living room, where Seth, Toby, and Milo were huddled around the table, hunching over Toby's laptop.

"What did I miss?" Evan asked, yawning.

"There's a fresh pot of coffee, and the guys brought doughnuts from that bakery in town," Seth said, smiling to see Evan up and around. "How do you feel?"

"Better," he replied. "Mostly normal. But I really need that coffee."

From the size of the mugs the others were using, Evan suspected this was already the second pot. He poured himself some java and grabbed a doughnut, then padded out to the table. Seth scooted over to make room, and Evan slid in next to him, pressing them together from hip to knee.

"What's so interesting?" Evan took a sip of his coffee and swallowed cautiously. The warmth felt good on his tender throat.

Seth gestured toward the laptop, which was angled so that they could all see. "Milo and Toby have been digging into more about Sturdevant."

"Tell me." Evan needed something to get his mind off Alice's ghost. He'd slept hard, but nightmares had still woken him more than once. Thankfully, Seth didn't mention it, but the look in his eyes said he'd noticed.

"Like the other witch-disciples, he changed names about every twenty years," Milo said. "He was Albert Olsen back in 1900, and he became Isaac Saunders at the forestry school. Conroy was the next name change, and that lasted from the twenties to the forties."

"In the fifties and sixties he changed names again and passed himself off as a private nurse," Toby added. "Probably because record-keeping and insurance were going to make it impossible to keep posing as a doctor."

"It also kept him low profile, so he could outlast people who might have remembered him in an old persona," Seth said. "He could have even gone back to get certified, because in the seventies and eighties he was doing physical therapy at an upscale assisted living facility. Smart move, since the people who got to know him wouldn't be around long to identify him, and with his medical training, getting certified shouldn't have been hard."

"Did he become Ira Sturdevant in the nineties?" Seth asked. "Because if so, he should be about ready to go to ground again."

Milo nodded. "Yes—and, you're right. Which is why I'm glad you're coming after him early. Once he moves and changes names, it's possible he could slip by us."

"What's Ira's cover story?" Evan held his mug with both hands, enjoying the warmth. He already felt the sugar jolt from the chocolate-frosted doughnut and debated going back for another.

"He moved around the area over the years—Asheville, Banner Elk,

Black Mountain, Maggie Valley, Boone, Blowing Rock. Far enough away so that he could avoid running into people who knew him before, but close enough to keep tabs on the Henshaws," Seth said.

"And early on, people didn't travel that much, so he probably was pretty safe," Evan added.

"Exactly." Toby got up and walked to the kitchen, then returned with the coffee pot and the rest of the doughnuts. Conversation paused as they all refilled their mugs and grabbed another treat.

"So how did he end up being a guy who runs a wilderness adventure company?" Evan asked before he bit into the maple-iced doughnut and closed his eyes in sugary bliss.

"I thought I was the only one who put that look on your face," Seth murmured in his ear.

Milo elbowed Toby. "Told you he'd make some 'O-face' joke."

Evan felt the heat rise in his cheeks. Seth groaned. "You didn't need to say that out loud, guys."

"Sure we did," Toby chortled. "It's our job."

Once they had finished their doughnuts, the conversation returned to Sturdevant and Evan's question.

"With computers and linked databases, we figure he couldn't get away with much in the medical field anymore," Milo said. "But he probably had a lot of money socked away. Immortality seems to be good for that."

"He also bought land when it was cheap and tied it up in so many trusts and dummy corporations that it was hard to trace back who really owned it, but I managed," Toby added with a triumphant smile. "The land he's using for his new venture was purchased back in 1927."

"I'm betting that he went with a non-profit to build goodwill," Seth said, leaning back, so he bumped shoulders with Evan. "He doesn't have to be seen much—a charity dinner now and again maybe, and he can use the same photo for anything in the news, so no one will expect him to look different. And since his company takes young people on wilderness adventures, he gets a reputation as a nice guy and a pillar of the community."

"So…how are we going to kill this upstanding local citizen?" Evan asked.

Everyone's expressions soured. "We're, ah, still working on that part," Seth admitted. "I was hoping that since we knew who both the witch and the victim were this time around, we could draw Sturdevant into the open."

Evan's eyebrows shot up. "You want to use Kyle as bait?"

Seth grimaced. "It sounds bad when you put it that way. Not exactly."

"Tell me a way that sounds good," Evan challenged. Having been in Kyle's shoes himself, he wasn't crazy about this plan.

Seth fidgeted, but Milo spoke up. "We know that the old forestry school was—and probably still is—where Sturdevant hides the bodies. But we don't know the ritual space yet. It wasn't the school or the sanatorium."

"And there's always an anchor and an amulet, because that's what stores his power and helps him access Gremory's magic when he does the ritual," Seth said. He set his empty cup aside and shook his head when Toby offered more.

"I think that the amulet is probably on him," Milo mused. "That's held true for the first two, and it makes sense. That plaque you brought from the hospital might be the anchor."

"Would he have just left it in an abandoned building if it was that important?" Evan asked. "That seems a little risky."

Toby shrugged. "Hiding in plain sight. Sturdevant is on the board of the development company that owns the land, so no one is going to swoop in and bulldoze the place without him knowing about it. No one goes there, and I'd guess that the only reason Seth was able to steal the thing is because he drew a null symbol on it."

"But that plaque went up in the 1930s," Evan protested. "He would have needed an anchor before that."

"Nothing says the anchor can't change shape," Toby replied. "Sturdevant's a witch. He could have manipulated whoever made that metal plate to incorporate the original magical anchor into it."

"Where's the plate now?" Evan glanced at Seth.

"In a lead box, in the truck's storage compartment," Seth replied. "Safest place we've got."

"What about the Brigadoon Coin?" Evan hadn't been able to stop thinking about the strange relic since they'd seen it at Mystery Mountain. "Could it be the anchor?"

"Doubtful," Toby said. "Those coins have one purpose—to cause a temporal distortion. You wouldn't want that to be part of the anchor—too much of a chance for magical cross-wiring, so to speak."

Seth's phone rang, and a glance at the screen revealed the caller. "Hi, Simon," he said. "Hold on—I'm going to put you on speaker so everyone can hear." He set his phone in the middle of the table.

"Hi, everyone." The voice on the other end of the line had just a hint of an upscale Southern accent. "Simon Kincaide. Seth asked me to look into a couple of things, and I emailed him a file, but I figured you might want the Spark Notes version."

"Thanks, Simon," Seth said and helped himself to another dough-nut. Toby reached to do the same, and Milo gave him a look. Toby withdrew his hand with a scowl that promised the two would have words when Seth and Evan were gone. "What do you have for us?"

"First off, Cassidy's friend can definitely take care of that Brigadoon Coin. He'll handle it, but I sent you some lore about the magic involved. And in case someone else gets the brilliant idea to move it, just realize that it'll take a box that is made of lead and iron and etched with binding runes. Knowing Milo, I included that too," Simon told them, a hint of snark coloring his tone.

"Wise move," Seth said, grinning at his mentor. "What else?"

"The short answer on the anchor question is, yes. The shape can change as long as the spell and material remain intact. Of course, it takes a higher level witch to change things around and not mess some-thing up, which is why most of them probably won't try. But theoreti-cally, it can be done. Gave you the details in the email."

"You're the best, Simon," Toby said.

"The real win was on that word you gave me. I checked out 'Nowhere' in different languages and cultures. Turns out, the answer was a lot simpler," Simon reported.

"There's a road that was supposed to be built with a tunnel through the mountain back at the turn of the last century when a town was flooded to fill a reservoir. The reservoir was built, but the tunnel was never finished. Without the new road, and with the old roads flooded, the locals had to go a distance out of their way to get to the next town. Pissed people off. And the unfinished highway was known as the 'Road to Nowhere,'" he added, a note of triumph in his voice.

"You're a genius." Seth looked up with a broad grin.

"I won't argue," Simon joked. "More like I've got great databases and heavy-duty WiFi. Here's the thing—the partial road and the tunnel still exist. But since a different, longer road was eventually built that went around the reservoir, no one wanted to spend money putting the tunnel through the mountain, so it just got left as it was. I only found it on a few old maps, and it doesn't show up on anything printed after 1939. There were some geocachers who tried to use it and some urban explorers, but they got run off by the local police."

Seth exchanged a glance with Evan, and Evan knew they were both thinking of Chief Bondell.

"I'm guessing you gave us directions?" Seth asked.

"Sure did. No suggestions about how you stay clear of the cops though."

"I think, between the four of us, we can come up with something," Toby promised. "Five of us, if you count Scott Williams."

"I remember him. Good man," Simon replied.

"Anything else?" Milo set down his mug and stretched.

"Just a warning about that tunnel. It might be haunted. There's a story about using convict labor to build it—wouldn't have been unusual at the time—and that some of the prisoners died going back across the reservoir at the end of the day. Boat tipped over, and their chains dragged them down. I couldn't find official records, but that kind of thing could easily have been hushed up," Simon told them. "It could be just a story. But in my business, I usually find that there's a bit of truth in most tales if you know where to look."

"We'll keep a sharp eye out," Seth promised. "This is a big help. Thanks, Simon."

"You're welcome. And I'll send you the bill."

The call ended, and Seth looked up at the others. "Do you think that you and Milo—and maybe Scott—could find a way to keep Chief Bondell busy while Evan and I check out the tunnel tomorrow?"

Milo grinned. "I bet we could manage that, without getting ourselves arrested. You up to it?" he asked his partner.

"I'm in," Toby assured them. "I've wanted a chance to size up this Bondell guy before he tries to get in the way. We'll figure something out. How long do you need?"

Seth had already opened the files from Simon's email and scanned the pages. He studied the map and chewed on his lip. "Looks like it's out past the forestry school. That would put it on the edge of the reservoir, which would make sense. We can only get so close with the truck; after that, we're going to have to hike in."

"Okay. Give us this afternoon to come up with a plan, and we'll work out the details over dinner. Sound good?" Milo asked.

"Works for me," Seth replied, and Evan nodded. "I had a batch of those stuffed cabbage rolls you like in the freezer," he said to Toby. "I thought maybe you'd want to come over here for dinner, for a change."

Toby grinned. "You mean *my* stuffed cabbage recipe that I gave to you?"

"Of course. Best one I've ever eaten. But you don't have to make it, so that's a win for you," Seth teased.

"I'll make some cornbread," Toby promised. "I think we've got a plan."

7

────────

SETH

April in the mountains meant they could get all four seasons in one day. The morning began gray and rainy, just above freezing. By afternoon the forecast promised clear skies and warmer temperatures. Seth wasn't going to bet on it.

"What is it with these witch-disciples and tunnels?" Evan asked as they slogged through the underbrush. Seth had located the unfinished road on a satellite map, but reaching it from anywhere they could drive was a challenge.

"Abandoned tunnels. And it's probably a thing because it works," Seth replied. "Out of the way, no one around, nice and private. Unlikely anyone is going to find the evidence."

"I never knew there were so many."

"Look at the bright side—it gives us a first place to look."

They tramped on in silence until Seth held up a fist, the signal to stop. Evan froze in his tracks. Seth pointed to a wooden stake with a sigil carved into it and motioned for Evan to follow him as they backtracked, then moved off the trail. They stopped once more when Seth spotted another stake. It took four tries to find a path to the old tunnel. Evan stayed silent until they were finally standing on the old road.

"What were those things?"

Seth scanned the woods around them. "My guess? Magical alarms of some kind. Probably how Sturdevant knew to set the cops on the urb-exers and geocachers. I don't know for sure, but it seems like a good bet. I hope we didn't miss one and set it off."

Evan nodded. "Okay. I'll watch for more."

"We might be all right now that we're on the road," Seth said. "There's a fine line between building a security system that works, and one that gets in your own way."

They both kept a lookout for either stakes or sigils but found none. The tunnel came into view around a bend.

"Once upon a time, a tunnel was just a tunnel," Evan observed. "Instead of a soul-sucking portal to the infernal realms."

"Why do you think I plan our routes to avoid tunnels whenever possible?" Seth replied without looking over at him. "I think there's a word for tunnel-phobia."

"It depends," Evan said. "On whether you're also scared of bridges, or just of being trapped. And it's a really common fear in Norway." Seth gave him an incredulous look. "What? You think I can't use a search engine?"

"So, what's it called?"

"Which one?"

"Either. Both."

Evan rolled his eyes. "I'd have to look it up again. Both of them were really long. It doesn't matter. I'd say we've got more reason to be afraid of tunnels than most people."

"I'll agree with you on that."

Once again they moved in formation, with Seth taking point and Evan watching their rear. Aside from the looming dark maw of the half-finished tunnel, nothing seemed out of place. Birds sang, the wind rustled through the trees, and in the distance, Seth heard the running water of a creek.

"Not very original," Seth observed when they had gotten to the end of the tunnel. Daylight gleamed in the distance as they looked back at where they'd come, and it seemed much farther away than Seth remembered. Their high-powered flashlights only lit up a portion of the gloom at a time, enough to see the sigils painted on the walls, the large dark stone in the middle of the road, and the ominous stain that darkened it.

"Like you said—it works. If it ain't broke, don't fix it."

Seth turned in a slow circle. "Do you feel that?"

Evan met his gaze. "You mean like we're being watched?"

Seth nodded. "Yeah. What's your bet? Ghosts or witches?"

Evan shuddered. "It's crazy to say this, but I really hope it's ghosts."

The tunnel was chillier than the outdoors, but Seth bet the ghosts made it even colder than normal. "We're here to help," Seth called out. "We want to stop the killing. We know who's doing it, and we think we know how to end it, but we might need your help."

"Seth." Evan's voice held warning. Their breath came in white puffs, and a skim of frost formed over the damp tunnel walls.

"Henshaw men!" Seth shouted. "He's going to kill another one of you. All I want is your word that, when the time comes, you'll help us if you can."

"Look."

Gray mist grew more solid. Some of the ghosts appeared to be the long-ago workers who died building the tunnel. Others bore a clear family resemblance to Kyle Henshaw.

Seth turned to the workers first. "Your deaths were a tragedy that should have been recognized. I hope you can go in peace. If you stay, I hope you can help us stop the murders that have been happening here."

He turned to the solemn figures of nine men who stood in a circle around Seth and Evan. From their clothing, Seth could pick out the time periods when they died, from the early 1900s to a decade past. They all bore a strong resemblance to Kyle.

"He's after Kyle," Seth said to the forty-something man in a polo shirt and jeans that he guessed was Kyle's father. "That's who he wants next. We're going to save Kyle, and stop the killing for good. But, the witch is strong. When it all comes down, we might need your help. Can we count on you?"

One by one, the men nodded, then their forms thinned and disappeared, leaving Seth and Evan alone in a blood-stained tunnel.

"That was creepy as fuck," Evan said.

"Let's get the hell out of here. At least we'll know where we're going, when the time comes," Seth replied.

SETH AND EVAN TOOK A DIFFERENT ROUTE BACK TO THE CAR, ALERT FOR more witch-alarms. When they reached the Silverado without incident, Seth let out a deep breath and saw the tension ease from Evan's shoulders.

On the way back to town, Evan sat silently, staring out the window.

"Penny for your thoughts."

Evan shrugged, uncomfortable. "Just thinking about what a hard time I gave you when you were trying to save me."

"You had your reasons."

Evan's grimace dismissed Seth's words. "Yeah. But you weren't my ex. I shouldn't have let what he did to me color my reactions."

"Cut yourself some slack. We all do that. Toby calls it 'fighting the last war.' Applying the things you should have done the last time to a new situation, whether they fit or not. Let it go. You're safe, we're both alive, and we're here. Together." Seth reached over and clasped Evan's hand. "It worked out."

"I just hope that Kyle believes us when we try to tell him."

So far, Seth had agreed with Milo and Toby that they needed to hold off talking to Kyle. Scott knew and maybe that would help, assuming he agreed to talk to his son when the time came. But Seth couldn't shake the feeling that their presence could be the catalyst that made Sturdevant push up his timeline, and that as necessary as their research was, they needed to make a move or lose any advantage they might have had.

"Yeah. Me, too."

Seth's stomach rumbled when they pulled into town. "How about if I run into the diner and pick up something to go?" he asked. "Milo and Toby were planning to be out all day. Or, we could go back and have sandwiches for lunch in the RV."

They had avoided eating out because Boone was a small town,

and the four of them might draw notice, even in a tourist area. Off-season meant less chance to blend in with the other out-of-towners. But one of them running in for takeout wouldn't be notable, Seth figured.

"Sure. I'll stay with the truck. Make it easy—just get me a bacon cheeseburger with chips," Evan said.

"You got it."

But just as Seth reached for the door handle, a cruiser with its lights flashing pulled up behind him.

"Shit." Seth and Evan exchanged a glance, and Seth was careful to keep his hands on the wheel. He was glad that he'd taken the extra few minutes to lock their guns and gear in the false bottom of the storage box. The gun in the glove compartment, he had a permit for, but he still wasn't looking forward to the conversation.

Chief Bondell sauntered to the side of the truck. He was a stocky man in his early fifties, with a bit of a paunch, like an athletic build had run to fat. Aviators and the regulation brimmed hat completed the picture. "I've been looking for you boys," he said when Seth rolled down the window.

"Did we lose something, sir?" Seth asked, his face a mask of innocence. Evan, beside him, looked equally blank.

"Got a call about a couple of out-of-towers causing some problems, bothering people with questions," Bondell drawled. "What are you? Reporters?"

"I'm just looking into some family history, sir," Evan replied, leaning forward. "We were in town to do a little rafting, maybe a zip line or two, and I thought I'd see if I could find out information for my mom and grandma." He gave his most engaging smile. "She's got a thing for those computer family tree sites, you know?"

Bondell's eyes narrowed. Seth knew the chief didn't have anything on them, but that didn't mean the cop couldn't hound them and get in their way. Bondell opened his mouth to speak when another voice broke in.

"Seth!" A black-haired man strode over, ignoring the stink eye Bondell gave him. "Is that you?"

"You know him?" Bondell asked the newcomer.

"Sure do. We served together. What'd he do—forget to put quarters in the meter?"

"Will? Will Penrod?"

"C'mon, Seth! It hasn't been that long since Mosul, man. Or maybe it's the hair," Will said, grinning broadly. "Not the buzz cut we had, huh?" He ran a hand through hair that nearly reached his collar.

"I was just about to tell your *friend* to watch the speed limit," Bondell said, lifting his chin. "Wouldn't want any tourists getting hurt." With that, he walked back to his patrol car and drove away.

Seth and Evan got out of the truck. Will thrust out his hand for a hearty shake and pulled Seth in to slap his back. Seth returned the gesture, feeling a little disoriented. *Had Will ever mentioned a connection to North Carolina?* Now that Seth thought about it, he seemed to remember something, but he hadn't paid attention at the time.

"Seth, you son of a bitch! Good to see you."

Evan stepped up beside Seth, close but not touching, giving Seth plausible deniability. *Screw that.* "This is Evan Malone, my partner," Seth said, reaching for Evan's hand in case the word was ambiguous.

"You sly dog. Good for you." Will cocked his head toward the diner. "Have you eaten? Got a few minutes to catch up?"

Seth didn't like being so visible, but there wasn't a graceful out, so he shrugged. "Sure. We were just about to go in."

Will greeted the cashier like an old friend and knew the server's name as well. A couple of the locals nodded to him when they walked toward their table in the back. Seth and Evan took the seats with their backs to the wall, on one side of the table. Will sat down across from them.

"So, are you from here?" Seth asked. "You seem to know everyone."

Will laughed. "Close enough. I've had family around these parts since, well, almost forever. When I got out, I thought about trying to get a job in Charlotte, but then a friend of my uncle's fishing buddy had an opening at his zip line attraction, and I ended up coming home."

He gave a self-conscious shrug. "It doesn't sound like much, but the place is a family-run attraction, and you'd be amazed how busy it is in the summer. We've added three new ropes courses, and this year a couple of escape rooms. I started out as a ropes flunky, and worked up to being a site manager." Will smiled, looking relaxed and satisfied. "It's not what I thought I'd be doing, but I like it. It pays well, and if we keep growing, it's got a future. How about you? Two," he added belatedly, with a glance at Evan.

"We're here on vacation," Seth replied. He slid a hand beneath the table to rest on Evan's knee, reassuring him that the good-looking, very straight, man across from them wasn't a threat. "I'm in computer security. Evan's a graphic designer. We can work from anywhere, so we like to move around. See the sights."

"I'm a little jealous," Will said. "I'm stuck here in the Blue Ridge, all year round." His voice made it clear that he relished his work. He leaned forward. "A word of advice? The chief takes his speed limits very seriously, especially for out-of-state license plates, if you know what I mean. And he watches anyone under forty like a hawk. Thinks we're all druggies or something. Just try to stay out of his way."

"Thanks," Seth said. "We will."

Seth and Evan both went with the bacon cheeseburger, while Will ordered a Reuben. Evan stayed quiet, letting them talk. Seth was eager to know what Evan's take on Will would be, once they were back in the truck.

"You hear anything from the other guys, from the unit?" Will asked.

Seth knew his smile didn't reach his eyes. He had only been home for a short time before Jesse was murdered, his parents died, and his home burned. Keeping in touch with old friends hadn't been high on his priorities.

"Nah. I'm not big on email and shit like that," Seth deflected. "I did my time. Got out in one piece. Not really looking to relive the glory days." Those last two words carried a touch of bitterness.

"Oh." Will looked unsure before his smile returned. "Yeah, I get it. I swore I wouldn't be like my grandpa, hanging out at the VFW with the guys he served with, talking about the good ol' days when they were young and horny—and being shot at."

"Do you? Hear from anyone?" Seth tried to make small talk so they could get the hell out of there without their departure looking odd.

"I hear from Tyler and Dequawn now and again. Ran into Carl on vacation in Vegas, of all places," Will replied. "Marriages, divorces, kids, job changes. The usual."

They managed to kill another fifteen minutes with excruciatingly trivial chit-chat before Seth glanced at his phone. "We've got spa appointments," Seth said with a sigh. "Over at Chetola." He flashed a smile that he hoped didn't look too fake. "Vacation splurge." Seth pulled out enough bills from his wallet to cover his meal and Evan's, plus a generous tip.

"Enjoy. I hear it's a nice place," Will said. "Let me give you my number. Never hurts to have a friend in town—or someone to make bail." Seth entered the contact, and they walked to the curb together.

"Great to see you," Will added, slapping a hand on Seth's shoulder. "Nice to meet you, Evan. Sorry we talked your ear off. Probably bored you to death—good job at sleeping with your eyes open. You had me fooled," he joked. "Give me a call if you want to do the ropes courses —or just need restaurant recommendations." He waved and headed off on foot toward town.

Seth and Evan got into the truck. After their run-in with the chief, Seth expected to find a parking ticket under the wipers but found a pizza coupon instead.

"Was that as weird as it seemed?" Evan asked as Seth headed for the campground.

Seth grimaced. "Actually, weirder."

"Were you and Will..." Evan didn't need to finish his sentence.

"Will? God, no. He's straight, as far as I ever knew. Never wanted to find out," Seth said. "We were all in the same team, back in the army. Ran missions together, and everyone hung out together because that's who was there. But we didn't have anything in common except that we were all a long way from home."

"Should we be suspicious that we ran into him here?"

Seth shrugged. "Probably not. Now that I think about it, I remember him saying he was from the Carolinas, in the mountains. He helped us out with the chief. And it might not hurt to know a local. Could come in handy."

Evan frowned. "Maybe." He sounded unconvinced.

Seth slid him a side-long look. "Jealous? Don't be. Like I said—Will's straight."

Evan chuckled. "No. Not jealous—except that he's known you for a lot longer than I have."

"In a place where people kept shooting at us and trying to blow us up," Seth reminded him. "I'm glad you missed all that."

"You think Bondell is going to be a problem?" Evan changed the subject.

"I think the guy's a dick," Seth said. "As long as he doesn't connect us to Sturdevant, he'll probably not be any more dickish than usual."

"That's not comforting."

"I'm not planning to be here long enough to care," Seth said as he made the turn to the campground. "We need to get to Kyle, convince Scott Williams to back us if necessary, and then go after Sturdevant. The sooner, the better."

8

EVAN

Evan had zoned in and out of the conversation that night at dinner with Toby and Milo. He felt edgy and restless and wasn't sure why.

"Figured we'd better check out that bridge because everyone says it's haunted," Toby said. "Turns out, not so much." He paused to take another mouthful of stuffed cabbage and washed it down with a swig of beer. "More like the local make-out spot, from the look of it."

"But on the plus side, down the road a piece we ran into our very own phantom hitchhiker," Milo added.

"Those are real?" Evan couldn't contain his surprise.

"This one was." Milo helped himself to another serving. "White dress, long dark hair, all bedraggled-looking and helpless by the side of the road."

"And after you threw salt at her, it was a good thing she vanished, because if she'd been real, she probably would have reported you for harassment," Toby replied, chuckling.

"Can you banish something like that?" Evan's curiosity got the best of him.

"Probably, if we found out who she was, where she's buried, how she died," Toby said. "It's just a type of repeater ghost. Thing is, she's not really dangerous. And that's not why we're here."

"Yeah, getting caught burning her bones would blow the surprise for Sturdevant," Milo agreed. "Priorities."

"Anyhow, we ruled out the bridge," Toby said.

"Tomorrow, I want to go to Elk Mountain Manor," Evan said. "The mansion that Sturdevant built back in the day. It's a museum, and it's supposed to contain original furnishings. We might pick up on something."

"Fine by me," Seth replied. "And then I vote for going to see Kyle and Scott. Get Kyle to safety. I can't shake the feeling we're on borrowed time."

"You think he'll listen?" Toby asked.

"Scott knows what we do," Milo answered. "And I told him Kyle was in danger. His boy is in love with Kyle. He asked me to keep them both safe. So yeah, I think he'll listen, but before we go WITSEC on him, we need to have a plan."

Seth looked up. "Taking Kyle is the plan, isn't it? Once he goes missing, Sturdevant has to come looking for him, or his schemes go up in smoke. We have his anchor, and we'll go after the amulet when we corner him. We just need a secure place to stash Kyle—and Steve—until it's over."

"It makes sense," Toby said, "but I doubt it'll be that easy."

"It never is," Milo muttered.

"Sturdevant isn't expecting us," Seth said, eyes shining with excitement. "We're early for his cycle by more than a year. He's got his eye on Kyle, just waiting for the right time. Then Kyle vanishes, and Sturdevant is going to have to make a move or lose his chance to level-up."

"Kinda hard on Kyle's family for him to just vanish." Toby leveled a look at Seth.

"Better than claiming his body at the morgue." The light dimmed in Seth's eyes, and Evan knew his partner was thinking about having to do just that, for Jesse. He reached over and took Seth's hand, gave his fingers a squeeze.

Toby held up his hands in surrender. "Okay. Okay. It's just a piss-poor brainstorming session if we don't look at things from all the angles."

"And we're also going on the assumption that Sturdevant either doesn't hear from the other disciples or doesn't spy on them, so he hasn't heard about the two we've already killed," Evan pointed out.

That, to him, was the wild card. Even if the witch-disciples hated each other and saw one another as competition, he had trouble believing they didn't keep tabs on the others, if only to watch their own backs. Then again, maybe creatures who were more than a century old thought about things differently, since they weren't a product of traffic cams, security systems, and GPS tracking.

"No way to know," Seth allowed. "So, we control what we can, and make the rest up as we go along."

Evan could see that Seth disliked not having all the bases covered. So did Milo. But Toby met Evan's gaze and gave him a nod in support, letting him know that the two of them were in sync about going with the flow. That's what made their partnerships work so well, the way their strengths complemented each other's.

Toby and Milo made an early night of it and returned to their cabin. Evan grinned at the memory of seeing Toby grab a handful of Milo's ass in the kitchen and the kiss that Milo thought he stole when no one was looking. He hoped he and Seth were just as hungry for each other when they got to be that age, whether or not they were still hunting.

After he and Seth cleaned up in the kitchen, Evan realized he was missing something. "I left my phone in the truck," he said. "I'll be right back."

The day had warmed from its chilly start, enough that Toby and Milo had opened windows in the cabin. Evan heard the conversation when he went out to the truck, and for a moment, feared he might be overhearing them getting it on.

"…I said I'm fine!" Milo sounded pissed.

"…you're not fine! You're supposed to take it easy. And you skipped your pills today." Toby's voice had risen, but instead of anger, Evan heard fear.

"…I'll take my pills. I get them most days."

"Most days isn't good enough! If we don't control your blood pressure, you're going to have another incident," Toby countered, sounding on the verge of tears. "Don't do this to me, Milo! I will not survive burying you. Please."

"I'm sorry." All the anger had drained from Milo's voice. "You're right. I'm a pig-headed old fool. Come here, Sweetheart. I'm not going anywhere."

Evan stood, transfixed. He knew he shouldn't be eavesdropping, but he couldn't make himself leave. When the conversation moved away from the open window, he finally got into the truck as quietly as possible and came back with his phone. Seth was watching him from the window.

"What happened out there? You froze like a deer in the headlights."

Evan blushed, embarrassed. "I overheard Toby and Milo fighting. And I was nosy."

"You've heard the phrase 'bicker like an old married couple'? I think they had Toby and Milo in mind when they came up with that."

Evan shook his head. "No, it wasn't that kind of argument. Toby didn't think Milo was taking care of himself, and he was really upset about it."

Seth pulled Evan to sit on his lap in the big recliner chair and turned on a movie they'd seen before. A press of a button dimmed the lights. Evan snuggled against Seth's chest, and Seth's strong arms closed around him, pulling him tight.

"Milo's had some heart scares," Seth said quietly. "Toby called me when Milo wasn't home. I don't think Milo knows I know. They're both from a generation that doesn't like to admit they're not bulletproof."

"That kind of stuff happens, when you get to a certain age," Evan replied. "And that's on top of a dangerous job." He hoped that he and Seth made it to mid-life, alive and together. Worrying about weight gain instead of wendigos sounded like a great goal.

"It's worse for Toby, after losing Ray," Seth added. "He fusses over Milo. Milo lets him, and I think he enjoys it up to a point, but then it ruffles his feathers, and they have a spat. Toby just can't help it."

"Do you think Milo's okay?" Evan hadn't known the two older

hunters long, but he was already fond of them, despite their curmudgeonly ways.

"I hope so," Seth replied, stroking Evan's hair. The movie played on in the background, an action flick they both knew by heart, comforting and familiar. "They aren't that old. Hunting goes hard on you. I don't like to think about it."

Seth probably dreaded losing his surrogate fathers after having to bury his own family the way Toby feared being a second-time widower. They all came into hunting with scars and gained more from the job. Maybe the only strange thing was they weren't all barking mad.

THE NEXT MORNING DAWNED CLEAR AND WARM. EVAN SHOULD HAVE taken that as a good sign, but he shared Seth's sense that time was running out. They grabbed a breakfast of cold cereal and coffee, then headed over to Elk Mountain Manor. Evan couldn't explain his hunch that touring the old historic house was important, but he was grateful that Seth followed his lead.

"Nice place." They parked in the gravel lot and followed the path to the ticket office. The huge, stately house had a wide front porch with columns, a testament to Victorian elegance and propriety.

"He built it when he was still Isaac Saunders. Maybe he hadn't figured out the need to hide yet," Evan said. "Saunders never married or had children—big surprise. The house and land belong to a private historic trust."

"So, Sturdevant still controls them."

"Probably. Yeah."

Tourists were sparse, so the tour group only had a few other people aside from Seth and Evan, a group of two retired couples who arrived together. "Someday, I want to go to a place like this without looking for ghosts or monsters," Evan said.

"How about New Orleans?" Seth suggested. "No promises about ghosts, but plenty of pretty old houses."

Evan smiled at him. "I'd like that. I'll hold you to it."

Ann, their tour guide, welcomed them inside. "With a smaller group today, I have time for more questions. If you hear something and you want to know more, just ask."

Ann brought them in through the back door, entering the big kitchen. She explained the old-fashioned appliances and how cooking was done a century ago before leading them through a pantry and into a formal dining room.

"He had good taste," Evan said under his breath.

"Maybe he thought this was the payoff for services rendered," Seth replied. One of the older women glared at him, and Seth shot back a fake smile.

Next was the parlor, a fancy room ready to welcome company. Evan could imagine men in their high collars and dark suits sitting on the stiff-backed sofa, and women with full skirts and tight corsets prim and proper—and damnably uncomfortable.

Everything in the parlor made a statement about the owner's wealth, from the Kilim rugs to the expensive clocks, glassware, and figurines that sat on the mantle. A huge Victrola gramophone took up a corner, while heavy velvet draperies hung over the windows. Saunders wanted to make it clear to anyone who visited that he was a man of money, taste, and education.

"Seth. Look."

Seth followed Evan's gaze to the painting over the fireplace. They had managed to find a few photographs of Ira Sturdevant in his various personas, all of them poor quality. Perhaps as time went on, Sturdevant learned to hide and conceal his face. But in this painting, Isaac Saunders stood proud and arrogant. The old-style haircut and sideburns disguised the resemblance, but not completely.

Then again, Evan figured, the long-time families in these parts were all probably intermarried enough to make resemblances common. No one would think much about the fact that the mansion's original owner bore an uncanny likeness to a present-day philanthropist.

"The medallion," Seth murmured, risking the wrath of the grumpy tourist lady.

"The amulet," Evan whispered. "There it is."

Hanging from a silver chain around Saunders's neck was a silver sigil. Evan didn't recognize it, but he knew it was ancient, associated with dark powers. In the painting, Saunders flaunted his arcane power the same way he showed off his wealth, and the self-satisfied half-smile on his face told the world that he got the joke that they all missed. Evan stepped in front of Seth to keep the tour guide from seeing Seth take a picture of the portrait with his phone.

Neither the guide nor the cranky lady seemed to notice when Seth and Evan slipped out of the back door, leaving the tour early.

"Well, we got what we came for," Evan said as they left the parking lot.

"You didn't want to finish the tour? It was a pretty nice house." Seth smirked. "Might give you ideas about how to spruce up the RV."

Evan laughed. "That's it. We should get a formal oil painting for over the electric fireplace. Make a statement."

Seth grinned. "It certainly would say something, although I'm not sure what."

Evan settled in for the drive to Blowing Rock. "I made some calls yesterday, following up on a few of the leads we got at the archive. Some of the people I'd spoken to earlier, and they said they'd look up the information I wanted. When I called them back, they either pretended they'd never heard of me or swore they couldn't find anything. A couple of them said that they had pulled the records I wanted, but then the files had been misplaced."

"That's a lot of coincidences—or rampant stupidity."

"Or tampering." Evan gave voice to his suspicions. "If Sturdevant figured out why we were here, it wouldn't take much to block us. A little stonewalling, a little gaslighting, and we hit a dead end."

"Emphasis on *dead*."

Seth picked up speed on a long, straight stretch, to help get them up the winding mountain highway. Evan enjoyed the view since Seth didn't dare take his eyes off the road. The whole valley lay spread out, rolling hills and trees just coming into bud.

As they crested the rise, Evan heard a thump, and the car swerved.

"Fuck," Seth muttered. His hands tightened on the wheel, and his jaw clenched. "Hang on."

The Silverado usually handled smoothly, but now Evan saw Seth struggling to keep the truck in its lane. Losing control here would be deadly.

"There!" Evan said, pointing to a runaway truck turnoff. He held on tight as Seth cut the wheel, and the Silverado plowed into the sand, hitting the soft speed bumps designed to stop an out-of-control eighteen-wheeler. Evan pitched forward, hard enough that the seatbelt cut into his chest, then slammed back against the seat as the truck came to a halt.

"You okay?" Seth asked with a worried glance. His hands gripped the wheel, white-knuckled.

"Yeah," Evan replied, deciding not to mention how hard his heart jackhammered. "I'm good."

Seth climbed from the cab, and Evan scrambled out as well. Seth stared at the front wheel, which canted at a strange angle. "That thump was the wheel coming loose. If we hadn't been able to pull off, we would have probably lost the whole wheel before we got to the bottom of the hill—and there's no way I could have held us on the road."

"Fuck," Evan muttered, feeling exposed as cars and trucks zipped by on the highway. "You think one of Sturdevant's goons tampered with it?"

"Don't you?"

"Yeah. Now what?"

"I'll call a tow truck, and have us hauled into Blowing Rock," Seth said with a sigh. "I'm glad we're alive. But this is going to be a pain in the ass."

An hour later, the tow truck finally arrived. Seth had waved off several well-meaning motorists who had tried to offer them rides. They couldn't risk the kindness of strangers, since they had no idea who might be working for Sturdevant. Seth fretted while the driver hooked up the Silverado, double-checking to make sure the tow connection wouldn't damage his truck.

Evan and Seth climbed into the back seat of the tow truck cab, sitting silently for the rest of the drive to Blowing Rock.

"Assuming nothing else was damaged, the guys in the garage said they should have you fixed up in three hours, max," the driver said. "If they find more, they can handle that, too, but it'll cost you extra."

Seth swore under his breath. Evan bumped his shoulder and offered what he hoped was an encouraging smile.

Once they reached the garage, Seth filled out the paperwork while Evan ran across the street to grab drinks and cookies for both of them from a nearby coffee house. When Evan returned, Seth looked resigned but calmer.

"The good news is they can get it done pretty quick," Seth said. "The bad news is the bill."

"I've got a new design job coming in next week," Evan replied. "It'll cover the cost. Just remember—it could have been worse."

They sat out the repair at the diner a few doors down, figuring that they might as well get lunch during the downtime. Evan could tell from the way Seth picked at his food that his partner wasn't all right.

"Talk to me," he said, reaching out to brush his fingers against Seth's.

"We could have been killed."

"I think that was the general idea."

"He knows."

Evan nodded. "Or he strongly suspects. At the very least, he's made us as hunters."

"That means he'll make his move, and we're stuck here, waiting."

"We'll go see Scott and Kyle right after this, and we already warned Milo and Toby. If Sturdevant is still warning us off, it might mean we still have time."

The look in Seth's eyes said otherwise, but Seth didn't argue, and Evan took it as a win.

Whether the garage just happened to have a slow day, or Seth's offer of an extra hundred dollars to speed things up made a difference, the Silverado was ready to go two hours later.

"At least Sturdevant didn't fuck up being able to get a tow or have it fixed," Seth said, looking relieved to be back in the driver's seat.

"Which means he isn't perfect. He was so sure he'd kill us that he didn't plan for other outcomes," Evan pointed out.

"Or he's toying with us, waiting to see what we'll do."

"Or that," Evan reluctantly agreed.

Twenty minutes later, they pulled into Scott Williams's driveway.

They'd driven by the police station but hadn't seen the chief's truck parked in the lot.

"Why is he home in the middle of a weekday?" Evan asked as they walked onto the porch.

Before Seth could answer, Scott Williams opened the door. "Evan. I was just about to call Milo. Come in." His tone made it a summons, not an invitation.

"Chief Williams, this is my partner, Seth Tanner."

"Call me Scott," the chief said, shaking hands. "Milo has told me a lot about you."

Scott looked haggard as if he'd aged in just the few days since Evan had seen him before. "What's going on?" Evan asked.

"We came to talk to you before we go see Kyle," Seth added. "We think the creature is about to make its move, and we want to get Kyle —and Steve—to safety."

"You're too late," Scott said, a bleak look in his eyes. "They're both missing."

Evan's head snapped up. "What? When?"

Scott waved them into the living room. "Liz is out putting up fliers like he's a runaway dog," the chief said, dropping into a chair. "But it gives her something to do, and it can't hurt. I was out all night, along with my deputy, checking the hospitals and morgues. They weren't there, thank God. I got a caffeine boost, and I'm heading out again. Surprised you caught me here."

"Are we talking kidnapping or did they run?" Seth asked, meeting Scott's gaze.

The chief lifted his chin. "I don't know. But they're gone. And I think it's about time you told me the whole story about this 'creature' you're hunting."

Scott listened as Seth and Evan tag-teamed the story, only leaving out the details that would earn them felony charges. Evan felt certain Scott could fill in the blanks on his own.

"Jesus H. Christ and all the fucking archangels," Scott muttered when they finished. "If I hadn't seen what I saw when I worked with Milo, I'd be getting you a room at the psych ward."

"Just one of the reasons we don't usually overshare," Seth replied.

Scott leaned forward with his elbows on his knees. "This isn't something I can pull my officers into, not on the record. And the boys can't be declared officially missing this soon."

"Probably not a good idea," Evan agreed.

Scott raised his head, and Evan could see the strain in his eyes. "That's my son out there, and a boy who's like a second son to me. And if some sorry son of a bitch took them, then I want in. I don't know much about monsters, but I can shoot, and I know the area. And I've got plenty of favors I can call in if it helps. Just tell me what to do."

"We'll take you up on that," Seth said. "But your wife is safer if she doesn't know the full story."

Scott looked sucker punched. "You want me to keep the details from Liz? Steve is her son, too."

"She's a civilian," Evan countered. "Treat it like any other case. How would you handle it, if the missing men weren't Steve and Kyle? And if the 'monster' was a mobster or a drug lord?"

Scott swallowed hard and closed his eyes. In a moment, he met Evan's gaze. "All right. Do you think she'll be safe here?"

"Sturdevant wants Kyle. You're only involved because Steve got tangled up in whatever happened. Sturdevant doesn't want you or Liz. He wasn't after Steve, either. He just wants Kyle."

"To kill him. Like he's killed the others."

"Yes," Seth replied. "But we're going to keep that from happening. And we could use your help."

9

SETH

"Did we cause it?" Evan asked as they drove back in the darkness.

"Cause what?" Seth still felt shaken from what happened at the Williams house, and his mind spun trying to come up with a plan to find and rescue Kyle and Steve.

"Did coming here make Sturdevant move ahead of schedule? Would they have been safe...at least for a while longer...if we hadn't stirred things up?"

Seth had been asking himself the same questions, but hearing them from Evan brought sudden clarity. "Maybe. Then again, if he heard about what happened in Richmond and Pittsburgh, he might have decided to move the date up regardless to raise his mojo, even if we weren't here. And if we hadn't come, Kyle and Steve wouldn't have anyone to fight for them."

Evan swallowed hard, then nodded, as if settling an unspoken, inner debate. "All right. What now?"

"We regroup with Toby and Milo, figure out where to look."

"The tunnel?"

Seth shook his head. "Probably not until right before the ritual. But maybe. Sturdevant might not know that we know about it."

"And Scott?"

"Milo said he was good in a fight. If he wants in, he's in. It's his kid."

"Well, that makes five of us, against a dark warlock and a corrupt police chief."

"It'll have to be enough."

When they reached the campground, Seth slowed the truck before they got to the cabin. "Do you see what I'm seeing?" he asked in a hushed voice.

"Yeah. What happened?"

Seth parked, and the two of them got out. "Someone vandalized everything they could reach," Seth said.

"But just near our cabin and RV. Nowhere else that I can see," Evan replied. Terra cotta pots filled with pansies were smashed, with the dirt strewn everywhere. Pieces of a broken birdbath and the wrecked decorative fencing looked like someone had taken a sledgehammer to them.

"We have wardings on the cabin and the RV," Seth said. "Sturdevant can't use magic against us, and the protections should hold off regular troublemakers."

"So it was a message."

"No, it was a threat." Seth felt his anger rise. "The only way he could be more clear would be if we got a police escort out of town."

"Be careful what you wish for."

Seth and Evan drew their guns and carefully walked the perimeter of their two campsites. The campground was nearly empty midweek in the middle of a cold, rainy spring. What had felt like safety and solitude now felt exposed and dangerously isolated.

They kept their guns in hand as they edged up and rapped on the cabin door. "Milo? It's us."

Milo checked through the peephole, and opened the door, waving them inside, then locked up behind them.

"What happened out there?" Evan asked.

"Freak windstorm," Toby replied, coming out of the kitchen with a beer in one hand and his gun tucked into the waistband of his jeans. "A rather specific one."

"You think it was Sturdevant, trying to scare us off?" Seth asked.

Milo shook his head. "I think he meant to do more than scare us. He just didn't think we'd be ready, and when he realized we were warded, he pulled back. He'll probably try again."

"I'm sure he will," Toby replied. "So we need to get gone."

Pounding shook the door. All four drew their guns. Toby moved to one side to look out. The others found cover, and Toby opened the door.

"We're looking for Milo Cornell. We need protection." Kyle Henshaw and Steve Williams stood in the doorway.

"Don't just stand there with targets on your goddamn backs." Milo grabbed Kyle and yanked him inside. Steve followed on his heels, and Milo slammed the door. Seth, Evan, and Toby lowered their weapons.

Kyle's eyes widened as he realized he'd walked into an armed stand-off. "What the hell?"

"What's going on? Where the fuck have you been?" Seth asked, pushing his gun into his waistband.

Kyle drew himself up, and Steve stood beside him, shoulder to shoulder, with a glare that said he was ready to protect his boyfriend.

"Stand down, both of you, before someone breaks a nose," Milo grumbled.

"Your parents are worried sick," Evan said to Steve. Steve's bluster softened to contrition. "And I bet your family is scared, too," he added, looking at Kyle.

Kyle shook his head. "My mom knows. I told her. I was working out what happened to Dad and the other men on the Henshaw side. And then when I figured out there was a cycle, she told me to run away and hide. So I told Steve what I was planning."

"And I said that he wasn't going anywhere without me," Steve said, still defiant. "I told him my dad knew people who could fight monsters. Dad told me about Milo. I just called around until I found out where you were staying."

Toby glared at his husband. "You used your real name?"

"Not the point right now," Milo muttered.

"Why didn't you tell your dad?" Evan asked Steve.

"Because if I told him, he wouldn't look scared enough, and no one would believe I was really gone. Anyone who knew about Kyle and me would know we're a package deal."

"We have to tell them," Seth said. "They've put on enough of a show. And we need your dad's help."

Steve's bravado crumbled. "I was trying to protect them."

Milo nodded. "Your dad will understand that. But we're going to need to leave here, and we need a safe house. He's the most likely one to know where we can hide, and then we'll bring him—and both of you—into the plan."

"Okay," Steve replied. Kyle gave him a supportive nod. Steve reached for his phone. Milo grabbed his hand.

"No. Use this." Milo went to a bag on the desk and dug out a cheap burner phone. "It's got no history, can't be traced."

Steve nodded and took the phone. He dialed and put it on speaker. "Watermelon."

Seth and the others exchanged confused looks. They could hear breathing on the other end of the phone.

"Listen and don't say anything," Steve said in a low voice, sounding more like a soldier than a runaway. "We're safe with your old friend. Need a new place, because this one's compromised. Do you remember fly fishing when I was ten?"

Scott grunted in response.

"Is the place still there?"

Another grunt, affirmative.

"I think I remember how to get there. Can you slip out and meet us? Make sure you're not followed."

Scott growled a few choice words.

"See you." Steve ended the call, looking suddenly tired.

"Watermelon?" Evan echoed. "What is that, some kind of code word?"

Steve handed the phone back to Milo. "When I was a kid, Dad was a little overprotective. Goes with being a cop, I guess. So we had some code words, in case I ever got kidnapped. 'Watermelon' meant it was really me."

"Your dad's a smart guy," Toby replied. "So where's this fly fishing place?"

Steve licked his lips nervously. Kyle moved closer in support and took his hand. "My mom's cousin owns a place out in Maggie Valley. Way out. No electricity, no phone line, been in the family for generations. It's got propane, and they keep it stocked, but they don't use it more than a couple of times a year. We can be there in around two hours."

Milo and Toby exchanged a look. "It hasn't changed hands in a long time, so there aren't any recent records of sale. No utilities. Off the grid. It could work," Milo said.

"Then let's get moving before Sturdevant strikes again," Seth said.

"Ira Sturdevant? The wilderness guy?" Kyle said, eyes widening. "He's the one who wants to kill me?"

"We'll explain later," Evan told him.

"Seth, Evan—grab what you need out of the RV. Figure we might be gone a few days," Milo said. "Bring all the weapons you can carry. We'll pack our stuff and grab some food, just in case, and then we'd better roll." He looked at Kyle and Steve, then glanced at the backpacks they carried. "You okay with what you've got?"

"For a few days, yeah," Steve said, and Kyle nodded.

"I'm going to pay the campsite through the end of next week," Milo said. "That way they'll be expecting us to stick around. Toby knows what to pack for me."

Seth and Evan headed over to the RV as Milo started toward the office. Seth had just unlocked the RV door when he heard Milo shout in alarm, then cry out in pain as wood splintered.

"Milo!" Seth shouted. He and Evan came running. Milo lay in the shallow stream bed, gasping, where he fallen from a decorative half-moon bridge that crossed the stream on the path. One leg was twisted at an unnatural angle where it had gone through the wood.

Evan moved to free Milo's leg. "Shit. Seth—someone sawed partway through the railing and the bridge. This wasn't an accident."

"Milo, can you walk?"

Milo closed his eyes and shook his head. "Don't think so. Fuck, this is bad timing. I think I broke a few ribs when I hit the railing before it gave, and the ankle's probably broken, too."

Seth looked to Evan. "Get Toby. Milo's going to need a hospital."

"You've got to get those boys out of here," Milo protested.

"And we will. Evan and I will get them there, and Scott will meet us. You'll join us when you're able."

Milo let out a string of curses. "We don't need this now."

"Never a good time for cracked ribs," Seth said.

"Milo!" Toby came running and stopped beside them. "I'm going to get you to a doctor." Without waiting for permission, he scooped Milo up as if the other man weighed nothing.

"Put me down."

"No can do," Toby said. Seth ran ahead to get the door to Milo's truck open and helped Toby get the other man inside.

"Take care of him," Seth said, meeting Toby's gaze. "We'll see you up in the valley."

They left Kyle's truck at the campground and drove the Silverado. Steve and Kyle sat in the back seat. For the first hour, Kyle and Steve peppered them with questions about who Sturdevant was and why the men in Kyle's family had died. Seth told them about Rhyfel Gremory and his disciples, and the cursed men of the posse that killed the warlock. After a while the questions stopped. When Seth glanced in the mirror, he saw that Steve had his arm around Kyle's shoulders while both dozed.

"What's the plan?" Evan asked, keeping his voice low.

"We get them into the cabin, make sure it's secure, ward it the way Toby and Simon taught us," Seth said, keeping his eyes on the dark highway ahead of them.

"And then?"

"We wait for Scott to show up, and for Milo and Toby to get there."

"Milo's out of the fight," Evan said.

"Down, but not out," Seth replied. "He's a stubborn SOB. I wouldn't count him out even if he was in traction."

Evan chuckled, but one look at Seth's expression quelled his laughter. "Seriously?"

"He's good. I'd take him beside me in a fight, banged up and bandaged, over most of the guys I served with."

"Huh." Evan nodded. "Then what?"

Seth let out a long breath. "Then, I come back to the RV. Wait for Sturdevant to make his move."

"You intend to be bait."

Seth answered with a shrug.

"I'm not staying in Maggie Valley without you."

"Evan—"

"No," Evan snapped, eyes blazing. "You listen to me. You think Milo's stubborn? Have you met me? If we're going to hunt these warlocks, we're going to do it together. I've got just as much skin in this game as you do. So stay or leave, we're doing it as a team."

Seth felt a rush of love mingled with sheer terror for Evan's safety. He wanted to keep Evan safe. He wanted to fight side by side. Both emotions were almost overwhelming.

"You're also a possible target. We don't know that this disciple couldn't power up from you as much as from Kyle."

"Or from you," Evan said, refusing to back down. "Because you were a target too. If we're partners, then we have to have enough faith in each other to believe we're harder to beat as a team."

Seth was silent for a few minutes. "Okay. You're right."

"How long do you think it'll take for Sturdevant to figure out Kyle and Steve aren't at the campground?"

"Maybe just long enough for us to do what we need to do."

Evan's expression suggested that wasn't nearly enough of a plan, but he didn't push.

They got to the cabin after midnight. Steve hadn't been kidding about it being off the grid. The Silverado's headlights were the only illumination, and this far in the woods, the night was true dark.

The one-story log cabin was a large square with a green tin roof and a wide front porch. A stone chimney ran up one side. A three-sided shed held neatly stacked cordwood, and a large propane tank sat behind the cabin, next to an equally large rainwater cistern.

"We're here," Seth said over his shoulder to the sleeping men in the back. Kyle and Steve sat up, groggy and sleep-mussed.

"You weren't kidding about it being a long way out here," Evan said.

"Let's just hope it's far enough," Seth replied. He looked at Steve. "Did you happen to swipe the keys when you took off?"

"No, but I know where they're hidden." Steve jumped out and shone the light from his phone on a small statue on the porch. He reached beneath it and withdrew a ring, letting the keys dangle.

Seth grinned. "All right. Let's get going. We've got work to do before we can sleep."

They moved their gear and weapons into the cabin, as well as an armful of cordwood. Steve and Seth got the propane lanterns working so they could save the flashlights.

"How about Evan and Kyle get the fire going and the lights on, and lay down salt and iron at all the doors and windows. Steve and I will set the outdoor wardings."

Both Steve and Kyle looked a bit gobsmacked, but they nodded and got to work. Seth pulled Evan to the side. "Go through the cabin, check everything for sigils, hexes, anything strange. You know what to look for. When you know it's clean, invoke the wardings the way Travis showed you. Make sure you show Kyle how not to fuck them up."

Evan nodded and started on his sweep. Seth gestured to Steve and headed outside. "We need to set protections," he said, setting his gear bag on the porch and starting to dig out what he needed. The full moon helped but didn't penetrate beneath the trees.

"You mean like traps? Tripwires? That kind of thing?" Steve looked confused.

"Sort of," Seth said with a tired smile. "Witch traps. You carry the bag. I'll do the trap setting."

They set down a circle of rock salt mix sprinkled with iron filings around the cabin. Seth pulled out half a dozen wooden stakes, marked them with protective sigils and sank them into the ground, evenly spaced apart. Once the stakes were in place, Seth walked counterclockwise around the circle, speaking a word of power and willing his intent to activate the sigils. Then he repeated the stakes and rote spells in an even larger circle so their vehicles would be protected.

"How did you learn to do all this stuff?" Steve asked, staring at Seth with a mix of curiosity and fear.

"From other hunters," Seth replied, as he placed a few battery-operated units along the driveway. They would set off an alarm inside if anyone broke the beam of light across the road. "Toby and Milo, and some of their friends."

"Is that what you and Evan are? Hunters?"

"Is that hard to imagine?"

"Actually, yes. I thought it was only something that happened in books or on TV."

"It's not exactly the kind of thing you put on a business card," Seth replied. "And we're not the only ones. Unfortunately, there's enough work to keep us all busy."

"How did you know to come to Boone?"

Steve wasn't much younger than Seth, but life had been kinder to him, and he still had an innocence that Seth could barely remember. The army had stripped away many of Seth's illusions, and whatever remained had been ripped out by Jesse's death and the aftermath.

"Research," Seth replied. "We tracked the descendants of the posse, and pieced together the identities of the witch-disciples."

"Most people's families don't stay in one place for that long."

"When descendants did move away, either the witches found a way to bring them back or followed them."

"So it doesn't work to just leave."

"'Fraid not."

"Are you going to kill him?" Steve met Seth's gaze. Not in challenge, but out of a need to know the truth.

"Yes. Because if we don't, he won't stop until he kills Kyle, and a dozen years from now, he'll come after Kyle's son, or cousin or nephew—whoever's the oldest male. He's killed nine of Kyle's ancestors—including his father."

Steve swallowed hard and nodded. "We figured out the pattern. That's when we realized that all the deaths couldn't just be accidents."

"We got rid of the disciple in Richmond who preyed on Evan's family. Evan and I are going after the rest of them. Throwing off the schedule. Sturdevant must have realized that, and decided to move up his timetable."

"Is Sturdevant human?"

Seth shrugged. "I'm not sure. As long as he can draw on Gremory's power, he's effectively immortal. Doesn't mean he can't be killed; it just means he won't age or die from natural causes."

"My dad is a cop. And you're talking about murder."

"Sturdevant might be human, but he's also a monster. He's killed at least nine men, probably more, and he'll kill again unless we stop him," Seth said. He and Evan had wrestled with the idea, and the answer always came up the same. "This isn't the kind of thing you can turn over to the state troopers, or the feds. So...hunters hunt."

"And my dad?"

"He understands what's going on. And he'll do what needs to be done to keep you and Kyle safe."

Steve looked stricken and walked off, pacing and running his hands through his hair. "I never meant to get Dad involved. Now I'm going to screw up his life."

Seth felt for the man. He knew from experience that this was a lot to take in. He'd had a hard enough time as a former soldier. "You chose to stand with Kyle. That's what you do when you love someone. Your dad is standing by his son. It's his choice." He heard the echoes of Evan's argument in his mind as he spoke.

"Do you think he can forgive me?" Steve's fear was clear in his eyes.

"Your parents can forgive you easier than they'd be able to live without you. When those are the only choices, the decision gets mighty clear."

"You make it sound easy." Steve sounded like he was at his limit, stress visible in every line of his body and in the way he moved.

"It's not. Evan went on the run with me when we'd known each other four whole days. We've been getting to know each other since then," Seth replied. "Same kind of thing happened to Toby and Milo. It's not normal, but I'd rather do it the hard way than not have him in my life."

"I love Kyle," Steve admitted. "I guess I never realized how much he loved me back until now."

"And when this is over, you can go back to your old lives. Ding dong, the witch is dead," Seth said with a smirk. "Forget all this ever happened."

Steve ran a hand over his face. "Yeah. Maybe. Probably not." He paused. "I just want to keep him safe."

"We will," Seth vowed. "Both of you."

Steve nodded. "Thank you. You came out here to save him, and you'd never even met him."

"Thank Jesse. He's the real reason."

Kyle and Steve had a right to answers, and Seth didn't begrudge him that. But talking about Jesse always made him melancholy. Maybe that would fade with time, or when the last of the witch-disciples was dead. But Seth both doubted and feared that it ever would. Doubted, because the loss ran too deep. And feared, because he didn't want to forget the brother he'd loved so much.

"Seth, Steve, you two okay? Need help?" Evan called from the doorway.

"We were just coming in," Seth called. He looked over to Steve. "You good?"

Steve nodded. "Yeah, I'm fine."

Seth knew he was lying. He felt a ripple of energy as he crossed the threshold, proof that Evan had done the wardings right. The fireplace cast a welcoming glow, and the warmth felt good compared to the chill outside.

"Kitchen's stocked with canned goods, powdered milk, pasta, and beans," Evan reported. "Even coffee. There's a well, and the water's good. Propane stove works. We won't starve."

"Good to know."

Kyle came out from the back hallway. "There are two bedrooms, and the beds are made up. The bathroom doesn't have the best water pressure, and the water's cold, but between the cistern and the well, there's enough."

Steve gave a tense smile. "If we have to hole up, it's not such a bad place."

"Are you kidding?" Kyle said. "This is great." He went to Steve, who gathered Kyle into his arms. "You just took charge when I was falling apart. Got us packed, found Toby and Milo, and thought of this place. I don't know what I'd have done without you."

Steve kissed the top of Kyle's head. "Just taking care of you, like I promised."

Evan pulled a deck of cards out of his bag. "I didn't figure we were sleeping until the rest of the crew got here. Anyone up for a friendly round of poker?"

Two hours later, the driveway alarms went off. "We've got company," Seth said, putting down his cards and moving to the window. He didn't pull his gun, but he had it in easy reach.

Steve went to the other window. "That's my uncle's truck." He grinned. "Wanna bet dad switched cars before he came here, in case someone was following him?"

Scott Williams parked next to Seth's truck. He brought his duffle bag with him and three bags of groceries. As soon as the door opened, he stepped inside, and Steve ran to him, hugging him tight. Kyle wrapped his arms around both of them, and Scott held on and closed his eyes, overcome.

"Thank God," he whispered. "I thought I was going to lose my mind, I was so worried."

"How's Mom?" Kyle asked.

"About as good as you'd expect," Scott said. "I told her I was going out looking for you. Aunt Jenny came over to stay with her."

"I'm sorry we worried you," Kyle said. "But we were afraid that if we didn't get out of there, and the witch came for me, he'd hurt you, too."

"You did the right thing," Scott replied, stepping back and letting go of them. "I'm proud of you. Now, how about helping me get the groceries put away. There's a cooler full of ice in the back of the truck."

Half an hour later, Scott had gotten settled and came to join the others in the living room. "The couch pulls out, so the cabin has beds for six," he said. "I brought a sleeping bag and a pillow. That should mean we've got room for everyone." He glanced at Seth. "Any word about Milo and Toby?"

Seth shook his head. "Toby knows where we are. He won't risk a call if he doesn't need to. They'll get here when they can. No telling how long it took at the hospital."

Toby and Milo rolled in after dawn. Toby parked and came around to open Milo's door, then helped him down. He wrapped an arm around Milo's waist and helped him limp to the cabin. Seth saw the way Milo held himself, a sure sign of cracked or broken ribs. The boot on his left foot and lower leg made walking difficult.

"Sorry we're late to the party," Toby said. "Took a while at the hospital, and we needed to get a few prescriptions filled since there's no telling when we'll get back to Boone. Grabbed some groceries, too."

Toby looked haggard. Then again, between worrying about his husband and pulling an all-nighter, Seth figured Toby had a right to look like death warmed over. He hurried to help Milo get to the bedroom they'd set aside for the two men, as Toby went back out for their bags and the food.

"We figured you'd do better in a real bed than a pull-out," Seth said, showing Milo to his room. "It's also closer to the bathroom, so fewer steps." He looked him up and down. "What'd they say at the hospital?"

Milo eased down onto the side of the bed. "Cracked the ribs, didn't break them, so no danger of puncturing a lung. Sprained the ankle, but didn't break the leg. So...I'm not going to be chasing through the woods for a while. But I still make a damn fine guard dog," he added with a tired smile.

"How's Toby?'

Milo rolled his eyes. "Damn fool kept trying to carry me. That's not good for his heart."

"He worries about you."

"The feeling's mutual," Milo groused.

Toby came in before either Seth or Evan could continue the conversation. "You've got to be beat," Toby said as if he wasn't equally tired. "Let me help you get ready for bed. We'll work out marching orders in the morning." He glanced to the window, where daylight seeped around the blinds. "Or, later this morning."

"Get some sleep," Seth said, clapping Milo on the shoulder. "Evan and I are going to take the back bedroom. That puts Kyle and Steve on the pull-out, and Scott brought a bedroll."

"Talk about cockblocked," Toby muttered.

Milo smacked him. "Hardly the time to worry about that." He yawned, looking wrecked. "Let me get some sleep. I had plenty of time to think while I was in that damn hospital waiting room. I'll fill you in over breakfast tomorrow."

10

EVAN

"I'm on family leave," Scott hunched in on himself, holding his cup of coffee like a lifeline. He grabbed a sweet roll from the box in the middle of the table. "So no one's going to expect me back for a while. My brother, Tom, and his wife, Jenny, are staying with Liz. Tom's an ex-Green Beret, so I think they'll be okay."

Toby nodded. "They will. I stopped by your place to put down wardings before we came here. Just tell her to stay put."

Scott looked relieved and grateful. "Thank you."

"Evan and I are going back to Boone," Seth said. "See if we can draw Sturdevant out. Either he'll come after us to get to Kyle, or he'll decide he can make do with two other intended victims."

"That's your plan?" Milo snapped. "Do you want me to paint targets on your backs before you leave?"

"What do you mean to do if you 'draw him out'?" Toby pressed.

"Get him before he gets us," Seth replied. "Simple as that. We have the anchor. We can get the amulet."

"You've never killed a witch-disciple when it wasn't in the middle of the summoning ritual," Toby said. Scott's head came up on "killed."

"We never had the luxury of time to do it differently," Seth countered. "It was pretty seat-of-the-pants."

"Is killing the only option?" Scott asked. "Can you, I don't know, exorcise him or something?"

Milo turned to his old friend. "Exorcism only works if the person is possessed. It won't do a thing for evil rooted in the heart. And that's what these witch-disciples are—evil. They were killers before Gremory was hanged, and in the century since then they haven't hesitated to kill whoever got in their way or could expose their secret, in addition to all the descendants of the posse that hanged their master."

"Sturdevant is coming into his weak period," Toby chimed in. "Now's the time to get him. He knows he's losing his mojo, and that might make him reckless. We can use that." He looked ragged, but he was up and moving, and Evan was impressed at the older hunter's grit.

"You're talking about murder," Scott said.

"Do you really want to try to arrest a dark warlock with more than a century of spell-casting experience?" Milo asked. "Read him his rights? Put him on trial? Try to convince a jury that he's over a hundred years old, passing himself off as different people because he doesn't age, sacrificing men in a local family to keep his fountain of youth? How well do you think that will work out?"

"I took an oath."

"To serve and protect," Milo replied. "And that's what we're going to do. We're stopping a supernatural serial killer. The only way we can."

Scott and Milo stared at each other for a moment. Finally, Scott looked away. "Okay. I get it. I'm in."

"All right," Milo said. He looked at Seth. "Go back to town, and keep us in the loop."

Toby walked up to Seth and Evan and clapped a hand on their shoulders. "Good luck. And—come back in one piece."

"Doesn't look like anyone's done more damage," Evan said, looking around the campground. "But I don't think we're going to get our security deposit back."

"Probably not."

They didn't need anything from the cabin or the RV, so they checked the locks and wardings and stopped by the campground office, offering to pay for the "storm damage." The woman at the counter accepted Seth's offer of an extra hundred bucks to cover the broken decorations and confirmed that their reservation was still in place.

"Well, if he comes looking, our story will check out," Seth said as they walked back to the Silverado.

"And now?"

"We go to town," Seth said with the cocky grin Evan knew he flashed when he was winging it. "We do what we've been avoiding—be visible. Go shopping. Eat at the diner. Be seen."

"You're daring Sturdevant to make his move."

"I can't come up with another way to flush him out," Seth replied. "Short of staking out Kyle's house for the next year, and hoping Sturdevant doesn't just kill us to keep us from getting in his way."

"You want to run the speed limit too, just to piss off Bondell?"

Seth glared at him. "There's a fine line between being bait and poking the bear."

"Oh, really?"

"If we end up in a cell, we're no good to anyone."

"Good point."

Evan fidgeted as Seth drove into Boone. The clear sky and sunshine promised a good day, but Evan's gut expected anything but.

"Relax. You look like you're going to face a firing squad."

"We're trying to provoke a showdown with Voldemort. Forgive me for being nervous."

"I think that's giving Sturdevant too much credit," Seth replied. "Let's not make him more of a threat than he is. As far as we can tell, we're the first ones to ever come after the disciples. So we're not the latest in a long string of tragic heroes who tried and failed."

"Comforting. Let's not be the first, either."

"I can agree with that."

They parked and strolled around downtown Boone. Old storefronts had been given an upscale facelift, and local artists had transformed formerly blank brick walls into works of art. On any other day, the picturesque tourist shops would have been fun to browse through, and Evan would have enjoyed window shopping. The RV didn't leave much room to collect "stuff," but Evan still enjoyed looking.

"Coffee's good," Seth said as they ambled out of a coffee shop.

"These are awesome," Evan replied, taking a bite from a chocolate chip cookie bigger than his hand.

"The outfitters have some nice gear," Seth remarked over a mouthful of snickerdoodle.

"I liked the galleries," Evan said. "Not that we've got walls to hang anything on, but they had nice artwork. Pretty stained glass. And the carved wood bowls were gorgeous."

"Do you mind not having a real house?"

Evan wanted to reach out and take Seth's hand, but while they hoped to draw out Sturdevant, he didn't want to provoke random local assholes. Evan sighed. He could hear the uncertainty in Seth's voice and didn't know how to make him believe.

"I had a house, back when I lived with my parents. Then they threw me out, and I didn't. I had an apartment in Richmond. But I wasn't safe there."

He turned to look at Seth and let their fingers brush. "I have a home now, with you, where I'm safe and loved. Screw artwork. I don't need knickknacks. Just because things are pretty doesn't mean I need to own them. Home is where you are."

The emotion in Seth's gaze told him the message was received. "Maybe someday, when we're done."

"Or not. We'll figure it out." Evan really hoped they'd have that chance.

They paused in a small park to drink their coffee, soaking up the sunshine. It should have been a nice day, but Evan kept waiting for the hammer to fall. He watched the tourists walk by, and had never felt more separate.

"Thoughts?"

Evan shrugged. "Just how tourist towns are all the same."

"They are?"

"Richmond got a lot of tourists, especially down in the Fan District, where Treddy's was," he said, naming the bar and the trendy neighborhood where he had worked and lived. "They were in town for a week or a weekend, looking to see the sights, drink too much, have a nice time, move on. Willing to be someone else for a few days, because none of it was real. And our job was to play along like we weren't in on the joke."

"What do you mean?" Seth shifted so he could see Evan better.

"People come here to be outdoorsy, get their nature fix, or have the celebrity treatment at the resorts. That's not who they are the rest of their lives, for most of them. It's a fantasy. They can be their alter egos, and it doesn't change anything. No harm, no foul."

"Okay," Seth replied, although Evan could see he didn't really follow.

"We kind of live our secret identities every day," Evan said. "When everyone else goes on vacation, they want excitement. They pretend to be someone more interesting than they are. When we go on vacation, we pretend to be normal and do regular stuff."

"Never thought of it that way."

"It's kind of cool, actually." Evan grinned. "Kinda makes the RV our Batcave."

"We are not wearing tights. No capes, either."

"Fine by me."

Seth finished his coffee and pitched the cup into a garbage can. "You know, when this is done, we'll have to get out of town pretty quick, I imagine. But we could head out on the Blue Ridge Parkway, find someplace to have a little downtime. We don't have to go straight to Charleston to take on the next one."

"I'd like that."

"Then we'll do it. Just you and me." His smile widened. "Maybe we can find a hotel with one of those heart-shaped bathtubs."

Evan rolled his eyes. "You're thinking of the Poconos."

"A pool with a hot tub?"

"I'm all for it."

Seth reached for Evan's empty cup and let his fingers linger against Evan's hand. Evan loved when they could be openly out, and he was proud of who he was. But he recognized the need to adjust to circumstances, and now wasn't the time or place to test the inclusiveness of this mountain community.

"Are you hungry?" Evan asked. "Because I've wanted to try that café since we drove into town." He pointed to a local place with a striped awning and bistro tables on the sidewalk. A reader board in front promised local produce and farm-fresh ingredients.

"Don't tell Toby," Seth replied. "He's never met a carb he didn't like."

They headed to the café and found it to be as charming on the inside as its window promised. Dark wood wainscoting, a pressed tin ceiling, and brass accents gave it the feel of a Victorian parlor. The hostess gestured for them to pick a four-top by the window, and they settled in across from each other.

"Everything looks good." Evan glanced over the menu. A note at the top said that items changed daily, depending on the season and local supply. "I'm going for the toasted pimento cheese sandwich and the tomato bisque soup."

"They've got a buffalo burger with blue cheese and fried onion strings," Seth replied. "Real buffalo. It's calling my name."

They placed their order, added iced sweet tea for both of them, and eyed the cooler full of homemade cakes and pies for dessert.

"I like this place." Seth shifted in his chair so that his knee bumped Evan's and their boots aligned under the table.

"Maybe we can grab another bite here on our way out," Evan suggested. "Because the menu says they change their desserts daily, too."

Conversation paused while they dug into their sandwiches, which were as good as advertised. Evan enjoyed the simple pleasure on Seth's face at his buffalo burger. They'd lived through enough bad moments—and Evan knew there were more to come—that he savored every good one.

"That was fantastic," Evan gushed when the server came to collect their plates.

"Did you save room for dessert?"

"Oh, yeah. I want a piece of that banana cream pie," Seth replied.

"And I'll take the coconut cake," Evan added.

"Coming right up."

"Seth! Evan!" Evan looked up to see Will heading toward them. "I wondered when I'd run into you two again. Have you already eaten? This place is amazing."

Seth grinned. "Yeah, it's really good."

Without waiting for an invitation, Will pulled out the chair next to Seth and sat down. "Did you get a chance to do some sightseeing? I can give you a discount on the ropes course or the zip line."

Everything coming out of Will's mouth sounded good, and his attitude seemed friendly and welcoming if a bit overly chummy. But Evan's gut tightened, and he had a sudden, weird urge to get the hell out.

A glance told Evan that the server wasn't on her way with their desserts yet. He'd already decided to ask for them to go, make up a reason, and hope Seth followed his lead.

"Let's see what the weather's like," Seth replied, glancing at Evan as if he could sense his partner's discomfort. A bump of his knee told Evan not to be jealous.

It wasn't jealousy. At least, Evan didn't think that was the problem. Seth had never given him reason to distrust him, never even flirted with anyone else since they had been together. He'd made it very clear that Will was both straight and just a friend. Still, Evan couldn't shake the feeling that they needed to get out of there.

"Here you go," the server said, laying down plates with two huge slices.

"Hey, could we please get those to go?" Evan asked, plastering on his best smile. Seth gave him a look but didn't contradict him.

The server looked perplexed but smiled and nodded. "Sure. I'll be right back."

"And we need our check, please," Evan added. His toe started to tap impatiently. Seth pushed his knee and gave him a look that was a silent *what the fuck?*

"You guys have places you need to be," Will said, annoyingly chipper. "Time for me to fly." He bumped shoulders with Seth. "Don't let me get in your way."

Evan thought he saw something drop when Will shoulder-checked

Seth. Will's expression didn't change, but in an instant, everything about Seth shifted. He straightened and moved his feet away from Evan's.

"What are you even doing here?" Seth snapped at Evan. Anger twisted his features, and his brown eyes were cold.

Evan's eyes widened. "We were eating lunch."

"You can't give me any space, can you? I don't have a moment's peace," Seth growled. "So damn needy. Always have to know where I am, checking up on me. I'm done."

"Seth—" Evan's heart raced, and he couldn't breathe. He swallowed hard and blinked back tears, feeling like the world had suddenly tilted.

"Didn't you hear me? I said, I'm done!" Seth's voice made patrons turn. Evan felt blood rush to his face as the whole restaurant stared.

Seth pushed his chair back, banging into the person sitting behind him. Will rose with him.

"I tried to let you down easy, Evan. I wasn't going to make a scene. But you just won't take a hint." He threw a few bills down on the table. "We're through." He turned and walked out without a backward glance. Will followed, and Evan knew he didn't imagine the smug look in Will's eyes.

The other diners turned back to their food. Evan stayed rooted in his seat, feeling like he might throw up. The server stopped beside him with a look of compassion.

"Do you still want the boxes?" she asked.

Evan stared blankly in the direction Seth had gone. "No. Just—give them to someone. My treat." He laid down money for his part of the bill. "Keep the change."

When he reached the sidewalk, Seth and Will were gone. Evan walked back to the park where he and Seth had talked about the future, flirted and laughed. He felt sick and angry and heartbroken, all at once.

Will did something. Evan remembered the shoulder bump, and the glimpse he got of something falling. That was the moment Seth's entire manner had changed. *Something cursed, haunted, or hexed. Magic. Shit. Will's working with Sturdevant. And now he's got Seth.*

11

SETH

When Will sat down at their table, Seth expected trouble.
Running into his old army buddy once wasn't too strange. But having
Will show up and act like his best friend, joining them at the café, was
definitely weird. Will had been friendly but distant back when they
served together. People could change—Seth certainly had—but his gut
told him that the situation was definitely wrong.

Then Will had done something—Seth still wasn't sure what—and
he was no longer in control of himself. White-hot anger surged
through him, fierce but meritless, aimed at Evan. He'd spewed all
kinds of awful things at Evan, who had just sat there and taken it, eyes
wide, looking like Seth had hit him.

Seth wanted to throw up. Under Will's spell—hex, curse, it didn't
matter—he'd broken up with Evan. Told him they were through. And
then he'd gone off with Will and left Evan in the café. Seth had the
keys to the truck, so he'd left Evan stranded in town, far from the
campground and the safe house. Abandoned Evan where he was
vulnerable to Sturdevant's attack.

"I didn't know that you'd be in town today," Will said as he drove
them out of Boone in his own truck. Seth had no idea where they were

headed. "But I figured that you'd show up sooner or later. It was my lucky day." He glanced at Seth. "Not so much, for you."

Seth opened his mouth to reply. Will shook his head, and Seth found his voice gone, although inside he screamed and raged.

"The Boss really doesn't care which one of you dies," Will went on as if discussing the weather. "You're all descendants. Whoever he doesn't get this time, he'll use later. Like backup batteries."

The Boss? Has to be Sturdevant. God, please don't let there be two witch-disciples in town.

"In case you're wondering, the Boss gave me a poker chit kind of thing with a spell on it. That's what I dropped in your pocket in the restaurant. It was supposed to make you mad at your boyfriend and make you do whatever I told you to do. Guess it works."

Seth wanted to throw himself at Will and wrest away control of the car. He was willing to take a chance on opening the door and jumping out, even while they were moving. It might kill him, but that would still be better than what Sturdevant had in mind. Instead, his body betrayed him, refusing to answer his commands. And inside, he howled and screamed, unable to make a sound.

"You're not going anywhere," Will said as if he could guess Seth's thoughts. "Not until I tell you to."

Seth just stared at him, wondering how a barely-there acquaintance had gone so wrong.

"Back in the army, you were the guy who had everything." Will's friendly tone had turned cold. "Looks, ability, smarts, and a family back home that sent you care packages every month and letters in between. And that was just normal for you. I'm sure you said 'thank you' because that's how you were raised, but it never really occurred to you that all those things weren't just supposed to be yours. That they weren't like that for everyone."

He turned to Seth with a look of pure malice. "Well, they weren't. My mom died from an overdose. I never knew my dad. Bounced around foster homes until I could finally go into the army. And there you were, taking everything I never had for granted."

Will gave a humorless laugh. "And you never had a clue how much

I wanted what you had. How much I resented you. Of course you didn't. That wasn't part of your safe, perfect little world."

Will's face contorted. "You didn't watch your mother go back to her dealer and her pimp over and over until she finally didn't come home. You knew who your daddy was. You didn't get smacked around by every drunken asshole who managed to fill out a foster parent form. They didn't want the kids—they wanted the money. Bet you never went hungry a day in your life. Fucking perfect."

Seth's heart hammered as Will spewed his rage. Back in the army, they had an acquaintance of convenience. He hadn't cared that he and Will didn't have interests in common. They'd been soldiers in a foreign land, comrades at arms, and in a war zone, that was enough. But as he listened to Will, the sick feeling in his gut grew. He'd thought Will was indifferent to him back then. Seth had never dreamed how much Will hated him.

"After I got out, I came here because I didn't have anywhere else to go. I needed a job, and I took what I could get. Let me tell you, starting out as a flunky at that ropes course sucked. Kids threw up on me, or I had to go haul their whiny asses down when they got stuck. Nothing but a bunch of rude, stupid people who didn't know how good they had it."

Will's smile was brittle. "And then, one day, Ira Sturdevant came to see the place. Turned out, he owned the company. That's when he noticed me. He took an interest in me. He cared." His voice grew louder, more insistent as if he was trying to convince himself as well as Seth.

"He hired me to do some extra jobs for him. Paid me. Appreciated me. Pretty soon I was his go-to-guy," Will bragged. "This big-shot honcho depended on *me*. And when I needed something—a car, a place to live—he took care of it. So when he started to ask for some extra things, I was happy to help."

Like murder? Seth wondered. *Hiding bodies? Luring victims?* He wanted to ask, but Will's control kept him silent.

"I showed him I could handle it. He could trust me. I wouldn't let him down. Proved my loyalty," Will rambled. "Pretty soon, he shared his secrets with me. With *me*," he repeated, his voice a mix of awe and pride. "I wasn't afraid when he told me he was a witch. Why should I be? Magic made him rich and let him live forever. He said he'd teach me. I could be his apprentice."

Shit. Will was Sturdevant's Igor, his Renfield. The poor, deluded sap had no idea that Sturdevant would chew him up and spit him out—or slit his throat and drain his blood—when Will stopped being useful. Even if Seth could have spoken, Will would never have believed him. He'd probably look dumbfounded when Sturdevant stuck the knife in his guts.

"He asked me to keep an eye on that guy, Kyle. The kid reminded me of you," Will said with a smile that showed his teeth. "Didn't know how good he had it, with mommy and the family business. And a pretty little boyfriend whose daddy was the chief of police. I figured he had it coming."

Seth could only stare in silence, as his stomach flipped and his jaw strained to open. Will had stalked Kyle, kept tabs on him for Sturdevant like grooming a prize turkey before Thanksgiving.

"And then you rolled into town. The Boss asked me to keep an eye on you, too. You and those old guys were slippery. But I saw enough. Enough to know you were dangerous." He glared at Seth. "I finally got something good that's mine, all mine. And I was not going to let you fuck it up for me."

The sheer venom in Will's voice turned Seth's blood cold. Seth had no doubt that if Sturdevant told Will to put a bullet in Seth's brain, Will would consider it a privilege.

Seth didn't recognize the road they were on. He thought they were heading out of Boone, but not toward the safe house in Maggie Valley. That was good. They were getting farther away from Kyle and Steve, and from Milo and Toby. For now, Seth's friends were safe.

But what about Evan? The look on Evan's face had shredded Seth's heart, even as more hateful words poured out of his mouth beyond his control. Evan wasn't safe; he was on his own in a town controlled by Sturdevant's stooge chief. Evan was in danger, and Seth had put him there.

"I enjoyed that, back at the café, you know," Will gloated. "Watching you go psycho on your boyfriend. Broke his widdle heart. I honestly thought he'd start boohooing, right there. He's so through with you now. Probably caught the next bus out of town. So don't expect him to come to your rescue. Not after the shit you pulled." He laughed. "The shit I made you pull."

If he survived—which was not looking likely—Seth would find Evan. Explain. Apologize. Beg, if he needed to. He'd make sure Evan knew how much he loved him.

If Evan would even see him. Before Seth, Evan hadn't had a great track record with his boyfriends. One had stalked him and tried to kill him. Another betrayed Evan and got him kicked out of his home. Evan had been wounded and wary when he met Seth. In the six months they'd been together, Evan had gradually learned to trust Seth. Seth had been so careful to earn that faith.

Then he'd burned it to the ground in the café.

"Your friends think they're so smart," Will said, picking up the one-sided conversation. "They're off hiding somewhere. But they'll turn up, sooner or later. Kyle won't leave his mommy. He'll think the threat is over and everything can go back to normal, and he'll come home. Right where the Boss can pick him like an apple, any time he wants."

Seth wondered what would happen if he gave in to his rising gorge and tried to throw up. Would Will pull over and let him puke, or make him choke on his own vomit? Seth willed his rebellious stomach to settle, not daring to take that chance.

"Of course, you won't really care at that point." Will shrugged. "You'll be dead. They won't find your body, assuming anyone looks. No one might care enough to try."

Will turned off the road, easing down a rutted driveway to stop in front of an old farmhouse. "Get out. Walk inside. Not too fast. Door's unlocked."

Seth found himself doing what he was told, although his muscles strained to rebel and his head pounded with the effort to break the hex that held him. The house was empty, and it stank of mice and mildew. Yellowed blinds covered the windows. Will lit a lantern, which only partly dispelled the shadows.

"There's a chair in the other room. Sit there until I tell you to move."

Seth sat on the wooden chair in the darkened room and tried to still his thoughts from racing. He didn't have any true magic of his own, but he'd learned a few rote spells from Milo, Simon, and Travis. They had always told him that the words of the spells were just a formality, that what mattered was willing all of his intention to manifest. Did he need to be able to speak to make a spell work?

He didn't know, but he intended to find out. Seth had nothing but time on his hands until Sturdevant decided to kill him. Might as well make use of it. Maybe he could still turn this around.

It was a long shot, Seth knew. But that beat having no shot at all.

12

EVAN

Scott answered when Evan pounded on the cabin door.

"Evan?" he asked as Evan strode past, hoping against hope Seth had somehow shaken off Will's control and managed to get there first. Despair coursed through him when Seth was nowhere to be found.

"Where's Seth? Have you heard from him?" Evan's heart hammered, as the full reality of the situation sank in.

Toby came running from the back. "What's wrong?"

"Seth dumped me and left me in Boone," Evan said. "I hitchhiked back."

Toby and Scott exchanged a glance. "Dumped you?"

"I'm pretty sure he was under a hex of some sort," Evan said, pacing. Kyle and Steve sat on the couch, watching him with concern. Toby and Scott didn't move closer, but Evan knew they were both worried.

"How about you take it from the top, Evan?" Toby used the tone he'd probably take with a freaked out witness. The look in his eyes was far from calm. He looked ready, willing, and able to kill whoever hexed Seth.

"Yeah. Okay." Evan took a couple of deep breaths, trying to calm down. He'd been in reaction mode since Seth had walked out of the diner. It had gotten him this far, but now the adrenaline left him shaky.

Milo came thumping out of the back bedroom, navigating with his cast and crutches. "What the hell happened, son? You look like crap on a cracker."

Evan gave them the whole sorry story, starting with Will's arrival at the diner. Heat filled his face as he recounted the breakup, ending with Seth walking out of the café with Will, and Evan hitching his way back to the safe house because he'd left his set of keys to the truck in his duffle bag.

"So we're compromised?" Scott said when Evan finished. "Whoever drove you here knows where we are."

Evan shook his head. "No. I switched cars four times. Told them to drop me somewhere, then picked up another ride. And I had the last one leave me off a mile up the road. I walked back. If we had a signal out here, I would have gladly had you pick me up." It had been lunchtime when Seth left him in the restaurant. He'd walked the last bit in the dark. That had been plenty of time to freak out, plunge into despair, feel numb, and gradually talk himself out of panic, knowing Seth needed him to keep a clear head to stage a rescue.

"Compromised?" Toby glared at Scott. "That's what you got out of his story? There's more at stake than where we sleep. Get your head out of your ass. Seth is missing."

Kyle got up and went to the ice chest, bringing Evan a beer and a piece of cold pizza. "Eat something," he urged. "You'll feel better." Kyle steered Evan to his seat on the couch, and plopped down in front of Steve, leaning back on his boyfriend's knees.

"Thanks," Evan said, although he had no appetite, despite the fact that hours had passed since lunch. He didn't meet anyone's gaze, still feeling the humiliation of admitting that Seth had broken things off. Hex or not, the words tasted like ash in his mouth.

"Do you have any idea where Will might have taken him?" Toby prompted.

Evan shook his head. "I don't know anything about Will except that he served with Seth in the army, and he works for one of the ropes courses. Not much to go on."

Milo leaned against the wall, taking the weight off his cast. Toby grabbed a chair from the kitchen and shoved it at Milo, who grudgingly sat as if doing so meant admitting weakness. "I think it's plain as day, the boy was hexed."

Scott looked from Milo to Toby. "Hexed? Is that even a thing?"

"Yes." Milo and Toby spoke in unison.

"Explain." Scott's snappish tone told Evan that the man was worried and feeling the lack of control.

"I think Will slipped something into Seth's pocket when he bumped against him," Evan said. "That's when everything changed, like flipping a switch."

"A hex is a malicious spell," Toby added, for the benefit of Scott, Kyle, and Steve. "It can be contained in a bag of ingredients with magical properties, or pressed into a clay chip, or engraved on a piece of metal. The important thing is, a witch sets the hex, and the item transfers it to the intended victim. It's nothing to fool around with. Hexes can kill."

"So what do we do about it?" Scott asked.

"How do we find Seth and save him?" Steve questioned. Evan could have hugged the guy for honing in on, what was to him, the most important thing.

"*You* don't do anything," Milo said. "That just plays into Sturdevant's hands. If he grabbed Seth, it's either to draw you out or because he knows Seth was the first-choice draft pick for the witch-disciple who killed Jesse."

"We need to do something." Evan lifted his head, defiant. "Because I've seen what happens to the disciples' victims, and I'm not going to let them do that to Seth." Whether or not Seth still wanted him. Even if the breakup was real.

"How do we break a hex?" Kyle asked.

"There are ways," Toby replied. "It would help to know more about what kind it is, but we can work on that."

"How are we going to do that?" Evan challenged, reaching his breaking point. "I can't even get one fuckin' bar on my phone."

Toby fixed him with a look. "That's enough. Freaking out isn't going to help anyone, least of all Seth. There are things called 'books.' Low tech. They work even if you don't plug them in."

Evan slumped, avoiding Toby's gaze. "Yeah. Okay."

"It's late," Toby said. "We're not going to do anything tonight." He held up a hand as Evan moved to argue. "Going looking for him in the dark, with no idea of where he is—that's not a plan, it's a suicide mission. So we'll pull things together tonight, and move on it tomorrow. But right now, you need to eat that pizza."

Toby led Evan into the kitchen. Milo clumped after them and sat down heavily at the table. They could hear Scott shuffling a deck of cards and starting up a new game of poker in the other room.

"Eat," Toby nudged.

Evan nibbled at his pizza and drank the beer. He didn't really taste either one, and he was surprised that his stomach didn't try to send them both back up. Every time he closed his eyes, he saw Seth walking out of the diner with Will, heard the words Seth hurled at him. And as much as he knew, intellectually, that the hex had forced the issue, he couldn't help worrying that a grain of truth remained.

"If you want to save Seth, you need to eat," Toby urged. "If we go in to get him and you pass out, I'm leaving your ass."

That made Evan crack a smile, even though he was certain it looked fake as all hell.

"Whatever Seth said to you, when the hex had a hold of him, it wasn't real." Milo dropped his voice so it didn't carry to the next room. He fixed Evan with his gaze.

"I know that, up here," Evan said, tapping his forehead. "But I'm not quite so sure, in here," he added, laying a hand over his heart.

Toby and Milo exchanged a look. "Seth loves you, Evan. A hex bag can't change that. It can make him say things he doesn't mean, but it doesn't change what's in his heart," Milo replied.

"He said that he tried to let me down easy," Evan said in a voice just above a whisper. "Maybe he was already thinking of backing off." He couldn't square that with the way Seth had acted all day, how casually comfortable they'd been together, but fear overrode logic.

"Bullshit," Toby said. "Look, Evan. I get the feeling you haven't had a lot of luck with the guys you went out with before. But Seth is not the love-em-and-leave-em kind. He's all in. And if that son of a bitch fed him a break-up script, then you'd better believe that wherever Seth is tonight, he's twisted up as fuck about what the hex made him say to you. I know my boy. He's as worried about you as you are about him."

"Thanks, Toby."

"Think about it this way. Here's your big chance to make a dramatic entrance and rescue the prince. It's your moment," Milo added.

"Yeah. Maybe." Evan felt exhausted and raw, hollow inside. He was running on fumes and starting to crash.

"You're not alone," Toby said. "We've got your back—and we're going to get Seth out of this."

"What if we're already too late?" Evan spoke his worst fear aloud. "What if they did the ritual tonight? What if he's already gone?" He couldn't keep his voice from cracking on the last word.

"Then we avenge him," Milo said fiercely. "And we put that warlock bastard and his lackey down like rabid dogs."

"Don't cross bridges until you get to them," Toby warned. "I don't think Sturdevant is going to move that fast. I'd be surprised if his Renfield was supposed to make his play just yet. I bet Will jumped the gun. Now he's forced Sturdevant's hand, and the boss man might not be too happy about that. Magic isn't random. Sturdevant might not need to wait for the anniversary to sacrifice his victim, but it can't be done at the drop of a hat."

"Thanks." Evan wasn't sure he completely believed Toby, but the words were nice to hear.

"Get some sleep," Toby said. "Tomorrow, we'll figure everything out."

Evan nodded and tossed what was left of his pizza into the garbage with the beer bottle. He nodded to the crew in the living room and passed by them to the bedroom he was supposed to share with Seth. Moonlight streamed through the window, giving him enough light to strip off his clothes and crawl into bed.

Evan knew that Seth's rejection had to have been orchestrated by the hex, but the words still stung. Worse was the fact that despite all that had happened between him and Seth, enough old insecurities still lurked beneath the surface to make him worry that Seth's reversal hadn't been entirely caused by the spell.

That was on him, his own issue to deal with. Knowing that didn't make the pain less real. Seth was a captive, in the hands of a warlock who had every reason to want vengeance—if not for the intended strike against him, then for the deaths of his one-time allies. There was a very real chance that Evan might never see Seth again. And the thought that the last words between them renounced their bond left Evan utterly bereft.

He turned his face into his pillow, grateful that he did not have to bear up to anyone's scrutiny. He finally broke down, feeling the fear and grief and despair wash over him. When he drifted off, too spent to cry any more, he was acutely aware that the other side of the bed was cold and empty.

Evan woke a few hours later from a troubled sleep. He wandered into the kitchen, poured some of last night's pot of coffee into a cup and drank it down, then started to boil more water to make a fresh batch. The caffeine did little to clear his head. He grabbed a slice of pizza from the box in the cooler and sat down at the table with a stack of Toby's books and a tablet.

The yellowed pages held diagrams and drawings, along with tightly spaced lines of explanation. Half of it was in Latin. Travis had suggested that Evan take an online course, and Evan had gotten a few months into it, but he had no idea about some of the vocabulary in the old book. *Imagine that,* he thought. *The course didn't focus on spells and curses.* Still, he made headway, chasing threads of ideas and following footnotes to other sources.

"Doin' it old school?" Toby asked from the doorway.

"Trying to." Evan blinked dry eyes and took another slug of java. "Where'd you get these books, anyhow?"

Toby shrugged as he walked over and poured what remained of the cold coffee into a cup, then joined Evan at the table. "Some of them came from other hunters. It's common to will each other weapons and hard-to-find materials—since they shouldn't get into the wrong hands. The rest came from estate sales, eBay, used books stores—people don't realize what they've got. Found a book of demonic summoning rituals at a yard sale in suburbia," he said with a chuckle. "The lady thought it was a gaming manual."

"I miss my laptop."

"Not much good for research with no signal. The kind of information we'll need to stop Sturdevant is more likely to be in these books than online," Toby said, reaching for one of the tomes. "He's drawing on old magic. Stuff that's been around for a long, long time."

"Here's what I've got." Evan shoved the tablet filled with his scribbling over to Toby, who read through the notes, his frown deepening.

"Not too shabby, for a newbie," Toby said, giving Evan an approving grin. "Guess that Latin's paying off."

"I'll do more when I get to the 'summoning and spells' advanced class," Evan replied, but his heart wasn't in the sarcasm.

"Get the basics, and I'm sure Travis and Simon will tutor you."

"About that. I've got an idea, and I'd like to run it by Simon. Do you think I'll give away our location if I walk out to the main road and try to make a call?"

Toby shook his head. "I doubt Sturdevant has enough juice to hack every wireless call. He's a witch, not the NSA. Go ahead and call. I'll go with you. Put it on speaker, and I'll be glad to give you my two cents, for what it's worth."

Toby told Milo where they were going, then he took a handgun from the weapons bag near the door, and handed a shotgun to Evan. They walked in silence down the long dirt road, alert for trouble. The cold morning air cleared Evan's head. When they got to the blacktop road, Evan checked his phone.

"One bar," he said, staring at the display.

"Might as well try, seeing as we came all the way out here," Toby replied.

Evan crossed his fingers and hit speed dial. Simon answered. "Evan? Do you know what time it is?"

"Seth's been taken. He's hexed, and the witch-disciple has him."

"Shit. Okay. Give me a minute."

Evan heard muffled conversation and suspected Simon was briefing his partner Vic, a homicide detective. He heard clothing rustling and then footsteps, followed by the sound of a chair being pulled across a tile floor.

"All right. I'm up and I've got coffee. What happened, and how can I help?"

Evan hadn't met Simon in person yet, but he'd come to depend on him for lore and supernatural history. Before Simon moved to Myrtle Beach and opened Grand Strand Ghost Tours, he'd been a professor at a university in Columbia, South Carolina. When the father of a student confused "folklore" with "witchcraft" and got Simon fired, he'd started over, relying more on his gifts as a psychic medium than his Ph.D., started the shop, and met the love of his life.

Simon listened as Evan recapped the hunt for the latest witch-disciple and the clusterfuck at the café.

"Definitely a hex of some kind," Simon said. "Your hunch about a chit or a bag is probably right."

"How do we break it?" Evan felt his heart speed up.

"Remove and destroy the item that carries the hex. That usually works. Unfortunately, part of the geas the hex places on the victim keeps them from doing that. Except—"

"What?"

"Really stubborn people are hard to hex for long. The same thing that makes them ornery makes them reject efforts to control them."

"Milo ought to be completely un-hexable, in that case," Toby muttered.

"It's one of those bugs that turn into a feature," Simon replied, chuckling. "So given enough time, Seth may be able to break free, or at least make the hex-caster fight for every inch. No way to know for sure, but don't count him out just yet."

"About that Brigadoon Coin," Evan said, running with a crazy idea that had come to him in the night.

Toby looked up sharply. Evan intentionally didn't meet his gaze.

"Yeah? What do you need to know? When you jump into some-thing, you go with both feet, don't you? The coins are complicated. Best avoided. That's why I've got a specialist ready to get rid of it."

"Can they be safely grabbed and transported?" Evan asked. He felt Toby's glare.

"Define 'safely.'"

"Hunter safe. Not regular people safe."

"That leaves plenty of room for interpretation," Simon replied. "I've never tried to handle one. Until a year or so ago, I didn't think they were real. My cousin says the person who's coming for it has very specialized skills."

"I want to steal the coin from Mystery Mountain, to keep Sturdevant from using its stored energy when we go up against him at the Nowhere tunnel."

"Evan—" Toby began. Evan shook his head, refusing to be derailed. "That's dangerous."

"This whole thing is dangerous."

"It's all kind of crazy, even by hunter standards."

"What can I say? I'm a quick study." Evan met Toby's gaze, feeling like he was in a middle school staring contest. Toby blinked first.

Simon let out a long breath. "Why do I have the feeling you're going to do this, with or without my help?"

"Because you're psychic," Evan said with a smirk.

"Funny," Simon replied sarcastically. "Tell me what you're thinking, and I'll try to tell you the odds of it getting you killed or sucked into a time warp."

"Comforting—not." Evan pulled in a deep breath. "All right," he said. "Here's what I'm thinking—and I'm going to need Toby's help to pull it off."

"IF THIS GOES SIDEWAYS, MILO IS GOING TO KILL YOU—AND I'M GOING TO haunt your ass." Toby paused by the back door to Mystery Mountain that night while Evan used the "unlock" rote spell to open the door. Toby swung inside and used a similar spell on the alarm system, which blinked once and went dark.

"If it goes sideways, I'll probably be dead, too. So we can haunt each other."

Milo had opposed the plan, but couldn't come up with anything better. They didn't share the details with Scott, Kyle, and Steve, giving them plausible deniability for when the dust settled. Later, Toby and Evan would put the plan in action, while Scott and Milo guarded the cabin and protected Steve and Kyle.

What with Simon, Toby, the books they had with them, and a quick call to Travis after they got to town, Evan managed to come up with what he hoped would be their best shot of saving Seth and stopping Sturdevant. He felt a bit of pride that they'd pulled it all together and still had time before dawn to make the first move.

"Can you feel it?"

Evan knew Toby meant the slight time distortion that gave the Mystery Mountain its reputation. "Yeah. I feel it. Let's just hope it doesn't feel us."

Evan navigated through the dark rooms and led Toby to the glass case filled with oddities. He opened the lock and slid the door to one side. "Get the box ready." Evan took out the special gloves they'd prepared, and the iron tongs. Toby opened the lead and iron box with sigils carved all over its interior and exterior.

"Go."

Evan only needed to move a few inches, but he felt like the coin kept retreating from him and that everything happened in slow-motion. Instead of panicking, he recited the invocation Simon had found to negate the coin's effects for a few seconds. It took three repetitions to cover the short distance, but Evan felt the energy shift as soon as cold iron touched the fragile cage that held the coin.

"Don't break it," Toby warned as if Evan hadn't already thought of that himself.

"Yeah. I figure that would be bad."

Both men let out a whoosh of breath when the coin and cage were in the box, and the lid slammed shut. Toby spun the combination lock and invoked a binding spell. Evan met Toby's gaze. "This place feels different now."

"It's supposed to. Let's get out of here."

They made it to Toby's truck, and Evan breathed a sigh of relief as they pulled away. A brief stop in town let them retrieve the plaque Seth had pried off the wall of the sanatorium, the anchor for Sturdevant's magic, from Seth's truck, with the second key Evan retrieved from his bag at the cabin. The plaque was safe in its own lead box, for now. Evan didn't know how closely Sturdevant kept tabs on his "insurance policy" of the Brigadoon Coin or the anchor, but he hoped the warlock didn't have time to check on the items with everything else going on.

"When this is over, I want you to teach me to hotwire a car," Evan said.

"That can be arranged," Toby replied.

"What's that?" Evan asked as Toby left an odd black box beneath Seth's truck, which they left parked in a lot behind a stretch of shops and restaurants.

"My own little insurance policy," Toby replied with a wily grin. He set out another box in the tall grass near a cluster of stores at the edge of town. "In case we need to get Bondell's goons off our tail."

Dawn broke by the time they reached the road for the Nowhere tunnel. "Do you remember where the traps were?" Toby asked as he and Evan picked their way through the underbrush on the way to the tunnel.

"Yeah," Evan told him. "I'm bringing you in the way Seth and I came out." He tried to shut out the feelings that came from hearing his partner's name and slammed a mental firewall on the worry that they might already be too late. "It's the way we'll use tonight."

"What makes you think it'll be tonight?"

"You don't?"

"Just want to know how you think," Toby replied.

"I agree that Will probably forced his hand, and that you were right about nothing being ready last night. But Sturdevant isn't going to push his luck for long—holding Seth, keeping us holed up. He's less vulnerable if he makes a sacrifice, and he'll have had a whole day to get what he needs. He's been doing this for a century, so he knows how it works. I'm afraid to wait."

Toby nodded. "Makes sense. And for the record—I think your plan is crazy, but it's actually not half bad."

"Thanks, I think."

Evan and Toby reached the old road, and both men scanned the surrounding woods for signs of guards. Either Bondell was lazy, or

Sturdevant felt sure enough of his win that he didn't feel the need to guard his ritual site around the clock.

"Clear," Toby said, but they both kept their guns ready.

"Carrying a ladder through the forest isn't the easiest thing I've ever done," Evan said. "Let's just get where we're going."

"It's a step stool," Toby corrected. "It's only got five steps."

"Still not made for backpacking," Evan countered.

They stayed alert for traps and ambush, but the walk to the tunnel was uneventful. When they reached the back of the unfinished tunnel, Evan and Toby sized up the territory.

"I figure he uses that for the altar," Evan said, pointing at the large, raised, flat rock in the center.

"So we need to be right above it," Toby replied. "Gimme the ladder and the spray paint. You hold the light and stand guard."

Evan had no idea whether a containment spell would work on Sturdevant, or slow him down for long. But right now, with Seth a prisoner and Milo injured, they were down two on their team. That reduced an already narrow margin to a snowball's chance in hell. Evan was ready to count on long shots and Hail Mary passes, and hope for the best.

"Can't see the damn gray paint on the rock," Toby grumbled.

"That's the whole idea. Fluorescent red might have been a tip-off. We could put in a black light."

"Watch your mouth, smartass."

Under other circumstances, Evan would have been reassured by how easily he'd slipped into comfortable banter with Milo and Toby, like family. Now, he was too worried about Seth to be able to feel much of anything.

Decades of hunting meant Toby made short work of the sigil. When he climbed down from the ladder, Toby walked to the very back, pulled something from his bag and hid it in the rubble.

"What's that?" Evan asked, though he had his suspicions.

"Insurance."

Evan backtracked toward the entrance of the tunnel carrying the ladder. Toby used a branch from a bush to sweep away any trace of their presence, then ditched it in the thicket outside.

"Let's hope it works."

"I've been drawing sigils since before you learned how to spell 'cat,'" Toby replied, raising one eyebrow. "Near enough, anyhow. That one's a favorite. Easy to draw—relatively speaking—and the activation is simple to remember. We just have to get close enough without getting caught, and hope to fuck we're in time."

13

———

SETH

"You've made this far more difficult than it needed to be." Ira Sturdevant looked like his CEO picture from the website of the non-profit he ran. Except instead of a white shirt and dress slacks, tonight Sturdevant wore a dark T-shirt and jeans with a canvas jacket and boots. Sturdevant was dressed for a hike, and that told Seth that he'd run out of time.

Still under the hex, the most response Seth could manage was a curl of his lip.

"I wasn't going to come after you, or your boyfriend," Sturdevant said. "You won fair and square against my not-lamented colleagues. I staked out my territory a long time ago. Played by the rules. I didn't go out of bounds. Didn't poach from my brethren, didn't over-harvest to raise suspicions."

Yeah, you're a fucking philanthropist. Oh, wait. You are. Joke's on us.

"Then you two showed up. My people spotted you." He shook his head. "Hunters. They always think they blend in. And you might have —before you splashed your wardings and sigils all over your campsite."

On the other hand, it kept your goons from getting at us, so score one for our team.

"Kyle Henshaw still had almost two more years to live," Sturdevant went on. "I stuck to the schedule. I didn't take anyone before I needed to." He smirked. "Well, not any of the descendants. Now and then, a hiker or two might have gone missing, when I needed a power-boost. Nobody important. Nobody that mattered."

They mattered plenty. To someone.

"But you screwed that all to hell." Anger glittered in Sturdevant's eyes. He bore a striking resemblance to his portrait in Elk Manor, despite the stylish haircut and fashionable stubble, a handsome man, for a serial killer. Same high cheekbones and aristocratic features, same full brows and piercing, gray eyes. And the same amulet, which hung from a leather strap around his neck, which together with the anchor were essential to controlling his magic.

"Once you came here, the schedule was fucked. You were going to warn Henshaw, ruin a good thing. I needed to move things up a bit. But you got tricky," Sturdevant added with a nasty smile. "Or Henshaw wised up. Doesn't matter which. But it meant I had to improvise."

Seth mustered his best baleful glare, hoping that it promised slow, painful death if he had the chance to deal with Sturdevant himself.

"I thought about luring Henshaw back home with a bit of bad luck at the nursery. A fire, perhaps. An accident. He would have come running. And then you went walking around town like bait, two descendants for the taking. I imagine you were trying to draw me out, but it didn't work out quite the way you expected, did it?" Sturdevant looked pleased with himself as if he'd bagged a trophy.

Laugh all you want. Whether or not I make it out alive, Evan and Toby will have your head on a cursed iron pike.

"At first, I wasn't pleased that Will snatched you so far off schedule, but now I see it's for the best. Once the ritual is done, your friends won't be able to touch me. I could kill them," Sturdevant mused aloud. "After all, Malone is a descendant as well. And the other two are hunters—it would be a public service to exterminate them."

"But maybe they're more useful alive. Let them cull out the weak from my brethren. The world's grown smaller since we chose our territories. They don't seem as far away as they once did. And along the way, I have no doubt that one of the other disciples will end them."

You have no idea how many hunters know about you now. If we die, they'll take up the fight. Your secret is out.

Seth had strained at his bonds all day and tried to work a rote unbinding spell. He'd feared that the hex would cancel any spells he might attempt. Pulling at the ropes accomplished little except chafing his wrists raw. But when he worked the spell—limited to invoking it silently instead of speaking the words aloud—he felt the ropes give. That was just before Sturdevant came in to give his victory speech. He dared not try again in case the warlock could sense even the smallest bit of magic.

"Everything is ready, Mr. Sturdevant." Will came to the door, shouldering a canvas pack. Seth gave Will a death glare, but the traitor just smiled in response.

"Load that into the car. Let my men know we'll be heading out, and advise Chief Bondell that we're not to be disturbed. Then put our guest of honor in the back. Mind that you don't dislodge the hex."

"Of course, Mr. Sturdevant."

"I'll see you again, very soon." With that, Ira Sturdevant walked out, leaving Seth alone again.

This was probably his last chance to do anything unobserved. Seth invoked the unbinding spell again, investing the memorized words with all of his intent, his fear for Evan's safety, his desire to avenge Jesse and prevent more deaths. The magic that always came easily danced just beyond his reach, allowing him to touch just a spark of power instead of yielding to him. At this point, Seth resolved to take what he could get, and he felt the bonds ease a little more. They loosened just enough that he could twist his wrists but not pull his hands through.

One more push might do it. I'll save it for when the time is right, or they'll just tie me up again.

WILL MANHANDLED SETH INTO A LARGE SUV, PAIRING HIM WITH A

muscle-bound guard holding a gun. Another guard drove, and Will sat up front, while Sturdevant had the middle seat to himself. Two guards might not be impossible to overpower, Seth thought. He couldn't do it alone, but maybe his friends would have come up with a plan.

Seth wanted to believe Evan had gotten back to the cabin safely, somehow. He took comfort believing that if Will had captured or hurt Evan, he'd have run to make sure Seth knew about it. That neither Will nor Sturdevant gloated about catching Kyle, Toby, and the others also gave Seth hope. Whether they could stop his death or just avenge it, Seth knew the others would do their best to make sure Sturdevant never hurt anyone again.

The mountain road was so dark that Seth could see nothing but his own reflection from the window on his side of the SUV. He knew they were driving him to his death, and from the ritual he had interrupted in Richmond, Seth had no illusions that his end would be quick or painless. Whether backup arrived in time or not, Seth had made up his mind to give Sturdevant the fight of his life. He wasn't going to make it easy, even if he failed to stop the warlock in the end.

Cold resignation settled over Seth. He remembered it from his days on the battlefield. Once he surrendered to fate, worry receded, fear lessened, and only purpose remained. *Just like going into a firefight outside of Mosul. Maybe I'll come back. Maybe I won't. But I'm going to give it everything I've got and take as many of those sons of bitches down with me as I can.*

Seth didn't want to die, but he didn't fear death. He'd had to make his peace with the likelihood of dying bloody back in the army. He didn't regret spending the last nearly three years of his life trying to get the justice for Jesse and the other descendants that they wouldn't find elsewhere.

But walking away from Evan in the café, causing the stricken expression on his face with the words Will forced Seth to say? Seth would regret that with his dying breath.

Surely if Evan didn't realize Seth was bespelled, Toby or Milo would pick up on the clues when Evan recounted what had happened. Evan was smart, and he dove into studying the lore, so he could have recognized the signs for himself. He'd seemed anxious almost as soon as Will showed up, eager to leave, even asking for their dessert to-go. At first Seth thought Evan might be jealous and had tried to reassure him. But maybe Evan's instincts clued him in to danger faster than Seth's had, perhaps because he had no memories of false camaraderie to confuse him.

Seth hoped Evan could forgive him, and that he'd remember their time together fondly. Seth knew that these last months had been the happiest in his life, despite the dangers. He hadn't been lying when he'd told Toby that he wanted forever with Evan. Now, Seth feared, forever wasn't going to happen.

He swallowed hard, unwilling to give Will the satisfaction of knowing that he'd gotten to Seth. If he didn't find a way to survive this night, Seth told himself that Evan would be all right. Toby and Milo would see to that. Evan might not be welcome in his parents' home, but he had found a family in Travis, Brent, Simon, and others, people who would have his back and keep him safe. Evan could decide whether to continue hunting. He had his graphic design business, and he was welcome to Seth's truck and the RV. Evan was strong. He'd survive.

But Seth wasn't ready to give up quite yet. One more good push with the unbinding spell, and even with the effects muted by the hex, Seth thought it might be enough to free himself.

There would be a moment during the ritual when Sturdevant was vulnerable. Just as the witch-disciple's victory was imminent, as the ritual opened a rift that would enable him to gain power from the ghost of his dead master, the warlock would be so invested in working his own spell that he dared not spare thought or energy to defend himself. Isolated inside the warded circle, none of the guards would be able to intervene. If Seth could surprise Sturdevant and overpower him, wrest away his amulet and interrupt the transfer of power, he could shove the warlock into the rift and be rid of him forever. Even if to make it happen, Seth got pulled in as well.

A few times along the way Seth spotted local police cruisers. Sturdevant had Bondell running interference for him, which would make it that much harder for Evan and the others to get to the tunnel—if they even realized that tonight was the night. He counted on Toby to expect problems from the corrupt chief of police and for Scott to know how to work around the cops who were in cahoots. Seth couldn't control that, and he had plenty on his plate as it was.

This time, the ride out to the trail that led to the Nowhere tunnel seemed much shorter. *Time flies when you're dreading something.* He kept his wrists pressed tightly together when Will hauled him from the SUV, hoping no one noticed that the ropes had loosened. Will shoved him, making Seth stumble, then roughly grabbed his upper arm to steady him. Seth yanked free, but Will dug his fingers in tight enough to bruise, and Seth chose to pick his battles, waiting for the time to make his stand.

Sturdevant didn't need to fear being seen, not with the cops in his pocket. A guard led the way with a high-powered flashlight. Sturdevant followed, then Will steering Seth by the arm, then another guard. Now and then along the way, Sturdevant twitched his hand to one side or another, and Seth figured that the witch was turning the sigil alarms off and back on as they passed through.

The Nowhere tunnel loomed ahead. Their lights illuminated the stone arch entrance, making the void within seem even darker. Seth's heart thumped, and his mouth went dry. He'd cheated death three years ago when the disciple mistakenly killed Jesse instead of him. Maybe fate couldn't be denied, and he'd only managed to forestall destiny, instead of changing it altogether.

Stop that! he told himself. *Because if I can't change my fate, then we didn't change Evan's. And I will not let him die.*

Instead, Seth channeled the adrenaline that rushed through him at the prospect of imminent death into the hyper-focus he'd found so useful on the battlefield. Any small detail could be the thing he could use to stop Sturdevant and save himself. He dared not let his attention wander, or give in to fear.

Bits of rock and dry leaves crunched underfoot as they entered the unfinished tunnel. The air smelled of mildew and moss, and in the shadows, water dripped. The lead guard's flashlight punched a hole in the darkness, but couldn't illuminate the whole space. In here, without the rustle of leaves or a glimpse of the stars, they might as well have entered the underworld.

When they reached the back, Sturdevant turned to the two guards. "Leave your large flashlights in here, pointing up, one on each corner," he ordered. "Then go watch the entrance. Only use your penlights if you need to. We don't need any nosy hikers getting in the way." The guards' receding footsteps echoed in the man-made cavern.

That left Will, Sturdevant, and Seth. "Put those other two big lights on the front corners of the workspace," Sturdevant told Will, who still had a painfully tight grip on Seth's upper arm.

"Don't go anywhere," Will warned Seth.

Seth wasn't sure exactly how the hex that bound him worked, but Will's words had some effect. And Will had told him not to leave, but he said nothing about being able to move. As Sturdevant readied the materials he needed for the summoning, Seth gave another push with his weakened rote magic. The ropes slipped again, loose enough that Seth thought he could rip his hands free if he didn't mind leaving some skin behind.

Will set the flashlights, giving the tunnel a low-budget horror movie vibe. Sturdevant set pillar candles between the flashlights and lit them. He pulled a piece of charcoal from his bag and marked sigils and runes around the ritual space and on the slab of stone that would serve as the altar. Then he shook the contents of a velvet bag into a shallow stone bowl and lit the mixture, filling the blocked tunnel with the sickly-sweet smell of incense. A silver chalice and dagger at the foot of the stone slab left nothing to the imagination.

Since thinking the rote magic spells without saying them aloud had worked, sort of, to loosen his bonds, Seth decided to see if he could summon ghosts, too. Sturdevant's past victims probably weren't the man's biggest fans, and if Seth could wake them, they might help him beat the odds. He concentrated again, trying to infuse his will with his love for Evan, his intention to protect Kyle and the other descendants from the witch-disciples, and his fierce need to avenge his brother's death.

At first Seth thought the rote spell had failed. Then he felt the tunnel's temperature plummet, something that Will and Sturdevant, in their focus on the ritual, didn't seem to notice. The icy brush of dead fingers across his wrists loosened the bonds even further. He hoped he wasn't imagining things when he felt the air stir next to him and heard a voice whispering in his ear. *We are ready.*

Seth thought he glimpsed movement near the front of the tunnel, but he wasn't sure. Hoping against hope that it might be Evan and a rescue party, Seth managed the only distraction the hex permitted him and dropped to the floor.

"What's wrong with him?" Sturdevant snapped as Will came running. "What did you do?"

"Nothing, sir. He probably just fainted." Will grabbed Seth by the collar and slapped him across the face to rouse him. Seth did his best not to react.

"Fuckin' lightweight," Will muttered, backhanding Seth again. "Sac up and take this like a man." Another blow made Seth's ears ring, but he refused to stand until Will ordered him to do so.

"Get him on his feet and stop screwing around!" Sturdevant ordered.

"Stand up," Will yelled, and Seth had no choice except to obey. He got up as slowly as the hex would permit.

Sturdevant glared at him. "You and your troublesome friends destroyed my anchor," he growled. "It's an inconvenience, but it will not stop the ritual. Not when I've stored more power elsewhere. And when I meet my master again, I will gain all the power I need."

The witch-disciple raised his hands and chanted. A shimmering curtain of power rose around the circle the witch-disciple had marked on the tunnel floor. On the far side of the circle, a pinpoint of light appeared, and Seth knew it was the rift opening to wherever Rhyfel Gremory's soul had gone, the conduit for Sturdevant to renew his mojo in exchange for Seth's life. Seth smelled the incense and wanted to retch. He readied himself to make his final stand.

The curtain of light wavered. Sturdevant spoke the words of power again, but the energy did not grow stronger. Instead, it waxed and waned like a bad TV signal. Seth didn't know what was causing the disturbance, but he felt certain Evan and Toby had something to do with it. It might not save his life, but Seth took perverse enjoyment in seeing Sturdevant's frustration.

"It's time." Sturdevant looked at Seth and smiled. "Come to me. We'll cross the curtain together, and you will meet my master."

Seth mentally repeated the rote spell and tore his hands loose from the ropes. In the same instant Will dove for him, reaching out to grab Seth just as Evan sprang out of the shadows. Evan's knife sank into Will's side and Will screamed. A shot rang out, catching Sturdevant in the shoulder, and Toby stepped into view, raised his gun, and fired again at Sturdevant. The bullet glowed as it tried to cross the curtain of light, and angled away, striking the stone wall.

"Kill him!" Will roared at Seth.

In response, Seth spun and rounded on Evan. His hands were free now, bloodied at the wrists, and he fought the command as his body lurched toward Evan. He swung a punch, aiming for Evan's jaw, all the while screaming inside his own head to stop.

His fist connected, snapping Evan's head to the side and making him stumble backward. Seth's eyes widened with horror at his actions, unable to beat the hex. He followed, fist raised to strike again, but Evan went low, head-butting Seth in the belly, and grabbing for his hips. As they fell, Evan pulled something out of Seth's pocket and hurled it into the darkness at the end of the tunnel. Seth felt the hex fall away, finally back in control of his own body.

"I'm free!" Seth said to Evan.

In the background Sturdevant shouted the spell defiantly, and the candle smoke and incense made Seth's lungs burn.

"Free? You'll be dead." Will lunged at Seth, pulling him away from Evan. In Will's hand was the bloody knife he had tugged from his own side, raised to strike.

Seth tackled Will at the knees, and they went down, with Seth holding on with all his strength, trying to keep Will rolling so he couldn't strike with the knife. As they tussled, the temperature plummeted, and the ghosts of Kyle's father and ancestors made themselves visible.

To Seth's surprise, some of the dead workmen joined the melee, perhaps tired of Sturdevant making their tunnel into a place of slaughter. Several of the spirits piled onto Will, trying to pull him away from

Seth. Others tried to get to Sturdevant, but he held them off with a gesture.

"It's too late to stop me," Sturdevant growled. "The ritual has already begun."

Toby shouted words Seth didn't recognize, and a sigil glowed to life on the tunnel ceiling, right above the ritual area. Static rippled through the curtain of light as the two magics warred. The ghosts closed on Sturdevant, coming at him in waves from all directions, trying to slow his invocation.

"Evan! Get Seth and run!" Toby yelled.

Will twisted beneath Seth and sat up, knife raised. Evan appeared behind Will and brought a chunk of rock down hard, striking Will in the temple and knocking him to one side.

Sturdevant kept chanting, as if he considered the fight going on around him to be of no importance, despite the blood that soaked his sleeve, confident in his ultimate win. The pinprick of light had grown much larger.

Seth knew they were running out of time.

Toby aimed and fired again, and this time the shot took Sturdevant through the head, splattering the back wall with brains and blood. Seth sprang forward and grabbed the amulet, jerking it hard enough to break the strap, then shoved Sturdevant's body through the curtain of energy, toward the growing point of light that was the gateway for Gremory's power.

"No!" Will hurled himself at Seth, knocking them both off balance. Seth reacted on instinct, trying to keep the knife away. He ripped free of Will's grip and shoved hard, sending Will stumbling through the glowing curtain too. The nexus of light had stopped growing as soon as Sturdevant died, but that didn't end its power. It still pulled the sacrifices toward it, drawing them into its maw. Sturdevant's body was already halfway through, and Will screamed as he fought against a power he could not escape.

"We need to get out of here," Evan said, grabbing Seth by the arm and dragging him toward the tunnel entrance.

"Don't let the bad man out!" Seth shouted at the ghosts, who closed ranks around the ritual area, to keep Will from leaving the circle in pursuit, if he managed to escape the pull of the rift.

"Toby! Now!" Evan yelled, as the three of them scrambled the last few feet to reach the outside.

Toby's deep voice rumbled a command in Latin. Light flared and an explosion from inside boomed like a cannon, belching out a cloud of rock dust as the tunnel collapsed, sending the three of them sprawling.

Seth scrambled backward, staring in horror at the collapsed tunnel. A short distance from the tunnel entrance, Seth saw the bodies of the two guards, who were either dead or unconscious.

Toby lay on his back, staring at the night sky. "I can't believe that actually worked."

Seth stared at both of them. "What just happened?"

Evan pushed himself upright. "Toby and I were out here earlier today. Toby put a containment sigil on the ceiling, and a little bomb in the back of the tunnel. He said it was for insurance. Oh, and we stole the Brigadoon Coin. I didn't want Sturdevant to have any extra mojo to pull on. It's in a spelled box, back at the cabin. Milo and Scott melted the plaque on a bonfire about an hour ago, and we can melt down the amulet, too," he added, nodding toward the talisman that still dangled by broken straps clutched in Seth's fist.

"Look!" Toby pointed toward a gray shape that grew more solid as they watched. Jack Henshaw's ghost materialized and looked at them solemnly. The ghost placed his hand over his heart, then extended his open, upturned palm. Seth could only guess at the meaning. *Thank you for stopping him. Thank you for saving my son.* A moment later, the ghost vanished.

Toby climbed to his feet and yanked Seth up, folding him into a bear hug. "Glad to see you in one piece."

"Chief Bondell—" Seth began, still trying to grasp that he was alive and had been rescued.

Toby chuckled. "I used a couple of remote frequency scanners to set off every alarm in range when we drove through town. That tied up most of the local cops. Bondell himself was guarding the road to the tunnel. I took him down with a tranq gun before he even knew we were here. He's trussed up like a Thanksgiving turkey, and he'll have a hell of a headache when he comes around."

Seth turned just as Evan stood. Memories of how they'd parted flooded back. "Evan, I'm so sorry—"

Evan cut off his apology, slamming their lips together, and hauling Seth up against him in a crushing embrace.

Toby cleared his throat. "How about running away now, makeup sex later?"

Seth and Evan stepped apart, both wearing sheepish grins. "It wasn't you, at the café. I figured out about the hex."

"I love you."

Evan grinned. "I know. And we're good. I love you, too. But we'd better get out of here, because I don't think they'll let us bunk together in jail."

14

—————

EVAN

They made it back to the truck and were on the road, headed away from town before the rest of Boone's first responders arrived to check out the explosion. It took some navigating, but they made a large circle to get back to the cabin without risking an encounter with Bondell's cops. On the way, Evan and Toby took turns filling Seth in on everything that had happened since Will snatched him. Seth listened quietly, looking a bit shell shocked.

"Thank you," Seth said when they finished the story. "I really didn't know if you'd make it in time." He looked to Evan, worry clear in his eyes. "I wasn't sure you'd want to."

Evan reached over and took his hand, giving it a squeeze. "Of course I did. We all did."

Toby glanced back at them in the rearview mirror. "No makeup sex in the car, either. Just got the upholstery cleaned. You hear me?"

"We hear you!" Seth and Evan said in unison.

Seth pulled Evan close, and they wrapped their arms around each other. They were both covered with rock dust and smeared with dirt. Seth was smeared with Will's blood, and dried blood near Seth's nose and bruises on his face showed that he'd been smacked around.

Seth raised a hand and touched Evan's sore cheek with his finger-tips. "I'm sorry I hit you. I tried to fight the hex, but I couldn't ignore a direct command."

"Pretty sure you managed to pull your punch, because I know you can deck me," Evan replied. They sparred often, training for the hunt. Evan had learned a lot, but Seth was still a stronger, more seasoned fighter.

"Still."

Evan turned Seth's face, forcing his boyfriend to meet his gaze. "What you said at the café hurt at the time. I was blindsided. And what he made you say played to all my fears. Guess I'm still an inse-cure mess around the edges." He offered a teary smile, and Seth bent to kiss him again. This time, the kiss was gentle and reassuring.

"I was screaming inside," Seth replied. "I couldn't stop. Please believe me, Evan. I didn't mean any of it."

Evan searched Seth's eyes, looking for confirmation, and found love and worry. "I believe you."

Seth visibly relaxed. "I was so scared that Sturdevant would hurt you. Or that he'd find the cabin, and come after all of you."

Snuggled together in the darkness, the backseat seemed like a haven, both of them still clinging to one another as if they feared the other might vanish.

"You came up with a good plan," Seth said, kissing Evan again.

"I came up with a completely crazy idea," Evan admitted. "I'm just glad it worked."

It wasn't until Toby cleared his throat, startling them both awake, that Evan realized they had dozed on the trip back. "When we go inside, we don't need to share all the details of what went down. Scott's on our side, but I don't want to put him in a bad place, choosing between upholding the law and protecting us. So we just say that we got you out, and something triggered the cave-in. Sturdevant and Will were trapped inside."

"What about the bullet?" Seth asked. "Can it be traced back to you? Just in case anyone decides to dig them out."

"Not my first rodeo," Toby replied. "That gun's not registered to me. So, no. And if the body didn't get sucked through the rift before it closed, half the mountain came down in that tunnel. I don't think anyone is going to bother trying to dig."

"You're sure Bondell didn't see you before you took him down?"

Toby shook his head. "No. He never saw us. I'm sure. Not that he won't have his suspicions, but that's not the same as proof."

Seth had no idea what time it was when they finally pulled in beside the cabin. The door flew open, and Scott came out on the porch, gun in hand. He relaxed when he saw the three of them heading for the steps.

"Is it over?"

"It is," Toby said. "Terrible thing about those old tunnels. Never know when they'll just tumble down."

Understanding flashed in Scott's eyes, and he gave a curt nod. "Should have made that place off-limits years ago. It was an accident waiting to happen."

Scott cleared his throat and glanced behind him, assuring that the others were out of earshot. "I've been busy on my own project while you were gone. I walked down to the main road and had a long chat with Dan Peters, the county sheriff. He's been building a case against Bondell for a while now. He had plenty of evidence, but Ira Sturdevant gave a lot of money to some of the local officials' campaigns and pet projects, in exchange for making Bondell untouchable. Dan finally has everything he needs to go around Sturdevant's stooges, bring Bondell up on charges, and oust his cronies. Dan was going to make that his parting shot when he retired. Now, he's moved up his timeline to do it right away. He's on his way back to get things rolling. Getting Sturdevant out of the way just made that a lot easier."

Scott led the way into the living room. Milo's worried gaze went immediately to Toby, who crossed the room and leaned down to give him a lingering kiss, assuring Milo he was all right.

"Are we safe?" Kyle asked. He and Steve sat on the couch holding hands.

Toby gave an edited recap of what happened at the tunnel, including the help from Jack Henshaw's ghost.

"You've got nothing to fear from Sturdevant," Toby told them as he ended his story. He glanced at Scott. "But there are other disciples still on the loose. And although they each picked a single family to prey on, as we saw with what Sturdevant tried to do to Seth, they can use any of the descendants for the ritual."

"What does that mean?" Steve asked.

"It means we can't guarantee that you're completely safe, not until all the disciples have been dealt with," Seth replied. "That's going to take a while. The disciples staked out their territories, so if you stay here in the area, you're probably okay."

"Probably?" Scott's voice had a sharp edge.

Seth frowned. "We haven't seen any of the disciples go looking to poach descendants from each other. But it could happen."

"How do I keep them safe?" Scott asked.

Evan guessed that Scott wasn't used to being so out of his element.

"I can give you some tips on how to stay low profile," Milo offered.

"We can put up wardings and give you charms to help protect you, deflect interest," Toby added. "But there isn't a supernatural Witness Protection Program, at least not one that I've ever heard about."

"If you'd have heard about it, it isn't working," Milo grumbled.

"Thank you," Scott said raggedly, moving to shake each man's hand. Kyle and Steve did the same, but Kyle threw himself into Toby's arms, hugging the older hunter hard.

"You got the guy who killed my dad," Kyle said when he stepped back, tears streaking his face. "And all the others. I can't ever repay you." Steve moved to slip an arm around his boyfriend.

"You don't have to repay it," Toby said, and his usually stony facade softened. "That's what we do. And…you're welcome."

THE NEXT DAY, AFTER EVERYONE SLEPT IN, THEY PACKED UP THEIR THINGS, set the cabin to rights, and made a list of the supplies Scott said he'd replenish. Scott promised to see Kyle and Steve safely home, so Toby drove the four of them back to town, and Seth reclaimed the Silverado from where he'd left it parked in a public lot from the trip to the café. Toby detoured to pick up his black boxes, leaving no trace of what had transpired.

"Gratitude notwithstanding, I think we'd better get the hell out of Dodge," Milo said. "Those guards Toby tranq'd are going to wake up with a roaring headache, and I don't want to be in reach if Bondell and his boys come after us. I'm glad the county sheriff has them in his sights, but they're not fired yet."

Milo headed over to cancel the rest of their reservation, thumping along on his crutches. He carefully avoided the decorative bridge, which was still cordoned off with tape since it hadn't been repaired. Seth and Evan made quick work of hitching the RV to the trailer, then went to the cabin to help Toby pack.

"Wasn't much of a vacation," Toby said with a sigh, looking out toward the mountains. "But then we knew what we were getting into when we came."

"If you don't have to be anywhere right away, why not take a couple of days for a real break?" Seth suggested. "There are some pretty spots in Tennessee and Kentucky—you have to pass right by them on the way back to Indiana."

Milo had hobbled back by then, and he and Toby exchanged a look. "I like the sound of that," Toby said, winking at Milo. "Just what the doctor ordered."

Seth and Evan exchanged hugs and backslaps with Milo and Toby, and for once, Evan was at a loss for words. Both of the older hunters had come to mean so much to him in the short time they'd been here in Boone, and while they would continue to be in touch by phone and video call, he knew he would miss their crotchety banter.

"You take care of each other, you hear?" Milo said as Seth and Evan headed for the truck. "Don't make me come after you and smack you up the side of the head."

Seth and Evan laughed and waved, then climbed into the Silverado and headed out of town.

"I know you want to get to Charleston, to go after the next witch-disciple," Evan said when they hit the highway. "But I found a place outside of Asheville that says it's got great views of the mountains and the campground has a hot tub…if you're interested in taking a few days off."

Seth looked over in his direction and grinned. "Oh, I'm interested. Lead the way," he said, handing off his phone so Evan could put in the address to adjust their route.

That evening, after they got the RV situated and ate a good steak dinner at a local restaurant, Seth and Evan came back to the trailer and sat side by side on a picnic table, staring out at the mountains as twilight settled over them.

"They really do look blue," Evan marveled. "I thought the whole 'blue ridge' thing was just poetic."

"Pretty place," Seth agreed, pulling Evan close to fight the evening chill. "Pretty nice company, too." He brushed a kiss against Evan's temple. Evan slid a hand over Seth's thigh, and let a finger wander up and down his inseam.

"How about we go inside and have sweaty I'm-so-glad-we're-both-alive sex?" Evan proposed. "That's one of my favorite kinds."

"Oh, really?" Seth gave a throaty chuckle that went right to Evan's cock. "And what are your other favorites?"

"Hmm," Evan said, pretending to need to think about it. "I like morning sex and shower sex and makeup sex and sucking you or giving you a handjob while we watch movies…come to think of it, pretty much anything that involves getting naked with you."

"Then why are we still out here?" Seth had a wicked gleam in his eyes. "It's too cold, and there are too many bugs to get naked."

"I totally agree."

They stumbled into the RV, groping and kissing. Evan pushed Seth against the wall and rode Seth's thigh, grinding down with abandon, letting Seth know just how hungry he was. Seth gripped Evan by the hips, keeping him close, and kissed him hard, open mouthed, devouring him.

"I want you to fuck me," Seth said, coming up for air. He met Evan's gaze. "Please. Need to feel you in me." He shuddered. "Need you so bad."

They often switched, and a flip fuck was Evan's favorite thing, where they both got to give and receive. But when they weren't feeling especially acrobatic and just wanted simple, satisfying connection and release, Evan usually bottomed. Not that Seth wouldn't have if Evan asked, but that had just ended up their go-to position.

"Sure," Evan said, reaching up to cup Seth's face. "Always. I need you bad, too."

Ever since they'd left Boone, he'd sensed a new tentativeness in Seth, as if the whole ordeal had left him emotionally fragile. Evan could relate. He knew how he'd felt when Seth had saved him back in Richmond. It didn't escape him that most couples—non-hunter "normal" couples—probably didn't have a sexual protocol for near-death experience aftermath. *Their loss,* he thought. He and Seth rarely had fights that required real makeup sex, but prove-to-me-we're-both-still-alive sex seemed to be a habit.

Evan took Seth's wrist and led him into the bedroom. They fell onto the bed together, stroking and kissing, tangling long legs and dry-humping until they broke apart, panting and sweating. Seth's eyes were dark, his face flushed, hungry and vulnerable.

"Fuck me," he told Evan. "Fill me up, make me feel it tomorrow. Leave marks. I don't want to think about anything except me and you, and you in me. Please."

Evan kissed him, then sat back on his haunches and pulled off Seth's T-shirt. He kept eye contact as he unbuckled Seth's belt, and Seth arched up to let Evan pull off jeans and trunks in one move.

"Want you naked, too," Seth said and reached out to grab the hem of Evan's shirt. Evan shimmied out of his clothing, too aroused to make a show of stripping tonight. Seth started to turn over, but Evan pushed him down gently.

"I want to see your eyes," Evan said, tracing a finger down Seth's chest. "Want to watch you come."

Seth licked his lips and swallowed, nodding. Evan bent over to lap at first one nipple and then the other, reaching between them to fondle Seth's balls and stroke the taint behind them. He shifted so their erect pricks rubbed against each other, a delicious friction.

"Don't tease," Seth panted, and Evan saw desperation in his eyes. "Just fuck me. Hard."

Evan reached for the lube in the nightstand and slicked up his aching cock. Seth grabbed his legs under his knees and pulled them up, spreading himself open and begging to be taken. Evan pushed in with one finger, then a second, angling to hit Seth's spot and make him groan.

"Just do it."

"Not going to hurt you." It had been a while since Seth had bottomed, and as much as Evan knew Seth craved connection, he wanted to make this good for him. He added a third finger, stretching Seth's hole, and Seth started to fuck himself on Evan's fingers.

"God, what you do to me," Evan murmured, as he watched, discovering he could get even harder than he already was at the sight.

"Now. Please, Evan. Now."

Evan withdrew his fingers and saw the loss in Seth's eyes. He gave a reassuring smile, then lined up his cock with Seth's slick furl and pushed in, sliding all the way on the first thrust.

Seth groaned, and Evan stayed still, letting his lover adjust, trying to hold on to his own control at how hot and tight it felt to be inside Seth, how much he'd needed this himself.

"More."

Evan started to move, anchoring himself with one hand on Seth's shoulder and the other on his hip, pushing his legs up until Seth was nearly folded double. He set a pounding rhythm, hard but not punishing. Being rough wasn't the goal. Evan knew from experience how much Seth wanted the sensation to overwhelm him, to block out the memories and fears and sweep him away to somewhere outside his churning thoughts where all that mattered was pleasure and fusion. He leaned forward, trapping Seth's dick between them, wanting to give Seth the release he needed.

Seth threw back his head, biting his lower lip, eyes wide open and staring. He wrapped both legs around Evan, drawing him even closer.

"Hey. Look at me. I want to watch your face," Evan said, knowing he wouldn't last much longer. All the tangled emotions of the past few days fueled the fire inside him that seemed to start in his toes and crackled up through every nerve until his balls drew up and he felt his control slipping.

"Come for me, Seth. Show me."

Seth's whole body went rigid, and he cried out Evan's name as hot ropes of come spurted between them. Evan managed two more hard thrusts and then felt his own orgasm wash over him, sweeping him away as he kept on pumping into Seth until the last of his release had spent.

Evan dropped forward, resting his cheek on Seth's chest, breathing in the smell of sweat and come. He heard the thud of Seth's heart and smiled to know he'd had that effect on his boyfriend. Seth wrapped his arms around Evan, holding them together.

As good as it felt, after a few moments Evan knew he needed to move. "We're going to stick together if I don't get us cleaned up," he said, stretching up to kiss Seth. "I'll be right back."

His spent cock slipped free as Seth reluctantly uncrossed his ankles from behind Evan's back and let go with his arms. Evan immediately missed the connection. He forced himself to roll to his feet and went to the bathroom, returning with a warm cloth to wipe both of them up. Then he crawled beneath the covers and combed his fingers through Seth's hair, their faces only inches apart.

"We're really going to need to wash the comforter," Seth said with a completely straight face.

Evan threw his head back and laughed, and seconds later Seth joined in. The laughter was like a second climax, uncontrollable and freeing, clearing away the last of the tension and fear, and they were helpless to stop. They laughed until they couldn't breathe, tears streaming down their faces.

"It wasn't that funny," Seth gasped, winded.

"Sure it was," Evan panted. He smoothed away the tears from Seth's face and wiped his own with the back of his hand.

"No one ever has a laughing fit after sex in the movies." Seth pushed a lock of hair out of Evan's eyes. "Is this weird?"

Evan kissed him lightly on the lips, tasting salt and something uniquely Seth. "Not weird. Comfortable. Real. And…kinda hot," he added with a smile.

"Oh yeah?"

"Yeah." Evan loved the look in Seth's eyes that promised affection and forever. Gone was the uncertainty and fear that had haunted his gaze since they'd left Boone. "I love you," he murmured because he knew Seth needed to hear the declaration as well as read it in his face.

"Love you, too," Seth replied. "I want you, this, forever."

"Forever," Evan echoed, kissing him again. "Sounds like a plan."

AFTERWORD

Boone, Blowing Rock, and the beautiful Blue Ridge Mountains of North Carolina are real places, full of breathtaking scenery, natural wonders, and fun things to do. Many of the places mentioned were inspired by real points of interest, although I relocated some sites from elsewhere in the state for the sake of the story. Writer's prerogative! Others I renamed or reimagined out of respect for the property owners. But if you visit, you'll quickly spot the landmarks that sparked my ideas.

The shady cops were entirely a work of fiction because I needed additional henchmen. No disrespect is intended to any of North Carolina's finest.

Many of the other characters mentioned in this book have their own series. Simon Kincaide and Vic D'Amato are the main characters in my Badlands urban fantasy MM paranormal romance series. Travis Dominick and Brent Lawson star in my Night Vigil series (written under my Gail Z. Martin name) of dark urban fantasy. Mark Wojcik headlines the Spells Salt and Steel series with plenty of snarky humor, co-written with Larry N. Martin. Simon's cousin, Cassidy Kincaide, is the lead character in my Deadly Curiosities urban fantasy series (also written as Gail Z. Martin). Those series and characters cross over with each other, so there's plenty for you to explore!

ACKNOWLEDGMENTS

It takes a village to bring a book to life. Thank you to Larry N. Martin, my partner and co-author, for all the behind the scenes work that got this book ready to share. Thanks also to Jean Rabe, our editor, to our beta readers Andrea, Beth, Christopher, Donald, Laurie, and Sharon, and our launch team, Amy, Anne, Annemarie, Barbara, Candi, Carra, Cheryl, Chris, Christi, Christy, Darrell, Diane, Karolina, Lisa, Manda, Mary, Nica, Patti, Raven, Sandra, Sarah, Shannon, Shirley, Tekna, and Xochitl. Thank you also to my Shadow Alliance and Worlds of Morgan Brice street teams, who share the journey and the jokes along the way. And most of all, thank you to my readers. Because you read, I write.

Look for Seth and Evan to return in *Unholy*, set in haunted, historic Charleston, South Carlolina!

EXCERPT | BADLANDS

SIMON

At this hour of the morning, the boardwalk ghosts were silent. Simon Kincaide stared down the nearly empty, broad beachside walkway and breathed in the ocean air. Flags flapped in the breeze, waves pounded the shore on the other side of the dunes, and seagulls swooped. The tourists hadn't yet woken.

Simon looked, out of habit, to the places the spirits favored. The old man with his bicycle and his dog wouldn't appear until late afternoon, cycling down the boardwalk. Kevin, a dreadlocked man in his twenties, liked the stairs that led to the beach, perhaps near the spot where he drowned. Two children in Victorian clothing, spirits so faded that they could not even remember their names, would skip past near sunset. Other ghosts came and went, but Simon could set his watch by those appearances. Not everyone could see the ghosts—most of the people milling along the boardwalk could not and never would—but Simon did.

Sebastian Simon Kincaide had known he wasn't like other kids when he realized nobody else could see and hear the spirits he considered regular playmates. Discovering he got glimpses into the future from time to time made him even less like his friends at school. Figuring out that he was gay was just the icing on the cake. That all happened long ago, but the sense of being an outsider never really went away, Simon thought, not even now at age thirty-five, with a prosperous business and a few bestselling books to his credit.

He worked the key in the front door. Grand Strand Ghost Tours, a small shop on the Myrtle Beach boardwalk, shared a building with a beachwear shop but had a coveted location between the legendary Gay Dolphin Gift Cove and the popular Myrtle Beach SkyWheel mega-Ferris wheel. Simon paused in the doorway, letting himself enjoy a moment of pride and satisfaction in the business it had taken three damn years to build.

Simon collected the mail, pocketed his keys, and locked the door behind him since the shop wouldn't open for another two hours. He switched on the lights and music, then went to the back to start a pot of coffee.

His phone buzzed, and he answered. "Hey, Seth. What's up?"

Seth Tanner chuckled. "You haven't had your coffee yet, have you?"

"I'm working on it." Simon held the phone between his shoulder and ear as he readied the coffee maker. "What do you need?"

Seth sighed. "I'm looking into a vengeful ghost problem near Breezewood, up in Pennsylvania. Salt and iron aren't doing the trick, but I'm sure it's ghosts, not demons, so exorcism won't work, either. Got any ideas?"

"Find the anchor object the spirit is tethered to," Simon recommended, measuring out the coffee. "Might not be near where the appearances are happening. Have an officiant from the deceased's faith tradition say a blessing and urge the ghost to move on. If nothing else works, there's a banishment ritual, but it's brutal on the spirits. And no matter what you've seen on TV, don't get yourself arrested trying to dig up the grave to salt and burn the bones."

Seth chuckled. "I knew you'd have the answers. You're a rare medium, Simon. Well done."

"Ha, ha. As if I haven't heard that one before," Simon groaned, rolling his eyes. He pressed the button, and the coffee maker chugged to life.

"Seriously, thanks," Seth replied. "Send me the bill."

"When I have to do some research, I'll charge for the time. This, I can give you off the top of my head. Next time you're in the area, stop in and we'll do dinner. Your treat."

"You're on," Seth replied and ended the call.

Simon headed out to the main room and started to get the shop ready for business. Shelves in the front held books about ghost stories from all over South Carolina and the Lowcountry, but especially those with tales of spirits, pirates, or old scandals of the Grand Strand. Prominently displayed were the three books on local folklore and ghosts that bore his name as author. The glass case by the register held gemstones and silver jewelry for healing and protection, colored candles, and sealed bags of the most common dried plants and flours used in rituals and aromatherapy. Shelves behind the cabinet held an assortment of candles in tall glass holders with pictures of saints on the front. In the back, a table and two comfortable chairs supplied a homey place to do appointment-only psychic readings, and the table could expand to hold six people for a full séance.

A rack on top of the counter held brochures about the Grand Strand Ghost Tours that Simon led four nights a week, as well as the "Pirates and Scoundrels" special tours and the "Lowcountry Legends and Lore" talk he gave twice a month at Brookgreen Gardens. The large sign on the wall behind the counter advertised ticket prices for the tours and special events, with a prominent reminder to "ask about rates for private spirit readings and séances."

Display racks offered t-shirts with the Grand Strand Ghost Tours logo, while others bore catchy phrases like "Ghosts Gone Wild," "Grand Strand Spook-a-palooza," and his favorite, a cartoon of a ghost holding a beach drink that read "Chillin' Out." The nearby shelves that held cups, stickers, and shot glasses with the same designs were a concession to tourist tastes.

Simon straightened some of the merchandise when his phone rang again. "Mark! You're up early."

Mark Wojcik grumbled something in response, and Simon grinned. Mark hated mornings even more than he did. "No, I'm up late and still haven't gone to bed," Mark muttered. "And I'm bruised from head to toe after I got my ass kicked by a were-cougar before we brought it down, so forgive me if I'm not Mr. Sunshine."

Like Seth, Mark was a real-life hunter of things that went bump in the night; part of a loosely allied group of people who by talent or personal tragedy found themselves initiated into a shadow world most people could live happily never suspecting. Simon's gifts as a medium and clairvoyant—and his training as a folklorist—made him a part of that hidden network, and his research skills provided a second stream of income.

"I finished the research on the kelpies you asked for," Simon replied. "Sent the files to the secure share drive."

"Okay," Mark said. "That's what I was calling about. I'll shoot the payment back atcha. Thanks."

Simon ended the call and ran a hand back through his shoulder-length brown hair. Four years ago, if someone had told him that he'd be making a living taking beachgoers on ghost tours, giving readings, and selling tchotchkes, he'd have laughed. But how he'd ended up on the Grand Strand was not funny at all.

Three and a half years ago, Dr. Sebastian Kincaide held a professor-ship at the University of South Carolina in the Humanities Depart-ment, teaching folklore and mythology classes and writing scholarly articles on legends and lore. He kept his abilities as a medium and clairvoyant hidden, although his long-time relationship with another professor on staff had been openly acknowledged, especially after he and Jacen had announced their engagement.

Even now, the memory brought a sour twist to Simon's stomach. Emerson Baucom Tallmudge, the father of one of his students, turned out to be not only a donor and a board member for the university, but a hard-core fundamentalist as well, of the "thou shalt not suffer a witch to live" variety. Apparently, after he'd gotten a glimpse of his son's textbooks for the class, Tallmudge got his dander up and lobbied the board to be rid of such an "evil influence." Simon thought he had successfully placated the board, citing the importance of classical mythology in a well-rounded education, but then Tallmudge found evidence online that Simon admitted to being able to talk with spirits, and everything came crashing down.

The board dismissed Simon with a severance package that told him they also thought Tallmudge's complaints were bullshit, but in the end, the prospect of an endowment beat out standing up for one of their faculty. Then Jacen broke off their engagement, too afraid that Simon's dismissal would compromise his bid for tenure, and Simon's world went up in flames.

Alone, unemployed, and unable to find another teaching job, Simon drifted down to Myrtle Beach, intending to stay for a week or so to regroup and lick his wounds. When his aunt offered to sell him the cottage in Myrtle Beach where he was staying, Simon took it as a sign to rebuild his life from the ground up. He put his folklore background to use writing a book on local ghosts and used the self-published book to leverage himself into jobs as a tour guide, haunted attractions actor, museum docent, and speaker while he put his plan together. Grand Strand Ghost Tours wasn't just a shop; it was Simon's howl of defiance at a universe that had fucked him over.

And which was still doing so, since the coffee maker had not only failed to produce a cup of java-rich goodness, but had sent a gush of murky water and wet grounds all over the floor.

"Shit." Simon grabbed a handful of paper towels and began mopping. The smell of burned electronics told him without needing to use his psychic gifts that the coffee maker was dead. He dropped the machine into the trash on top of the sodden towels, ordered a new one on Amazon with expedited shipping, and then contemplated the prospect of a morning without coffee.

"Screw that," he said, glancing at the clock. He locked up, turned out lights, and headed for Mizzenmast Coffee.

Before he'd made it half a block, his phone buzzed once more. This time he smiled at the number that came up. "Hi, Cassidy. Everything okay?" His cousin, Cassidy Kincaide, ran an antique store in Charleston, just two hours south of Myrtle Beach. They hadn't been close growing up, but now that Cassidy had discovered her own ability to read the history of objects by touching them, they had bonded.

"Fine. Just busy. Mostly regular stuff, but some of the other too, if you know what I mean." Cassidy's shop proved to be the perfect opportunity to get cursed and haunted objects out of the wrong hands.

Simon and Cassidy often talked over whatever weird or supernatural situation they were currently navigating. Not to mention Cassidy had a gorgeous gay Weaver witch best friend as a partner in her supernatural escapades. It was another sign of the universe's contempt for Simon that Teag was already taken. "Is the store open yet? Can you talk?"

"I'm heading for coffee," Simon replied. "What's up?"

"I've got a carved mahogany trinket box with the name '*Jeremiah Holzer*' engraved on the bottom," Cassidy said. "There's a pretty nasty curse on it. I think Jeremiah was from the Myrtle Beach area, but Teag and I can't find anything about him online, and I thought maybe you could check some local archive stuff for me."

"Sure," Simon agreed. "How urgent?"

"We've got the box quarantined, so it's not doing any new damage, but two people were injured from the curse, and I have a feeling there's missing information that we need to break the bad juju. So, the sooner, the better."

"I'll work on it tonight, after the tour," Simon promised. "Say 'hi' to everyone for me."

"When are you going to come to Charleston? You know we've got the best restaurants on the Southeast coast," Cassidy replied. "Plus, Teag and Anthony have a couple of cute guys in mind they think you might hit it off with."

Simon cringed, glad Cassidy couldn't see his expression. Even after three years, he wasn't sure he was ready for a new romance. Perhaps he never would be. "It's the busy season," he begged off. "But maybe this winter. Or come visit me. Roads go both ways, you know."

"It's tourist season here, too," she reminded him. "But we'll get together soon, one way or another. And thanks for the research."

"You got that haunted painting off my hands," Simon replied. "I owe you." He hung up, but couldn't shake the melancholy that had settled in. A couple walked past, hands clasped, talking quietly, and an ache he didn't want to acknowledge flared in his chest. As much as he feared being hurt again, Simon couldn't deny the fact that he missed being in a relationship, having someone to wake up with every day and fall asleep with at night. For a while, he'd buried himself in his work, and that had dulled the loneliness. Now that he was no longer in survival mode, the evenings were not completely filled with busyness, and the nights stretched long.

Simon chuckled at his fears. *Here I am, backing up people who hunt real monsters, and I'm too chickenshit to go on a date. I need to man up and…man up.*

EXCERPT | TREASURE TRAIL

ERIK

"IF THE SHOW PROPOSAL GOES THROUGH, IT WILL REALLY PUT *TREASURE Trail* and Trinkets on the map!" Corinne Scott had the bouncy enthusiasm required of an agent, and it came across as clear over the phone as it did in person.

"It's exciting, but let's wait before we break out the champagne," Erik Mitchell protested. He had been dealing with the chaos of unpacking boxes and living out of a suitcase for two weeks, since his move to Cape May, New Jersey, and the complete uprooting of his life. "If they're counting on using my supposed notoriety to sell the show, they might be disappointed. There's a lot I can't talk about—and it's mostly the exciting parts."

"You traveled the world stopping art and antiquities fraud," Corinne continued, undeterred. "It's like something out of Indiana Jones."

Erik winced. Much as he loved those movies, Indy was more like the kind of guy he helped bust for swiping relics. "Um...not really. I spent a lot of time in the back rooms of museums going over old stuff with a magnifying glass. And I only got shot at a few times."

That was enough. A collector with a very rare Fabergé egg music box wanted Erik to authenticate the egg for the buyer. Unfortunately, there were other interested parties, and they all brought more muscle than brains. The deal went sideways when they decided to negotiate with guns; all hell broke loose, and Erik nearly died. He ended up with a concussion, a bullet wound in his shoulder, and nightmares verging on PTSD.

"This wouldn't be anything so dangerous!" Corinne was in full sales mode now. "It's only six episodes, and it's the local PBS station. All the crimes have already been solved. You're just on camera for the expert cameos, and to toss out some advice on how to avoid buying fake art or accidentally stealing priceless relics."

The longer Corinne talked, the more Erik became convinced the whole TV show was a colossal mistake. He had relocated to Cape May from Atlanta to get away from the sensational—and dangerous— aspects of his old life. Sure, chasing down art fraud had been his dream job, like something out of a thriller novel. His younger self had relished the constant travel and intermittent danger, and the work paid well—in headlines and in a very healthy salary.

Then there was the clusterfuck bust and Erik's injury. He realized that he was ready to move on, settle down, and step out of the spotlight. He'd thought his boyfriend, Josh, would be happy about the change. Then he got home a few days earlier than expected and found Josh banging Erik's personal assistant on the dining room table.

After all the shouting and tears were over, Erik found himself single and lacking an assistant. He'd decided right then to leave his old world behind. That meant getting out of Atlanta, out of the apartment he'd shared with Josh, and going somewhere he could get a fresh start.

He surfed real estate sites and found a beautiful Victorian in Cape May at a great price. Even better, it was part of a package deal and included an established antique store on the main floor, inventory included. Suddenly, the daydream Erik had indulged about starting a blog on trendy antiques and running a boutique service for designers all came together. The next thing Erik knew, he was standing in front of his new home and business with the keys in his hand, wondering whether he'd lost his mind.

Now, he was certain that the answer was "yes."

"Let's see if the proposal even gets interest," Erik protested. "And if it does, it's going to depend on what they actually want, and we'll take it from there."

"Party pooper," Corinne joked. "Fine. I'll let you know when I hear from the producers. But I'm telling you, Erik, this would be a great way to start your new business off with a bang!"

That's what I'm afraid of.

Corinne conveniently seemed to forget that some of the thefts, forgeries, and smuggling rings he'd helped bust had ties to the Mob and the cartels, or left a trail of pissed off billionaires who were used to getting what they wanted. Death threats had been common, and for a while he'd had a bodyguard. While Erik wanted his new venture to succeed, he didn't want to attract the wrong kind of attention.

"Look, I need to finish what I'm doing," Erik said. "Call me when you hear something. And…thanks." Corinne might be exasperatingly upbeat, but she had stuck by Erik through all the changes in his life, and she had been a good friend—especially when there was a commission in it for her.

Erik ended the call and slipped the phone into his pocket, turning to look around the downstairs of the grand old house. It had been updated by the prior owner to create a shop on the first floor and an expansive living area on the second and third floors. Boxes and packing peanuts littered the floor, along with crinkled paper shred. He sighed, completely overwhelmed.

"It can't be that bad." Susan Hendricks, Erik's new next-door neighbor, looked up with a grin from where she sat on the floor, helping to unpack some of the items Erik had shipped from Atlanta. His condo and office had been full of antiques he had bought in his travels, but he'd decided to sell them all and start over, using his personal collection as part of the inventory for Trinkets. "You've got some real pretty pieces here."

"I'm just feeling a little out of my depth," Erik admitted. Susan was probably the same age as his mother, but far more energetic and approachable. Her short salt-and-pepper hair framed a youthful face, and he suspected her wardrobe of T-shirts and yoga pants saw real gym time. She'd been the first person other than his real estate agent to

welcome him to Cape May, and won him over with her genuine friend-
liness and no-bullshit attitude.

"I couldn't help overhearing," Susan said. "There's nothing wrong
with spreading things out instead of doing everything all at once. You
don't have to say no or yes…you can say 'later.'"

That sounded like the best thing Erik had heard all day. "Thank
you. You're a genius."

Susan laughed. "No, I've just felt overwhelmed a time or two
myself, and I'm happy to pass along the tricks that worked for me, for
what it's worth."

If I just take one room at a time, it might be all right, Erik thought. The
front parlor was the main showroom, and the furniture was already in
place, providing plenty of places to display the additional inventory he
had brought with him. He bent down to pick up a vase, trying not to
wince at the thought of the pricy piece sitting on the floor.

"You might change your mind about only being open by appoint-
ment," Susan said as she carefully unwrapped a vintage tea set. "The
folks who visit Cape May have refined tastes—and money."

Erik figured he would get everything safely off the floor and out of
boxes and rearrange them for maximum impact later.

"I know. Just trying not to bite off more than I can chew. I want to
get the blog up and running because that will not only bring people
into the store, but it should attract decorators and curators looking for
the perfect piece. If I can attract those folks, they'll be steady business
even in the off-season." Given his knowledge and reputation, Erik's
collection was likely to attract attention from museums looking to
round out their collections, and designers searching for eye-catching
and unusual items for their clients' homes. He could make more
money with less overhead.

"Sounds like you've thought everything out," Susan said, wiping
some stray paper fibers from an inlaid music box.

"Not really, but it's nice of you to say so." Erik felt like he'd been
careening from one major life decision to another since he'd woken up
in a hospital in Antwerp with a concussion and a gunshot wound, and
decided the paycheck and fame weren't worth dying for. Now here he
was, relocated, single, a new homeowner, taking over a business and

finding his way in a vacation town he vaguely remembered from a few trips when he was a kid. He'd been outrunning his dumpster fire of a life, and Erik was ready to slow down and try to find some kind of new normal.

"Have you done anything except unpack, move furniture, and work on your website since you got to town?" Susan raised an eyebrow to tell him that she already knew the answer.

"Guilty as charged. But there's so much to do, and…"

"And you know what they say about all work and no play," Susan said with a grin. "You need to go out, meet some people, let the town get to know you. Maybe meet a cute girl—or guy," she added with a wink.

"Definitely guy," Erik replied.

"Well then, you've come to the right place. Cape May is very welcoming. My son is probably a few years younger than you, and he and his friends never seem to have any trouble finding dates."

Erik's escape plan hadn't been quite as headlong as it sometimes felt. He'd done his research on Cape May, a town he visited several times vacationing with his aunt, uncle, and cousins when he was in middle school. He remembered the beach and all the classic Victorian houses—and the ice cream. When he went looking for a place to relocate, he checked out the town on a whim and discovered it was gay-friendly and eclectic. While that was definitely true of his former home in Atlanta, the same couldn't be said about everywhere else in Georgia, or in his native South Carolina.

At thirty-five, Erik was ready to put down roots, settle in, and settle down. He never really liked hookups, even before his relationship with Josh, and while Josh's betrayal had rocked Erik's confidence, he still hoped that there was someone out there for him.

"Don't worry. All in good time," Susan reassured him. She got to her feet with a gracefulness that only came from hours of asanas and dusted herself off. "Let me help get everything up on shelves, and by then the meatloaf in the slow cooker will be done. I don't know about you, but I'm starving!"

"It does smell good." Erik knew he'd lucked out with a neighbor like Susan. She had refused any pay for helping him unpack and insisted on bringing over dinner. He'd been wary about her friendly overtures at first, but she quickly won him over.

"It was one of Keith's favorite recipes," Susan said, and her smile grew wistful. "Nothing fancy, just good comfort food." She had mentioned her husband's death to Erik not long after they met, and they had commiserated about how scary it was to get back into the dating game.

"I just bought ice cream, so I can at least contribute dessert," Erik said.

"Sounds like a plan," she answered. Together, they made quick work of moving the antiques out of harm's way and cleaning up the packing materials. Then Erik led the way into the next room, where the slow cooker sat on the table, along with the paper plates and plastic utensils Susan had brought. A two-liter bottle of soda and red cups made for a picnic-style supper.

Susan filled plates while Erik brought chairs. He had to admit that the smell of a home-cooked meal made the place feel more welcoming. He'd been surviving on takeout subs and pizza delivery.

"Tell me about Cape May's ghosts," Erik asked as they sat down to eat. "I've read that local ghost whisperer's books, and I've got to admit, I'm very curious."

Susan wiped away a bit of tomato sauce. "Oh, there are plenty of them, enough to go around, if all the tales are true. It's almost a point of pride to claim you've got a resident ghost."

Erik ate and listened as Susan recounted what she knew. Most of the stories told of victims of swimming or boating accidents who never left, or jilted lovers who died of grief or by their own hand. The fierce storms that had pummeled the beach town added a few more spirits to the tally, as did old local scandals.

"But you know, I think the biggest ghost story in Cape May isn't a 'who.' It's a 'what,'" Susan said with a conspiratorial smile. "A big old hotel that took up two city blocks—the largest hotel in the United States when it was built back around the turn of the last century."

"A hotel?"

"The Commodore Wilson Hotel was quite the showplace back in the day, and everyone who was anyone stayed there. But the hotel was snake-bit from the start. Or cursed, maybe. Ruined everyone who owned it and seemed to be a magnet for tragedy."

Erik vaguely remembered seeing the hotel mentioned when he had researched Cape May, but hadn't seen anything that resembled what Susan was describing. "Where is it? I can't believe I missed it!"

She paused to take a few bites of meatloaf. "Oh, they finally tore it down years ago. It was a grand place in its prime, and it was a shame to see it fall into disrepair. In the end, no one could afford to fix it, so they brought the hotel down with dynamite, and the whole town held a wake."

Erik made a mental note to do some online digging. The Commodore Wilson sounded like the sort of hotel he always sought out when he traveled, a place with a rich history and the kind of architecture no one could afford to build anymore. "You said the place was cursed?"

Susan shrugged. "Maybe that's not literally true, but it sure seemed like it. Five owners went bankrupt. A mobster got gunned down in the lobby. Several celebrities committed suicide there. Its real heyday was probably during Prohibition and the Second World War, but it was still *the* place to be seen into the seventies. Then a shady televangelist bought it and brought all his followers in for big events. It was all fun and games until he up and vanished, leaving a pile of debt and a bunch of pissed off followers—and a lot of unpaid taxes."

"Did they ever find him?" This story was better than anything on the History Channel.

"Nope. Hard to imagine someone who'd had his face all over TV like that could just disappear, but everyone figured he probably went to Brazil or somewhere else without extradition," Susan said. "If so, I guess he was smarter than that TV preacher from South Carolina. He went to jail."

Erik remembered. He'd grown up in Columbia, South Carolina, and the infamous preacher's scandal had unfolded when he was a child, but it had been impossible to live in the state and not know. For a while, it seemed like all anybody talked about.

"Wow. That's a lot of excitement packed into one building," Erik said. "But I hate to see landmarks like that destroyed. They're a part of history."

Susan grinned. "Oh, the Commodore was so much a part of this town's history I swear it's like a ghost itself. Everyone who grew up here had a story about the hotel—working there, wedding reception, going to prom, drinking too much in the bar, spotting someone famous. And after it closed there were paranormal investigators and urban explorers—and local kids who dared each other to go inside and bring out a souvenir."

She sighed. "You should have seen the crowd when they finally sold off all the Commodore's stuff. People who used to live here or stay at the hotel came from all over the world to buy a memento. Monogrammed china sets, silverware, knick-knacks, even the metal fobs for the room keys. It was quite the media circus."

Erik grabbed another slice of meatloaf and gestured for her to continue. "Sounds like my kind of event."

Susan raised an eyebrow. "Actually, you'd have been right at home. Even at the end, there were rumors that some of the artwork and antiques were fake. So many of the hotel's owners were strapped for cash, I wouldn't be surprised if they'd sold the originals and put good forgeries in their place."

"It happens more often than you'd imagine," Erik replied. "I've had to break the news to European nobility that their 'priceless' Monet or Rembrandt was just a very good copy."

Susan sat back and took a sip of her soda. "So, you're interested in ghosts? See any yourself?"

Erik hesitated, but figured that in a place like Cape May, where the local spirits were practically celebrities themselves, it wouldn't hurt to tell the truth. "I've seen a few," he admitted, although the real number was more than he could count. "Guess it goes with knocking around museums and historic old mansions. I can't talk to them or hear them say anything, but I've seen some things I can't really explain."

He didn't mention his odd hunches, the ones that always seemed to know the forgeries from the real deal. They were never wrong. Erik also didn't mention his second sight, the way some objects gave him flashes of their history, showing the world as the object had seen it, a window in time.

Thank God that didn't happen with everything. But it occurred often enough that he usually wore gloves to handle new acquisitions, until he could check them privately to avoid an embarrassing incident. He'd only told one person about that ability, Simon Kincaide, a grad school friend who was a psychic medium. Simon had understood. Erik knew others wouldn't.

"I believe. In ghosts, I mean," Susan said. "There are plenty of things about the world we don't understand. Seems a little arrogant to think we've got it all figured out, don't you think? I don't understand why some people can see ghosts and others can't, but I know enough people who have that I can't dismiss it."

Erik relaxed a little. Susan set him at ease. Most of his friends in Atlanta and on the cases he had worked were situational, so when they weren't forced together by circumstances, the connection withered. He could count the friends who didn't fit that pattern—Simon included—on one hand. It felt good to make a new friend who liked him just for being him.

"So every now and then, I pick up a hint of a drawl from you," Susan said, going back for another small slice of meatloaf. "I get the impression you're not a Jersey boy."

Erik usually didn't say much about his family, but he appreciated that Susan hadn't just Googled him. "I'm from Columbia, South Carolina. State capital and all that. But I've been gone for a long while, and I've lived in New York, London, Rome, and Atlanta. I think the accent comes out most when I'm tired." Or stressed or hurt, he didn't bother to add. Josh had always chided him when his drawl slipped out, calling him a "redneck" and spewing bigoted stereotypes.

And yet, I sat there and took it. So what does that say about me?

"Your parents must be so proud. I imagine they'll be the first to tune in if your TV show comes through."

Susan meant well, but she didn't know his family. "My sister was an Olympic athlete—brought home two silvers and a bronze in gymnastics—and now she coaches. If the TV is on at home, it's usually because Macy has a televised meet."

"That sounds exciting." Susan didn't press for more, and Erik got the impression that she read between the lines.

When Erik was growing up, Macy was being groomed for gold medals. All of his parents' time and money went toward coaches, lessons, and going to competitions all over the country and later, the world. That usually meant no one was around to go to his high school plays or other events. Erik had worked part-time jobs and gotten scholarships to put himself through college and graduate school. He loved his sister, and he did his best not to hold his parents' favoritism against her, but they weren't really a close family.

"How about ice cream?" Erik asked. It wasn't the smoothest segue, but it worked to get past an awkward moment. It wasn't Susan's fault that a question normal people could answer without blinking was such a minefield for him. Even now, with all his accomplishments, Erik had to remind himself that he wasn't as invisible and replaceable as his parents' indifference always made him feel.

"Count me in!" Susan replied with a grin. "And I know it's still off-season, but once everything opens up for the summer, there are some fantastic local ice cream shops that make everything from scratch. I'll have to take you!"

"You're on." He ran upstairs to get the ice cream out of the freezer and returned a few minutes later with a scoop and bowls.

"I'm really looking forward to seeing the town wake up from its winter nap," he said as he set out generous portions of vanilla bean for both of them, finishing off what was in the carton. Once he got settled, he'd have to see about adding toppings to his grocery list. "I know a lot of shops and restaurants close in the off-season. I'm looking forward to getting the whole Cape May experience!"

He had fond memories of the seaside town with its stately Victorian homes and yellow-striped beach tents. Aunt Karen and Uncle Jim included Erik whenever they could in their vacations, saying it was because he was the same age as their boys. Now that he looked back on it, Erik guessed that they were doing their best to make up for his parents' indifference. Their visits to Cape May had left a lasting impression.

"Oh, you'll love it," Susan gushed. She was definitely the town's biggest booster. "I mean yes, there's more traffic. But there's also a lot more energy. Plus even more theater and music, live bands in the bars, fireworks—I wouldn't want to live anywhere else!"

They chatted about favorite kinds of ice cream and desserts, fun topics without any stress. Once Susan scraped her bowl clean and licked every drop from her spoon, she sat back with a satisfied sigh.

"This has been fun. Thank you."

Erik gave her a perplexed look. "You volunteered to spend an afternoon helping me unpack and brought dinner. I owe you a big thank you!"

Susan shrugged. "I enjoyed the company and got to see some lovely antiques up close. I stay pretty busy, but it's nice to get out. Tank and Ziggy are good company, but the conversation gets a little one-sided." Erik had already met Tank, the bulldog, and Ziggy, the black cat.

"Anytime," Erik said. "This was fun." Once he unpacked his kitchen boxes, he'd have to find the few recipes he could make well enough to serve to company and repay the favor.

Susan helped clean up the garbage and went to grab the slow cooker. She divided the leftover meatloaf and put half into a plastic container for Erik. "Here. It makes great sandwiches."

"I never turn down good food," he assured her. "Thank you—for everything."

She grinned. "You're very welcome. Don't forget it's Friday night—why don't you wander into town and see if there's anyone worth meeting? You never know if you don't try!"

With that, she was out the door and across the yard. Erik watched out the window to make sure she got in safely, still thinking about her words. Before he could second-guess himself, he pulled out his phone and downloaded a dating app. As soon as the app registered his location, he uploaded a photo and sketched out a quick bio.

He hesitated, staring at the photo, worried it might not attract interest. He considered his looks fairly average, and he hadn't devoted enough time to the bar or club scenes to gauge his effect on other men. He hadn't had difficulty finding casual boyfriends in college and graduate school, but then he'd connected with Josh and taken himself off the market.

His light blond hair had a bit of a wave no matter how he styled it. Erik had always considered his blue eyes to be his best feature. They were dark like sapphires, and he thought they made up for other unremarkable features. At five foot ten, Erik wasn't short, but he wasn't terribly tall, either. Running and lifting weights kept him in good shape, although he doubted anyone would mistake him for an underwear model. His build remained on the slender side, even now that he was in his mid-thirties. He'd discovered long ago that he preferred men who were taller and more muscular, and had found that interest was often returned.

Erik paused. He really wasn't looking for a quick fuck. The appeal of hookups had gone cold in grad school. Trying not to overthink this, he dismissed the profiles that made it clear they were "one and done." Whether they were telling the truth, a few of the profiles indicated they wanted friends with benefits or were willing to start slow and see where it went.

For once, his intuition wasn't telling him a damn thing as he looked through the remaining profiles. He picked one for "David," a good-looking man with dark hair, a muscular build, and the promise of intriguing tattoos peeking from beneath the sleeves of his T-shirt. Then Erik gathered his courage and hit "send."

ABOUT THE AUTHOR

Morgan Brice is the romance pen name of bestselling author Gail Z. Martin. Morgan writes urban fantasy male/male paranormal romance, with plenty of action, adventure, and supernatural thrills to go with the happily ever after.

Gail writes epic fantasy and urban fantasy, and together with co-author hubby Larry N. Martin, steampunk and comedic horror, all of which have less romance and more explosions.

On the rare occasions Morgan isn't writing, she's either reading, cooking, or spoiling two very pampered dogs.

Watch for additional new series from Morgan Brice, and more books in the Witchbane, Badlands, and Treasure Trail universes coming soon!

Where to find me, and how to stay in touch

Join my Worlds of Morgan Brice Facebook Group and get in on all the behind-the-scenes fun! My free reader group is the first to see cover reveals, learn tidbits about works-in-progress, have fun with exclusive contests and giveaways, find out about in-person get-togethers, and more! It's also where I find my beta readers, ARC readers and launch team! Come join the party! www.Facebook.com/groups/WorldsOf-MorganBrice

Find me on the web at https://morganbrice.com. Sign up for my newsletter and never miss a new release! http://eepurl.com/dy_8oL. You can also find me on Twitter: @MorganBriceBook, on Pinterest (for Morgan and Gail): pinterest.com/Gzmartin and on Bookbub https://www.bookbub.com/authors/morgan-brice

Enjoy two free short stories set in my Badlands series. Read *Cover*

Me here for free: https://claims.prolificworks.com/free/iwZDEP9Z and *Restless Nights* here: https://claims.prolificworks.com/free/js6x0fq8

Start Seth and Evan's adventure from the beginning with *Witchbane*! And please check for excerpts from the other series. You can explore the supernatural side of Myrtle Beach with psychic medium Simon Kincaide and skeptical homicide detective Vic D'Amato in *Badlands* or take a walk on the wild side of Cape May with Erik Mitchell, a former art fraud investigator, and Ben Nolan, a burned-out ex-cop from Newark, in *Treasure Trail*.

Support Indie Authors

When you support independent authors, you help influence what kind of books you'll see more of and what types of stories will be available, because the authors themselves decide which books to write, not a big publishing conglomerate. Independent authors are local creators, supporting their families with the books they produce. Thank you for supporting independent authors and small press fiction!

ALSO BY MORGAN BRICE

Witchbane Series

Witchbane

Burn, a Witchbane Novella

Dark Rivers

Flame and Ash

Badlands Series

Badlands

Restless Nights, a Badlands Short Story

Lucky Town, a Badlands Novella

The Rising

Cover Me, a Badlands Short Story

Loose Ends — *Coming Soon*

Treasure Trail Series

Treasure Trail